Dark Spy's Mission
THE CHILDREN OF THE GODS
BOOK THIRTY-SIX

I. T. LUCAS

Dark Spy's Mission is a work of fiction! Names, characters, places and incidents are products of the author's imagination or are used fictitiously and are not to be construed as real. Any similarity to actual persons, organizations and/or events is purely coincidental.

Copyright © 2020 by I. T. Lucas

All rights reserved.

No part of this book may be reproduced in any form or by any electronic or mechanical means, including information storage and retrieval systems, without written permission from the author, except for the use of brief quotations in a book review.

Published by Evening Star Press

Also by I. T. Lucas

THE CHILDREN OF THE GODS ORIGINS
1: Goddess's Choice
2: Goddess's Hope

THE CHILDREN OF THE GODS

Dark Stranger
1: Dark Stranger The Dream
2: Dark Stranger Revealed
3: Dark Stranger Immortal

Dark Enemy
4: Dark Enemy Taken
5: Dark Enemy Captive
6: Dark Enemy Redeemed

Kri & Michael's Story
6.5: My Dark Amazon

Dark Warrior
7: Dark Warrior Mine
8: Dark Warrior's Promise
9: Dark Warrior's Destiny
10: Dark Warrior's Legacy

Dark Guardian
11: Dark Guardian Found
12: Dark Guardian Craved
13: Dark Guardian's Mate

Dark Angel
14: Dark Angel's Obsession
15: Dark Angel's Seduction
16: Dark Angel's Surrender

Dark Operative
17: Dark Operative: A Shadow of Death
18: Dark Operative: A Glimmer of Hope

19: Dark Operative: The Dawn of Love

Dark Survivor
20: Dark Survivor Awakened
21: Dark Survivor Echoes of Love
22: Dark Survivor Reunited

Dark Widow
23: Dark Widow's Secret
24: Dark Widow's Curse
25: Dark Widow's Blessing

Dark Dream
26: Dark Dream's Temptation
27: Dark Dream's Unraveling
28: Dark Dream's Trap

Dark Prince
29: Dark Prince's Enigma
30: Dark Prince's Dilemma
31: Dark Prince's Agenda

Dark Queen
32: Dark Queen's Quest
33: Dark Queen's Knight
34: Dark Queen's Army

Dark Spy
35: Dark Spy Conscripted
36: Dark Spy's Mission
37: Dark Spy's Resolution

Dark Overlord
38: Dark Overlord New Horizon
39: Dark Overlord's Wife
40: Dark Overlord's Clan

Dark Choices
41: Dark Choices The Quandary
42: Dark Choices Paradigm Shift
43: Dark Choices The Accord

Dark Secrets
44: Dark Secrets Resurgence
45: Dark Secrets Unveiled
46: Dark Secrets Absolved

Dark Haven
47: Dark Haven Illusion
48: Dark Haven Unmasked
49: Dark Haven Found

Dark Power
50: Dark Power Untamed
51: Dark Power Unleashed
52: Dark Power Convergence

Dark Memories
53: Dark Memories Submerged
54: Dark Memories Emerge
55: Dark Memories Restored

Dark Hunter
56: Dark Hunter's Query
57: Dark Hunter's Prey
58: Dark Hunter's Boon

Dark God
59: Dark God's Avatar
60: Dark God's Reviviscence
61: Dark God Destinies Converge

Dark Whispers
62: Dark Whispers From The Past
63: Dark Whispers From Afar
64: Dark Whispers From Beyond

Dark Gambit
65: Dark Gambit The Pawn
66: Dark Gambit The Play
67: Dark Gambit Reliance

Dark Alliance

68: Dark Alliance Kindred Souls
69: Dark Alliance Turbulent Waters
70: Dark Alliance Perfect Storm

Dark Healing
71: Dark Healing Blind Justice
72: Dark Healing Blind Trust
73: Dark healing Blind Curve

Dark Encounters
74: Dark Encounters of the Close Kind
75: Dark Encounters of the Unexpected Kind
76: Dark Encounters of the Fated Kind

Dark Voyage
77: Dark Voyage Matters of the Heart

PERFECT MATCH
Vampire's Consort
King's Chosen
Captain's Conquest
The Thief Who Loved Me
My Merman Prince
The Dragon King
My Werewolf Romeo
The Channeler's Companion

The Children of the Gods Series Sets

Books 1-3: Dark Stranger trilogy—Includes a bonus short story: **The Fates take a Vacation**

<u>Books 4-6: Dark Enemy Trilogy</u> —Includes a bonus short story—**The Fates' Post-Wedding Celebration**

Books 7-10: Dark Warrior Tetralogy

Books 11-13: Dark Guardian Trilogy

Books 14-16: Dark Angel Trilogy

Books 17-19: Dark Operative Trilogy

Books 20-22: Dark Survivor Trilogy

Books 23-25: Dark Widow Trilogy

Books 26-28: Dark Dream Trilogy

Books 29-31: Dark Prince Trilogy

Books 32-34: Dark Queen Trilogy

Books 35-37: Dark Spy Trilogy

Books 38-40: Dark Overlord Trilogy

Books 41-43: Dark Choices Trilogy

Books 44-46: Dark Secrets Trilogy

Books 47-49: Dark Haven Trilogy

Books 50-52: Dark Power Trilogy

Books 53-55: Dark Memories Trilogy

Books 56-58: Dark Hunter Trilogy

Books 59-61: Dark God Trilogy

Books 62-64: Dark Whispers Trilogy

Books 65-67: Dark Gambit Trilogy

Books 68-70: Dark Alliance Trilogy

Books 71-73: Dark Healing Trilogy

MEGA SETS
INCLUDE CHARACTER LISTS
The Children of the Gods: Books 1-6
The Children of the Gods: Books 6.5-10

PERFECT MATCH BUNDLE 1

CHECK OUT THE SPECIALS ON
ITLUCAS.COM
(https://itlucas.com/specials)

FOR EXCLUSIVE PEEKS AT UPCOMING RELEASES &
A FREE I. T. LUCAS COMPANION BOOK

Join my *VIP Club* and gain access to the VIP portal at itlucas.com

To Join, go to:
http://eepurl.com/blMTpD

Find out more details about what's included with your free membership on the book's last page.

TRY THE CHILDREN OF THE GODS SERIES ON
<u>AUDIBLE</u>

2 FREE audiobooks with your new Audible subscription!

Kian

Kian turned his office chair around and looked out the window at the wet pavement below. The rain had started about an hour ago, chasing away the café's customers and whoever else had been enjoying the village square.

The gloomy atmosphere was not conducive to work.

Instead of analyzing the file that Shai had put on top of the stack, he would have much preferred to go home to Syssi. The sticky note his assistant had attached to the file said 'read first,' and he'd been right about the property having great potential for development. But it didn't excite Kian as it normally would.

The problem was not with the deal, it was with the lack of motivation that had been plaguing him since he'd come back from vacation.

Kian wondered whether the rain was affecting his mood, or his mood was making everything seem glum.

The truth was that he was tired.

He should have felt energized after the vacation, but the break in routine only made it harder to get back to it.

Not that anything about his days was routine.

There was always something going on, and it usually had absolutely nothing to do with the business conglomerate he was running.

Like the three new potential Dormants hiding in the keep, who might also be spies for the government program he'd freed them from. Then there were the ten paranormal talents that he'd left behind, which bothered his conscience.

Kian hoped to someday free them as well, but that wasn't a sure thing.

Then there was Kalugal to worry about, a powerful immortal who might become either an ally or a foe.

Jin was the perfect spy to send after him, but she was young and inexperienced, and Kian worried about the thousand and one things that might go wrong with that plan.

That was why instead of calling it a day and going home to his wife, Kian was still in the office, waiting for Turner to arrive so they could brainstorm the plan.

Just another ordinary day in his hectic life.

How the hell was he going to add fatherhood to the mix?

Kian didn't want to be the kind of dad whose only interactions with his child would be a good morning and a goodnight kiss.

"Good evening." Turner walked into the office, put his briefcase down, and removed his dripping jacket.

"Thank you for coming." Kian pulled out a box of cigarillos from the drawer. "Do you mind accompanying me to the roof?"

"It's raining." Turner smoothed his hand over his wet hair. "I still expect to find a bald head when I do that. When I got out of the pavilion, I braced for my scalp to get hit by the rain. I was pleasantly surprised when my hair got soaked instead."

"You were human and bald for much longer than you've been an immortal with a full head of hair. Don't worry about getting wet, though. I have a big-ass umbrella up there."

"Then lead the way." Turner lifted his briefcase and put it under the chair. "I'll leave it here."

That was out of character for the guy. Turner was the definition of paranoid.

"I can put it in a drawer if you wish. Or hide it in the fridge." Kian walked over to the minibar and pulled out four miniature bottles of whiskey.

Turner chuckled. "You would need to make more room in there. And what's the deal with those miniatures? Did you pilfer them from the plane?"

"I have better taste than that. Shai got them for me. He's always coming up with ways to make my life easier. Instead of carrying a large bottle and a couple of glasses to the roof, I can just slip several of those into my pocket. But if you want, I can move things around and stick your briefcase in the fridge."

Turner shrugged. "I'm not worried. The only people who might be able to hack into my laptop are William and Roni, and I trust those two to stay out of my business."

"That's good to know. I thought that you didn't trust anyone."

Turner followed him out of the office. "I trust you."

"Thank you. I'm touched."

As Kian opened the rooftop door at the top of the stairs, he got pelted with raindrops, not because it was raining more heavily, but because it had become windy. Rushing, he and Turner took cover under the umbrella, and Kian turned on the outdoor heater.

"Every time I come up here, there is an additional improvement to the setup." Turner sat on one of the rockers. "Did you find out who is doing this?"

"Anandur promised to snoop around, but so far no one is taking credit. The prime suspect is Shai."

"A smart way to get a promotion or a raise."

"Not if he does it anonymously." Kian handed Turner one of the bottles. "Shai is just looking out for me."

Turner unscrewed the cap and took a sip. "Are you ready to brainstorm?"

Kian nodded. "I told Jin about Kalugal, and she agreed to do it. She suggested taking Jacki along because the girl is an immune, but I don't trust any of the three newcomers."

"You shouldn't. But do you have a concrete reason to mistrust them?"

"Just my gut feeling."

Turner cradled the bottle between his palms and leaned closer to the heater. "Jin is a smart girl. We haven't made any plans about her actually approaching Kalugal, but we need to take into consideration that he can thrall or compel her and get any information he wants out of her. I hope that you followed the same protocol with Jin as you did with the other three."

Kian frowned. "She is Mey's sister and a sure Dormant. It didn't occur to me to hide the keep's location from her. But I don't think it's a problem. We got there in the middle of the night, and she was half asleep. I don't think she paid attention to where we were going."

Turner shook his head. "You should have considered who you wanted to send her after. She knows that the keep is in downtown Los Angeles, and she knows it's a high-rise. Kalugal could show her an aerial map, and she might be able to narrow it down for him to just several buildings."

"You're right. I wasn't thinking. It was late, and the other three were sleeping, so I didn't even bother with going to the building across the street first and using the tunnel. I told Okidu to go straight to the clan's parking level in the keep." Kian pulled out a cigarillo and lit it. "You are worried about the worst-case scenario that is not going to happen. All Jin needs to do is touch Kalugal once. He'll think nothing of it. Just a random human girl touching his arm for a brief moment won't even register."

Turner chuckled. "And how long do you think she is going to stay human?"

"That's a good point. I think something is going on between her and Arwel. I need to have a talk with him."

That wasn't a conversation Kian was looking forward to. The Guardian's sex life shouldn't be anyone else's business. Except, it was when it could induce Jin's transition prematurely.

Perhaps Bridget could do that? Coming from the doctor, it would be less embarrassing.

"I hope that you are not too late." Turner crossed his legs. "The rumor machine has it that they are already together."

"They only met two days ago."

Turner arched a brow. "And your point is?"

"What have you heard?"

"Bridget was gushing about how happy she is that Arwel has found a mate, and how deserving he is. I guess she heard something. Don't forget that Jin is a millennial, Kian. She is not a damsel of yesteryear who expects her first time to be on her wedding night."

"Right."

The current generation of young humans was as casual about sex as the immortals had always been.

"I will talk to him."

Turner nodded. "When you send Jin after Kalugal, you should give her a substantial Guardian backup. The problem is that they can't be anywhere near her when she approaches him. I wish I could go with her, but, unfortunately, this is not going to be a quick one-day mission, and I have several projects I'm working on that require my presence. Weeks might pass before Kalugal is spotted in a place appropriate for Jin's tethering."

Kian hadn't considered Turner accompanying Jin, but he was starting to realize that he should have. Not only was the guy a blank as far as projecting emotions, but he was also an immune. The question was whether he was immune to Kalugal's mind tricks as well.

Annani was the only one who could test immortals for immunity, and he should have asked her to check Turner's.

Taking another puff, Kian leaned closer to the heater. "If Kalugal realizes that Jin has information he can use and decides to take her, Guardians are going to be useless because he can thrall and compel other immortals. Our only chance is her tethering the guy without him noticing it."

Turner put the empty miniature bottle on the side table. "I don't like depending on luck."

"Neither do I. Regrettably, you can't go with Jin. Still, I should have asked Annani to test your immunity to mind manipulation as an immortal. Other than Navuh and Kalugal, she is the only one who can do it to other immortals."

"I'm pretty sure that I'm still immune. I wasn't susceptible as a human, so there is no reason to think that I am as an immortal. What about Jacki?"

Kian shrugged. "I don't see how she could be helpful. Even if she is immune to Kalugal's compulsion, it's not like she could prevent him from abducting Jin. She could raise the alarm, but Kalugal would just compel the Guardians to do nothing about it."

"You could put a tracker on her."

"What for? We know where he would take her. What would we do? Storm the place?"

"As a last resort, yes."

Kalugal

"Welcome home, Professor Gunter." The immigration officer returned Kalugal's passport.

"Thank you, young man." Kalugal pushed his wire-rimmed glasses up his nose and smiled. "Have a pleasant rest of your day."

When disguising himself to look like an old man, the thing to remember was to talk and walk accordingly. He affected a heavy German accent, hunched his shoulders, and walked slowly.

Unfortunately, when traveling through airports a shroud was not enough. He had to put on the old, distinguished gentleman disguise as well. There were cameras everywhere, and the security personnel was actually watching, especially those travelers returning from places like Egypt and Iraq, both of which Kalugal visited often.

The cameras saw what was really there, not what he was projecting into the minds of the humans around him.

Those sitting in the security office might be miles away, which was too far for his mind to reach.

He was continually working on improving the range, as well as the precision, but the skill was far from perfected. And then there were the rare immunes whose minds were not susceptible to manipulation.

"Professor Gunter, over here!" Rufsur waved at him.

His second-in-command was standing among the other limousine drivers, holding up a cardboard sign, and trying hard not to laugh.

Pushing the cart with his luggage, Kalugal ambled up to him. "After all these years, you still find this funny?"

Rufsur shook his head, took the cart from him, and started walking toward the exit. "I think that, while you are wearing the disguise, you actually turn into the old professor. You've developed a split personality."

"It's called good acting. But you are not entirely wrong. After two full weeks of this, it becomes second nature, especially since it's my third archeological dig this year. Sometimes I catch myself thinking with a German accent."

"Did you find anything interesting this time around?"

Kalugal shrugged. "I always find something, but regrettably not what I'm looking for."

"You know what I think." Rufsur stopped at the pedestrian crossing. "Everything was destroyed when Mortdh dropped the bomb on the gods' assembly. The entire city was wiped out of existence."

"Those gods didn't all live in one place. Most of them had their own homes and temples in other cities, and some of their possessions must have survived. I just need to keep on looking. The problem is that Professor Gunter is getting old." Kalugal stuck out his fake belly and patted it in a grandfatherly gesture. "In a few years, I will have to switch to Gunter Junior. I'll have the old man die and his son take over the research."

As they reached Rufsur's car, he popped the trunk and hefted one of Kalugal's suitcases.

"Careful with that!"

"Don't worry. By how heavy it is, I figured that you brought artifacts back with you again."

"Naturally. I love seeing my collection grow."

After Rufsur had loaded the suitcases, Kalugal added his leather satchel and closed the trunk. "I probably have the largest collection of Sumerian artifacts outside of a museum."

It had started as a curiosity some twenty years ago and had quickly turned into an obsession. Kalugal's fortune allowed him to finance private archeological digs and, thanks to his thralling and shrouding, he could get the artifacts out of the country with ease. His original goal had been to find more information about the gods and their technology, but it was no longer just about that. He loved discovering new things about the past. With many of the pieces missing, putting the puzzle together was an intellectual challenge, and it fed Kalugal's thirst for knowledge.

Besides, if he ever decided to sell his collection, it could also be highly profitable. Not that he had any intention of doing that.

It was priceless.

It was his passion.

"I still don't know what you are hoping to find." Rufsur drove toward the exit and stopped to pay the parking fee. "If the gods had advanced technology, it has turned to dust by now. All you are going to find are clay tablets that humans wrote their impressions of the gods on. It might be interesting, but it's not worth the effort and time that you are putting into it."

His deputy was a pragmatic male, and seeking knowledge for its own sake seemed pointless to him. Unless there was a profit to be made or power to be gained, he considered it a waste of time.

"One of their tablets must have survived. My father used to rant about Annani and how she and her clan had an unfair advantage over the Brotherhood. He was convinced that she must have taken one of those tablets with her when she escaped."

Rufsur arched a brow. "With all due and undue respect, Navuh is unhinged. Annani and her clan probably have nothing to do with the humans developing new technologies. If the knowledge came from her, the industrial and technological revolutions would have happened much sooner. Why would she wait so long to give the technology to humans?"

Kalugal shrugged. "Maybe she thought that they weren't ready. Or maybe she didn't understand the technical information contained in the tablet and had to wait until one of her descendants managed to decipher it much later. My father is a power-hungry despot, but he is not crazy. I believe him about the tablet. He said that Mortdh had one and that he used it to communicate with Ahn and to record his thoughts and plans. Given that Navuh told me about it many years before iPads and other tablets were invented, he couldn't have made it up. Mortdh's tablet was just such a device or maybe something even more advanced."

Rufsur waved a hand. "That only reinforces my opinion that you are not going to find anything in those digs. The tablets of today are not designed to survive a decade, let alone thousands of years. If Annani indeed has one, she must guard it like a precious treasure and take excellent care of it. That wouldn't be the case with a device that was left to disintegrate in the ground. After so many years, there would be nothing left of it. Not even a scrap."

"You are probably right. But that's not the only reason I keep digging for artifacts. I find it exhilarating."

Rufsur shook his head. "I don't get it. Working in the dust and the heat while wearing the professor's disguise cannot be pleasant."

Kalugal smiled. "But then I get to go home with my loot, deposit it in my perfectly air-conditioned underground bunker, and work on putting the puzzle pieces together. That's my hobby. It gives me a pleasant respite from my day job of taking over the world." He lifted his chin and affected a haughty expression. "Mwahaha."

"Speaking of conquering the world, did you hear the news about your main competitor for the position?"

His levity gone, Kalugal grimaced. "I thought that I had more time, but it's like someone in the Chinese government is reading my mind and implementing my ideas before I even have time to think them through." He shrugged. "Then again, they might be unwittingly putting my plan into action for me. I just need to figure out a way to hijack it from them and improve upon it."

Rufsur smirked. "Payback is a bitch. I would love for them to get a taste of their own medicine. They've been stealing technology for decades. Now it's their turn to develop a brilliant plan to take complete control of their population and have it stolen from them."

Jin

"Is everyone here?" Amanda looked around Mey and Yamanu's living room.

The place seemed to be bursting at the seams with people, but not because there were so many of them. The dungeon apartment was small, and it felt even smaller after Amanda and the makeup artist had put down the two huge trunks they'd wheeled in.

Since there weren't enough seats for everyone, Jin vacated her spot on the couch and sat in Arwel's lap. She had expected some raised eyebrows or snarky remarks, but everyone ignored it as if she and Arwel becoming a couple was old news.

The question was how had they heard about it so soon?

This morning, when she'd made Arwel recite the proclamation about them hooking up to Mey and Yamanu, none of her new friends had been there. So, unless her sister and her fiancé had been calling everyone in the village to tell them the news, Jin couldn't figure out how they'd learned about it.

Since she was quite sure that Mey and Yamanu hadn't been the culprits, Jin lifted her eyes to the surveillance camera mounted near the ceiling and wondered whether the security personnel were behind this.

That was just as unlikely, but she couldn't come up with anything else.

Still, the fact remained that no one had batted an eyelid when she had plopped onto Arwel's lap.

Except for Richard, who seemed uncomfortable and was doing his damnedest to avoid eye contact with her.

It was a weird situation.

Up until two days ago, Jin and Richard had been a couple. And even though they had both realized that their feelings for each other had been the result of compulsion, they had some history together. Thankfully, Jin had held off on the sex. It would have been doubly awkward for everyone involved if she and Richard had done the deed.

Especially for Arwel, who was showing possessive caveman tendencies.

Richard's life would have been in danger, or at least the integrity of his face would have been.

The surprising part was that she didn't mind Arwel's attitude. In her former life, Jin would have dumped a guy for acting like that faster than he could blink. But for some reason, she liked Arwel's possessiveness.

Maybe because with him it went both ways. She felt just as possessive about her guy as he felt about her.

Amanda put her arm around the makeup artist's shoulders. "Let me introduce Eva. She is going to do your makeup."

Eva dipped her head.

"And this is Jin, Mey's sister, and over there at the table are Jacki, Wendy, and Richard."

Eva waved. "Hello, everyone."

Amanda continued. "You all know Callie, so I don't need to introduce her. I will be in charge of cutting the hair, and Callie will style it."

Callie lifted a blow-dryer and a brush. "I'm armed and ready."

Yamanu got up. "I'll leave you ladies to have your fun."

"Stay!" Amanda pointed at him. "The guys are getting makeovers too."

Stifling a chuckle, Yamanu bowed his head. "I don't need a makeover. I'm perfect the way I am."

"I agree." Mey crossed her arms over her chest. "It's crowded in here. I think the guys should go hang out somewhere else."

"I want a makeover," Richard said. "I'm staying."

"No one needs to leave," Eva said. "We can use the bedroom for the makeovers, and the living room for those waiting their turn."

"I still don't want anyone touching this." Yamanu flipped his long hair back. "It's the source of my power." He winked at Mey.

"You can watch," Eva said. "Who wants to go first?"

"I do." Jin lifted her hand. "I want to look like a completely different person. Nothing permanent, though. I'm fine with wigs and makeup, but I don't want you to cut my hair."

Per Kian's instructions, Jin hadn't told any of her friends about her upcoming mission, so they wouldn't understand why Eva was changing her looks so drastically.

"Why do you want to look different?" Wendy asked. "You're beautiful."

"Thank you. But this is for fun. Eva is a professional makeup artist, and I'm curious to see what she can do."

Wendy shook her head. "I don't want to look like someone else. I just want to look pretty and glamorous."

"No problem." Eva patted the girl's arm. "I promise that you will be happy with the results."

"I'm going to put the trunk in the bedroom."

Yamanu lifted Eva's trunk, but when Richard grabbed the other one, he almost keeled over. Gritting his teeth, he braced it on his chest and followed Yamanu.

"Poor guy." Amanda cast Arwel an accusing glance. "You should have grabbed it before he had a chance. He saw me lift it off the cart, so he thought that it wasn't heavy."

Chuckling, Arwel tightened his arms around Jin. "I couldn't get up without dropping my precious cargo."

Jin kissed his forehead. "Your precious cargo needs to get up anyway."

Reluctantly, he loosened his arms and let her go.

Pulling out a chair from the dinette, Eva took it to the bedroom and put it in front of the bed. "Come and sit over here." She motioned to Jin.

Amanda closed the door. "What look are we going for?"

"Can you make me look not Asian?" Jin asked. "My height and ethnic features give me away."

Eva snorted. "Easily. I can do it just with makeup. I don't even need prosthetics."

"What about the hair? A blond wig would look weird on me."

"An Afro?" Amanda suggested.

Both Jin and Eva grimaced.

"It was just a suggestion. What about dreadlocks?"

Eva shook her head. "They would attract too much attention to Jin. We don't want to make her look pretty, she already is. We want to make her look drab and not as noticeable."

"That's no fun." Amanda plopped on the bed. "Makeovers are supposed to be about making people look better, not worse. Ella looked adorable when we changed her looks. The disguise didn't make her ugly."

Jin frowned. "Why did Ella wear a disguise?"

"It's a long story." Eva pulled out a fluffy brush from her case. "But since this makeover is not going to be quick, we have time."

Arwel

"How about a game of cards while we wait?" Mey put a deck on the coffee table.

Lifting it, Wendy examined the design. "I don't know any card games that are played with real cards. Do you have Uno?"

Mey shook her head. "That's all I have."

"Can we play charades instead?" Wendy put the cards down.

"That's a great idea." Mey smiled. "I haven't done that since Jin and I were kids."

The last thing Arwel wanted was to play silly games, but some form of distraction was needed.

Richard was casting him accusing glances, and the guy's emotional grid was all over the place. He appeared to mourn the loss of his relationship with Jin, even though it hadn't been love, but he also lusted after Jacki, who was ignoring him.

In fact, she was acting strangely.

Staring into the distance, she seemed to be somewhere else. If Jacki were the quiet type, her behavior wouldn't have attracted Arwel's attention, but normally she had an opinion on everything and wasn't shy about voicing it.

Was she having a vision?

The only other clairvoyant Arwel knew was Syssi. Her visions were sporadic, and when they happened, they were hard to miss. She looked like an epileptic having a seizure.

Jacki just stared with unfocused eyes. But when he tried to tune into her feelings, he couldn't get a read on her because she was sitting next to Richard, whose strong emotions overwhelmed her muted ones. Later, when there weren't so many people around, he could ask what was bothering her. Was she scared? Worried about her future?

Since he couldn't tell her anything about immortality yet, assuaging her fears would be difficult, but he could at least reassure her that she would be taken care of.

When the bedroom door opened before his turn for charades arrived, Arwel counted himself lucky. It had been almost an hour since Jin had entered the bedroom with the self-appointed makeover specialists, and except for him and Jacki, everyone else had already had their turn at playing charades.

"Attention, everyone." Amanda clapped her hands. "Get ready to be wowed."

When Jin made her entrance, Arwel's eyes widened. How the hell had Eva accomplished such a transformation?

As the rest of the makeover crew came out, Yamanu started clapping, and then everyone joined him.

A chin-length auburn-colored wig covered Jin's long hair, and heavy makeup obscured her Asian features while making her look a decade older. The baggy, shapeless dress added to the illusion of a thirty-something suburban mom.

Arwel didn't like the new look, but it was one hell of a disguise.

"Amazing," Jacki murmured. "I wouldn't have recognized you on the street."

Richard grimaced. "It's unattractive."

Arwel seconded that opinion, but he was smart enough to keep his mouth shut. No woman wanted to hear that even when she was making herself look worse on purpose.

"I agree," Mey said. "But as a disguise, it's perfect." She got up and walked over to Jin. "The makeup is fantastic. But I doubt you can do it without Eva's help."

Eva shook her head. "Jin doesn't need to go that far when she does it herself, and I can teach her how to do a simplified version. Thankfully, her disguise doesn't have to be as complicated as the one I did for Areana."

"Who is Areana?" Jacki asked.

Eva cast her a suspicious glance. "Someone who also needed to change her looks."

Anyone else would have been intimidated, but not Jacki. "You must be doing a lot of those to be so amazingly good at it."

"I'm a private detective. My work often necessitates elaborate disguises. This is nothing compared to what I do for myself."

"Cool. Is there a school for that? Or are you self-taught?"

Eva narrowed her eyes at the girl. "Why do you want to know?"

Jacki shrugged. "At some point, I will need a job, and this seems like fun. I wondered if I can go to school for it and how much it costs."

Evidently, he'd been right about what had been troubling her. Jacki had been thinking about her future.

"I'm self-taught," Eva said. "But there are schools for stage makeup and costume design. I have no idea how much they cost, though."

Jin tapped Eva's shoulder. "Can we take it off now and make me look pretty?"

"Sure." Eva smiled. "Unlike this, making you pretty won't take long because you already are."

Just as promised, ten minutes later Jin walked out looking like herself again, with just a little color on her lips and barely-there eye makeup.

"That's much better." Arwel got up and pulled her into his arms for a quick hug.

Amanda tapped his shoulder. "Your turn."

"Are you going to make me look like a grandpa?" he joked to cover his embarrassment.

Fates forbid that anyone should find out about him asking Amanda to help him out with his looks. The Guardians would never let it rest.

"No, silly. I have something different in mind for you."

Jin

After Arwel left with the makeover crew, Jin sat next to Jacki. "Do you have a new career in mind?"

She shrugged. "There aren't many job openings for unreliable clairvoyants, and I don't have any other skills."

"What did you do before joining the program?"

"Mostly waitressing and some other occasional gigs. Basically, I did what I could to scrape together enough money for rent and other necessities."

Jin had a feeling that Jacki didn't want to talk about her past before the program. Every time she'd asked her about it, Jacki would answer in generalities and change the subject.

"I'm sure you made good money in tips."

"The tips were good, but not good enough. Besides, I want to do more with my life."

"Have you considered college?"

Jacki shook her head. "I can't afford it, not even with a full scholarship. I need to support myself."

It was so difficult to keep quiet and not tell Jacki about the possibility of her being a Dormant. When she turned immortal and joined the clan, all of the concerns that were troubling her so much would become irrelevant.

Instead, Jin patted her arm. "Don't worry. The solution will present itself."

"I'm in the same boat," Richard said. "I hope the organization will find jobs for us."

Wendy didn't contribute her opinion, but she didn't have to. Her troubled expression said it all.

The thing was, even if her three friends turned immortal, that didn't solve the problem of them earning a living. It wasn't like clan membership came with a free ride. Every member Jin had met so far had a job.

She and Mey should start working on the business proposal that Kian had promised to look over. If he decided to invest the clan's money in their business, they could offer jobs to her friends.

Doing what, though?

Richard was a hustler, so he could be the sales manager. Wendy could be the secretary, and Jacki could model. At five foot nine, she was tall enough for their fashion line, and even though she was much curvier than what models were supposed to be, that wasn't a problem either. The clothing line Jin and Mey had in mind was meant for real women who didn't wear size zero or two. The average was more like size twelve. And that was especially true for tall females.

Except, she couldn't even tell Jacki that. Her friend's lack of a college education wasn't the result of a low IQ. Jacki was smart, and she would wonder why Kian was making Jin and Mey such a generous offer.

It was better to bite her tongue and say as little as possible.

Then again, she could lie and say that Yamanu had money and was investing in Mey's dream. But to do so, she had to coordinate it with them first.

"I'm bored." Wendy got up. "Can I turn on the television?"

"Don't you want to play some more charades?" Mey asked.

"I'm too good at it, and it's not fun when I can guess it right away. I kept quiet not to spoil your fun."

Jin had been under the impression that Wendy had suggested the game. Why had she done it if she didn't like playing it?

The girl was weird.

"How about something to drink?" Yamanu asked. "There is enough left over to make several margaritas."

The bedroom door opened, and Amanda walked in. "Did I hear margaritas? Because I would love one. But first, let me introduce the new and improved Arwel." She waved both arms toward the door. "Please give him a round of applause."

As everyone started clapping, Arwel walked out with a shy smile on his handsome face.

Talk about a transformation.

He looked like a freaking GQ model.

His hair was trimmed and slicked back, which made his gorgeous eyes pop, and he was clean-shaven, which made him look even more kissable than usual.

But the best part was the change of wardrobe.

Gone were the baggy cargo pants and the oversized checkered shirt over a plain white T-shirt. Instead, Arwel had a pair of slim jeans on and an elegant button-down shirt, both fitting him perfectly and showing off his fantastic body instead of hiding it.

The man was mouthwateringly handsome, and he was all hers.

"You cleaned up nicely," Yamanu said.

"Thank you." Arwel wasn't looking at his friend when he thanked him. He was looking at Jin, waiting for her to say something.

"Wow," was all she could come up with.

What she wanted to do was take Arwel's hand, lead him out of Mey's room, take him to hers, and lock the door.

He wasn't going to stay dressed for long.

Arwel

Some might have scoffed at Arwel's efforts to look good for his mate as unmanly, but he didn't care what others thought. If he did, he would have taken care of his schlumpy appearance a long time ago.

The only person whose opinion mattered was Jin, and she seemed very happy with his new haircut and the well-fitting, elegant clothes Amanda had given him.

It was so worth it.

Smiling suggestively, she got up, walked up to him, and took his hand. "I'm tired of playing charades. I think I'm ready to call it a night."

"It's not even eight yet," Mey said.

Jin cast her an amused glance. "I didn't say that I was going to sleep."

Pulling on Arwel's hand, she led him out of the room to the sounds of snorts and chuckles.

"You look good enough to eat," she whispered in his ear. "I promise to be careful when I remove your beautiful new clothes."

Fates, he loved how bold she was.

"You know that most of them can hear you, right?" He used his phone to open her door.

"I don't care." Jin pulled him inside and pushed him against the wall. "Kiss me."

He pressed on the close icon, tossed the phone on the bed, and closed his arms around her body, palming her ass.

"Why don't you kiss me?"

"You are better at it." She touched a finger to his fang, sending a pulse of heat straight to his shaft. "Because of these."

Smirking, he turned them around and pressed his body to hers. "Happy to oblige." He took her mouth.

Soon, the kissing got frenzied, with both of them fumbling for buttons and zippers in their rush to remove the barriers between them.

And then his damn phone started ringing.

Ignoring it, Arwel pulled Jin's blouse over her head and cupped her breasts over her bra.

As she moaned into his mouth and attacked his shirt buttons with renewed fervor, he helped, shrugging the shirt off as soon as she popped the last button and pressing his bare chest to hers.

With the skin to skin sending another bolt of lightning down into his straining shaft, he kicked his boots off and was ready to push his pants down when the damn phone started ringing again.

"You'd better answer it," Jin murmured. "It might be an emergency."

"Someone else can take care of it." He reached behind her back to unclasp her bra.

The phone kept ringing.

With a curse, Arwel let go of Jin and walked over to the bed. His intention was to bark at whoever was calling and tell them to get lost, but luckily he stopped for a split second to check who it was.

"Fuck! It's Kian." He accepted the call. "What's going on?"

"I apologize for the interruption and for what I'm about to ask of you, but regrettably, I have no choice. You need to use condoms, Arwel. Jin can't enter transition before she tethers Kalugal."

"Noted."

"Goodnight."

Damn. He should have thought of that. Not only had they had unprotected sex already, but he hadn't gone out to buy condoms. Perhaps there were some left over in the old clinic?

"What's the matter?" Jin hugged him from behind, pressing her naked breasts to his back.

He put his hands over hers and turned his head to kiss her cheek. "Kian reminded me that we need to use condoms to prevent you from entering transition before you tether Kalugal."

She chuckled. "It might be too late. We didn't use them last night."

"Still, we need them now, and I don't have any."

"That's a bummer." She rubbed herself against him. "But as I said before, you look good enough to eat, and that's what I want to do. I don't think you can induce my transition like that." She nipped his ear.

His eyes rolling back, Arwel pulled Jin's arms tighter around him. "There might be some condoms left in the clinic. I can go check."

"You are not going anywhere." Turning him around to face her, she pushed him onto the bed. "Not right now, anyway."

When she kneeled on the floor and started tugging on his socks, he tried to stop her and do it himself, but she batted his hands away.

"Let me. This is my treat to you."

Leaning back, he groaned. "Fates, woman. What are you doing to me?"

She took a sock off and tossed it aside. "Pampering you." She pulled the other sock off and dropped it on the floor. "And pleasuring you."

Bracing on his arms, he lifted his ass and pushed his jeans and boxer shorts down his thighs.

Jin pulled them the rest of the way. "Oh, my." She licked her lips. "Now, that's a treat." She touched his erection.

His hips shot up. It was an involuntary action, but it seemed to please her.

"Excited to meet me, aren't you?" She flicked the head with her tongue. "I'm excited too." She licked all around it.

"Fates," he groaned.

"Jin would suffice." She smiled up at him and then opened her mouth and took him deep inside it.

His head dropped back, and he arched up into her mouth.

She took him even deeper.

Damn. He had to see that.

Lifting on his forearms, he looked at Jin's lips wrapped around his shaft. The dual sensation of feeling and seeing was enough to trigger his climax.

Sensing it, she tightened her hand and pulled back. "Not yet. I'm not done having fun with you."

Kalugal

After a shower and a short nap, Kalugal headed down to the bunker. Not trusting anyone else to handle his treasures, he hadn't allowed his men to unpack the trip's loot and was excited about doing that himself. There was nothing like coming home and going over his latest finds before putting them on display.

His best one was a small statue of a beautiful woman that was nearly intact. What fascinated him most about it, though, was that it looked a lot like a woman he'd seen on one of his trips to Egypt.

On the way back from one of his digs, Kalugal had passed the Colossi of Memnon, but even though he'd visited the statues several times over the years, something had prompted him to stop at the tourist attraction and have another look.

When he'd noticed the female, it was because of her height and her most unusual jade eyes. He'd been intrigued, but he'd had no intention of flirting with her while in his Professor Gunter disguise. Still, if she had been alone, he could've shrouded himself in a more appealing form and approached her, but since she hadn't been, he had just walked over to take a better look.

Something about her was different.

When he'd gotten closer, that elusive something had turned into a most interesting discovery. The woman was an immortal. His reaction to her had been much subtler than the one he'd had to her man, but both of them had caused the hair on the back of his neck to tingle in alarm.

As her senses had picked up on him as well, she'd turned to look at him.

Instinctively, Kalugal had shrouded himself in thin air, disappearing from sight. Since she could sense his otherness, even his Professor Gunter disguise wouldn't have been enough. The female would have wanted to check out who he was and why he'd triggered that particular response, or worse, send her formidable mate to investigate.

Then he had bumped into the two of them again at the airport.

Who were they?

If he had met the male alone, Kalugal would have assumed that he was a member of the Brotherhood sent by Navuh to search for him. But the presence of the immortal female precluded that. The two couldn't have belonged to the Devout Order of Mortdh.

They either belonged to Annani's clan or were an unaffiliated couple. In either case, he had no wish to engage, and not just because the male looked dangerous.

Kalugal's curiosity had been piqued, though, more on a personal level than anything strategic.

The clan played no part in his future plans, and they could do nothing to stop him, so he was perfectly okay with leaving them alone. But ever since he'd seen that couple and the loving way they had interacted with each other, he'd been having thoughts about finding an immortal female to share his life with, and the clan was the only community that had them.

"I knew that I'd find you here." Rufsur walked over to the worktable. "Pretty." He leaned to look at the small statue.

"Don't touch it." Kalugal cast him a warning glare.

"I know better than to breathe on your artifacts." Clasping his hands behind his back, Rufsur peered over the fragments of a stone tablet that Kalugal was carefully spreading over the table.

"Anything interesting happen while I was gone?"

Rufsur rubbed the back of his neck. "There was a small incident that I forgot to mention."

Straightening up, Kalugal narrowed his eyes at his number two. "What is it, and why didn't you call me right when it happened?"

"Relax, it's nothing. We had a woman stop by the gate and ask to see the grounds. She and her husband were looking for a house in the neighborhood, and she wanted to see the landscaping. Just in case, I had them followed and checked them out. They seemed to be precisely who they claimed to be. They were staying at a posh hotel, looking at properties during the day, and enjoying their evenings in nearby restaurants and bars."

"It could be nothing, and it could be something." Kalugal took his gloves off and started walking toward the security office. "I want to see the footage from when that woman stopped by the gate. Was she alone?"

"The husband stayed in the car."

That made it less suspicious. A woman alone wouldn't ring the bell on a stranger's estate and ask to come in. But a pushy one who had her husband as backup might.

"Hello, boss." Gabe turned his swivel chair around. "What brings you into my humble office?"

"I want to see the footage." Kalugal looked at Rufsur. "When did the woman stop by?"

"Twelve days ago. I think it was Thursday."

"I remember her." Gabe turned back to his monitor array. "A hot little number. I hope they find a house in the neighborhood and that her husband leaves on many business trips." He typed on his keypad, bringing up the gate footage from that day and then scanning it on fast forward to the right moment.

Kalugal leaned over Gabe's shoulder. "Freeze it and zoom in on her face."

She was petite and too skinny for his taste, but her face was beautiful. Her hair and the gentle expression on her face reminded Kalugal of his mother, and as always, the memory made his gut clench with sorrow.

Keeping him away from her was a sin for which he was never going to forgive his father.

"That's indeed a gorgeous woman. A trophy wife," he said to cover up for his momentary slip into sentimentality. "Let it play with the audio on."

Without consciously admitting it to himself, and for no reason whatsoever, he hoped that the woman also sounded like his mother, but she didn't. No woman ever had.

His mother was one of a kind. A gentle soul trapped by a despot whom she for some reason loved.

Was this woman who called herself Viv also married to a control freak?

"Can you show me the husband?"

Gabe switched to another camera. "Here he is. Nice car."

"Mercedes' finest," Kalugal said.

The top of the convertible was down, and the husband was clearly visible. The man was immaculately groomed and elegantly dressed. While his wife conversed with the guard, the guy was busy typing a message on his phone.

So far, everything had fit with who the couple claimed to be, but they also could have been well-prepared spies. People were curious about the mysterious owner of the estate, and ambitious journalists might have devised a plan to find out more.

"Can you zoom in on the phone? I wonder if I could read what he is typing."

"I can try."

The camera angle was such that it was impossible to read the message, but the phone itself was interesting. At first glance, it looked like the latest iPhone model, but upon closer examination, it didn't look like any of the major brands.

"Are either of you familiar with that phone?"

Rufsur leaned closer. "It looks like one of those cheap Chinese copies of an iPhone."

That was what had crossed Kalugal's mind as well, except it didn't fit the rest of the picture. The couple seemed rich. Why would the husband use a non-brand phone?

There were two possibilities Kalugal could think of.

One was that the couple had been journalists in disguise, using a rented Mercedes and expensive clothing as disguises, but not bothering with a small detail like a phone.

The other possibility was that the phone wasn't a cheap replica, but rather a special issue of breakthrough technology or powerful encryption, or both, like the ones he and his men were using.

"I want security increased, and I want you to report anything suspicious to me right away. And I mean everything, no matter how trivial you might think it is."

"Yes, boss." Gabe saluted. "Code red?"

"Code yellow will do."

Rufsur frowned. "Why? What did you see?"

"The phone. A guy wouldn't be driving a Mercedes and at the same time using a cheap Chinese counterfeit. I have a feeling that this device is a special issue, encrypted like ours."

Syssi

Amanda walked out of her office and stopped at Syssi's desk. "Let's have lunch at Gino's."

Syssi looked up. "We haven't been there in ages, and Gino is going to give us the look."

"What look?"

"The guilt-inducing sad one because we've stopped coming."

Amanda frowned. "We are there at least once a week."

"Precisely. But the last time was three weeks ago."

"We need to plan Kian's birthday, and that's the best place for it. I'll just give Gino a hug and all will be forgiven."

"Be careful." Syssi pulled her purse out of the drawer and pushed to her feet. "A hug from you might give him a heart attack. The old lecher has the hots for you."

Amanda shrugged. "And so do ninety percent of my male students and ten percent of the female."

"Yeah, but they are young. Gino is in his sixties, and he is about fifty pounds overweight."

"You've got a point. I'll just air kiss his ruddy cheeks and leave a big tip."

"That's better."

As usual, when they got to Gino's it was packed. The excellent home-style Italian food, combined with reasonable prices and big portions, attracted customers from as far as the university. Which meant that there was a chance that Amanda would bump into one of her students, something she tried to avoid on her lunch break.

Thankfully, Gino wasn't there to give them the look, but since all of his staff knew them, they still got the royal treatment.

"Follow me, ladies." Gino's nephew headed toward the back of the restaurant. "The only table I have available is in the private room on the second floor. I hope you don't mind. Otherwise, you'll have to wait."

"That's perfect." Amanda started up the rickety stairs. "Syssi and I need to plan my brother's birthday."

He turned around with a big grin on his face. "We could cater it. How many people are you inviting?"

"That's what we are about to figure out."

"Let me know when you have a number, and we can go over menu options."

"I will do that."

After he took their order and headed back down, Syssi leaned and whispered, "We can't have Gino cater the birthday."

"Why not?"

"Because after the party is over, we would have to thrall all the waiters."

Amanda shrugged. "I don't think it will be necessary. They won't notice anything. It's not like our guys are going to get aggressive or horny and start flashing fangs. They will get drunk and sing in Gaelic but that's fine. Just a bunch of guys having fun."

Syssi nodded. "I hope you are right."

"The question is where to do it and who to invite. I vote for the banquet hall in the keep. If we invite the Scottish arm of the clan and they all come, bringing them to the village would be a hassle, and housing them would be a problem as well. Also, the increased traffic to the village might get noticed. The keep, on the other hand, is close to several high-end hotels, and it's in the middle of downtown."

Amanda's mention of hotels lit up a bulb in Syssi's head.

Leaning back, she crossed her arms over her chest and smiled. "I have a better idea. Let's do it in the clan's hotel in Hawaii."

Amanda's eyes brightened. "You are a genius. Why didn't I think of that? It's perfect. Everyone loves Hawaii, and that way we won't risk exposing the village or the keep."

"That's just one of the benefits. Think about the weather and the beaches. It's going to be so much more fun than hanging around Los Angeles in the winter." Syssi looked out the window. "It's drizzling again."

Tapping her finger over her lower lip, Amanda squinted. "What about a cruise ship? We could rent one exclusively for the clan."

Syssi sighed. "The problem with that is the same as with my idea. Someone would have to stay behind and guard the village here and the castle over in Scotland, which means that not everyone will take part in the celebration, and that sucks. I want everyone to be there."

"Not everyone came to your wedding, or to Nathalie and Andrew's. That's just how it is."

"Maybe we could have two parties instead of one? That way everyone can participate."

"True, but then it's not going to be a clan-wide celebration."

"Right. There must be a solution; we are just not thinking creatively enough."

Amanda chuckled. "If the Perfect Match studios had enough devices, we could hook up everyone and have a virtual party."

"Maybe by Kian's third millennial party there will be one in every home."

Amanda laughed. "No one would ever leave. People would spend their lives inside virtual realities."

It was a scary thought, but Syssi doubted it would ever happen. "Real life brings endless scenarios and possibilities. The virtual world is limited by the designers' imaginations. Eventually, people would get bored."

"You think?" Amanda arched her brows. "For most people, real life is boredom and tedium. They get up in the morning, go to work, come back home, eat dinner with the family, watch some television, and go to sleep. Rinse and repeat. It's the same for us. It's not like every day brings new and exciting things, and when it does, they are rarely good."

Syssi nodded. "Kian would agree with you a hundred percent. There is always something going on, and it's usually trouble."

When the sound of footsteps announced their waiter's arrival, they paused the conversation and waited until the guy left.

"We've gotten sidetracked," Amanda said. "Back to Kian's birthday. Are we holding it in Hawaii, or are we renting a cruise ship?"

"I prefer Hawaii. Having most of the clan on one boat is dangerous. If word somehow got out, it would be very easy for our enemies to get rid of us with one freaking missile."

"Or a torpedo. And it's not like we can hire an escort of battleships to protect us." Amanda tapped her palm on the table. "So, it's decided. We are having the party in Hawaii."

"Yes."

"Now to the next item on the agenda. Do we tell Kian? Or are we going to surprise him?"

"Let me think about it. If we coordinate it well and get everyone to cooperate, we might be able to surprise Kian. I can tell him that I want to celebrate his birthday by going on a vacation to Hawaii. We will go first, and then everyone else will follow. I'm pretty sure Onegus can take care of the village's security. Except, Kian doesn't like surprises. I think he would enjoy the event more if he knew about it ahead of time."

Kian

"Good afternoon." Kian got up and pulled out a chair for Vivian.

When Magnus had walked into the office with his wife, Kian hadn't been surprised even though he hadn't invited her. Vivian had been an integral part of the operation in the Bay Area, providing cover for her husband. Her idea to walk up to the gate and ask to see the grounds hadn't been sanctioned, but it seemed as if no harm had been done. The tail that had followed them around for a couple of days had eventually given up.

"Thank you." She sat down. "I hope you don't mind me joining the meeting."

"Not at all. You were an unofficial team member, and your contribution was appreciated."

"That's so kind of you to say, but in retrospect, I regret going up to the gate and pressing that button. I thought that we could learn something by courting a tail, but you didn't want me to engage the guy following us. Then to keep our cover, we had to pretend to show interest in nearby properties. I enjoyed the house walkthroughs, but Magnus not so much."

Kian stifled a chuckle. That had been an accusation cloaked in an apology.

"We've found what we were after anyway, and you two got to see some nice houses for sale."

She smiled at her husband. "Magnus was bored out of his mind."

"I wasn't." The Guardian took her hand. "I just couldn't stand the realtor's endless prattle. Besides, it wasn't a total waste of time. One of the houses we saw has potential."

Kian frowned. Surely, Magnus wasn't thinking about buying it for his family or even as an investment. Unless he'd meant it had potential for the clan.

"How so? I typically invest only in hotels and office buildings, not in private houses."

"I meant as a stakeout house," Magnus clarified. "It's located at the end of the street Kalugal's mansion is on, but because it's a corner house, its front and its driveway face the other street."

Kian's curiosity was piqued. "Go on."

"The good part is that Kalugal's gate is visible from the home's second floor balcony. The bad part is that the property costs a fortune to lease. The quoted price was twenty-seven grand a month, and the minimum lease term was one year."

"We can thrall the owner to agree to a month-to-month."

"That occurred to me. But the owner lives abroad. Regrettably, we can't thrall humans over the phone."

Kian leaned back and smiled. "You are right about that. But Lokan can compel him. He proved that he could do it when he compelled his island manservant to send him Navuh's portrait even though it was not allowed."

Vivian shook her head. "Still, twenty-seven grand a month is a lot of money."

"It is. But that would be the best cover possible for our operation. Especially if you two moved in. Since Kalugal's men have already checked your story and found no holes in it, they won't find it suspicious that you rented or bought a property nearby."

Magnus didn't look convinced. "They might go for a more thorough investigation if we become their neighbors. Besides. We've been away from home for too long already. We can't leave Parker alone again."

"Can you take him with you?"

Vivian and Magnus exchanged glances, and then Vivian shook her head. "I don't want to expose Parker to even a whiff of danger. But if you think this will be helpful for the mission, I'm willing to accompany Magnus again. Ella is back, so she can take care of Parker in our absence." Vivian chuckled. "Not that he is thrilled about living with his sister. Parker prefers spending time with Merlin. If the doctor ever wants an apprentice, our son would jump on that."

Magnus grimaced. "Merlin fills Parker's mind with useless information instead of teaching him actual biology and physiology, things the kid could actually use in school."

"It's not useless." Vivian smiled shyly. "Merlin's potion is helping us to conceive."

Magnus's eyes softened. "I like the guy, and I want to believe that his potions actually work, but Syssi and Kian's success might have been coincidental. None of the other couples who have started the treatments have been successful yet."

"Give it time, love. It will happen."

"Fates willing."

Kian waited impatiently for the discussion between the mates to be done. It wasn't that he lacked sympathy for their cause, but it was irrelevant to what the meeting was about.

"Give me the house's details, and I'll arrange the lease. Get ready to go back on Thursday."

Vivian's eyes widened. "So soon? You can't close the deal so quickly."

"With Lokan's help, I can. Kri and Michael are going to join you there, and once Jin is ready, she and Arwel will stay with you as well. I haven't decided how many additional Guardians I'm going to send with her, but they are also going to stay at that house, provided that it's big enough."

Magnus nodded. "Six bedrooms and eight bathrooms. I think that should do it."

"Indeed. Given the cost of hotel rooms in the Bay Area and how many I would have had to rent for the mission, the house is probably a better deal."

Jin

"How did you enjoy the lesson with Dalhu?" Arwel looked at Jin's sketchbook expectantly.

She put it on the coffee table. "It was fun. You should have stayed."

Showing up mid-morning with a bunch of artists' sketchbooks and charcoals, Dalhu had surprised everyone, including Arwel. He'd murmured something about doing it because Amanda had demanded it of him and apologized for not calling ahead of time.

Arwel had arranged for them to use one of the classrooms, stayed for a little while to watch, and then left ten minutes into the lesson.

"I draw like a six-year-old." He glanced at her closed sketchbook again. "Can I see what you have in there?"

Jin shook her head. "I'm not much better than you. Mey is the talented one." She pulled a bottle of water from the fridge and joined Arwel on the couch. "Richard can't even draw a stick figure, and yet he stayed. Dalhu was very patient with him."

Snaking an arm under her, Arwel lifted her onto his lap. "Good for him. But I don't have the patience for it. My next chosen career is not going to be anything artsy."

He kissed her softly, his arms skimming over her sides and brushing lightly against her breasts.

It didn't take much for Jin to get excited. Turning in Arwel's arms, she straddled him. "Did you get condoms?"

It was a mood killer to talk about rubber, but she had to ask. For some reason, they had to use condoms until she tethered Kalugal. Arwel hadn't explained why, just saying that it was necessary.

Was Kian afraid she'd get pregnant and that it would interfere with her ability to tether people? Or maybe it was about the immortals' superior sense of smell. If they didn't use protection, could Kalugal smell Arwel on her?

Talk about gross.

Arwel smirked. "I did. There is an entire commercial-sized box of them in the clinic. Someone was very thoughtful."

The thought of having sex with a barrier between them was far from exciting, and using up an entire box before they could stop was depressing.

"Yeah, remind me to thank whoever left it there for us later." She looked down to hide the involuntary grimace.

Arwel hooked a finger under her chin. "You look upset."

"I don't want to make love to you with those things on. They take away from the pleasure. Besides, I don't understand how they will prevent me from entering transition. I was tested when I entered the program, and I'm clean, my birth control shot is good for another month, and after that Bridget can give me another one."

"It's not about preventing pregnancy or catching diseases. Immortals don't get infected, and we don't transmit either. Our bodies eliminate viruses and bacteria. But in order for you to transition, I need to bite you and to come inside you at the same time. It has nothing to do with getting you pregnant. It would be a miracle if I did."

Maybe for him, but not for her. Jin wasn't ready to start a family.

"I don't get it. You said that for guys to transition it's enough for them to get bitten during a fight. How come females need semen in addition to the venom?"

He shrugged. "I'm not a doctor, but I suspect that the venom's different composition has something to do with it. Maybe it's not as concentrated when used during sex, and to transition the extra chemical boost from semen is needed. Bottom line, experience has taught us that this is how it works, and as long as condoms are used, transition doesn't happen. And since it is important that you approach Kalugal as a human, you can't transition until you tether him."

"Then I don't want to wait. I want to do it as soon as possible and be done with it. I want us to make love with nothing to diminish the experience, and I want to transition."

He nodded. "I want that too, but I don't want to rush things. Kalugal is a dangerous man, and we should plan the operation carefully. I don't know whether Kian and Turner have finalized the details yet."

"What's to finalize? Their part is to locate him in a place where I will have access to him. Once I'm there, it can be all done in five minutes. Bada bing bada boom."

Arwel laughed. "Suddenly, you are enthusiastic about going out on a spying mission?"

She undulated, rubbing her center over his erection. "I have strong motivation. I want that bad boy in me without a raincoat. Call Kian and tell him that I'm ready to go."

Arwel arched a brow. "Now?"

"Yes. If he knows that I'm ready, he will finalize those details you are so concerned with."

Arwel frowned. "You are taking this way too lightly. So many things can go wrong. We need to use every precaution possible to ensure your safety. If anything happens to you..." He trailed off.

Jin cupped his cheeks. "I'm not stupid. I'm not going to rush into it or go in without backup. But this is not some dangerous mission that involves walking into the lion's den or crossing enemy lines. What's the worst that could happen? Kalugal walks away without me having a chance to tether him? Then we will do it again."

"What if he grabs you and runs? No one will be able to stop him because he can compel other immortals, and he can certainly compel you to go with him without a struggle."

"Why would he do that, though? Has he kidnapped random girls from clubs before?"

"Not that we know of."

"So he is not going to start with me." She reached into his pocket and pulled out his phone. "Call Kian. The sooner you do that, the sooner we can make love."

He chuckled. "Is that supposed to motivate me to make the call?"

"You betcha."

Arwel

Arwel dropped the phone on the couch beside him and put his hands on Jin's waist.

"What are you doing?" She batted them away.

"You told me to call Kian, and I can't do that with you sitting on me." He gripped her waist again and started to lift her.

She put her hands on his forearms to stop him. "Why not?"

"Because I can't concentrate when you are rubbing all over me."

Smiling evilly, Jin leaned to the side and picked up the phone. "Call." She handed it to him. "Let's test your self-control." She emphasized by twisting her hips and grinding against the club pushing on his zipper.

"You are evil."

"I'm a challenge."

That she was, and Arwel loved every moment of it. She was like no other female he had ever been with, and that was saying something when coming from an immortal who'd been sexually active for more than three centuries.

With an exaggerated groan, Arwel chose Kian's contact and then waited for the line to connect.

"He is not picking up." He disconnected the call.

"Give him a moment. Maybe he's in the restroom and is just zipping up."

Arwel shook his head. "I really don't want you thinking about Kian and zippers in the same context."

She chuckled. "Sorry. I just thought that if he was on the line with someone else, he could have paused, switched over to you, and told you to wait. But since he didn't do that, I figured he couldn't get to the phone."

As his phone started ringing, he arched a brow. "Maybe you were right." Planting a quick kiss on the tip of her cute nose, he answered. "Hi, Kian. Thanks for calling back."

"I was on another call."

Jin shrugged and made the zipping motion.

He mouthed, *naughty girl*. "I have Jin here with me. Do you mind if I put you on speaker? I'm calling on her behalf, and the door to her room is closed, so the others can't hear us. We can talk freely

"Go ahead."

She leaned into the phone even though it wasn't necessary. "Hi, Kian. How is your day going?"

"Very well. And yours?" He sounded amused.

"I'm ready to go after Kalugal."

"Don't you need to rest a little longer?"

"She is impatient to start her transition," Arwel interjected before Jin had a chance to blurt something about the damn condoms.

The girl really had no filter.

"I see," Kian said. "Can you be ready to leave for the Bay Area by Thursday?"

Arwel frowned. He hadn't expected Kian to be ready so soon. "That's only two days from now. Are there any new developments that I'm not aware of?"

"I spoke to Vivian and Magnus earlier, and they told me about a house for lease down the street from Kalugal's mansion. We are renting it starting Thursday. The place is fully furnished, so you can move right in. Since Vivian and Magnus have been pretending to look for a property in the area and Kalugal's men have investigated them already, they are going to be the official renters."

"How many Guardians are you sending with us?"

Arwel took it for granted that he was going, and if Kian objected, they would have a problem, because he wasn't letting Jin go without him.

"Kri and Michael are already there. I'm thinking of sending four more, but that might be overkill. You,

Magnus, and Kri, that's already three, and you can count Michael as half."

"What's half a Guardian?" Jin asked.

"Michael is still in training, but he is very good," Arwel explained.

Jin pursed her lips. "Then that's more than enough. You don't need to send any more people to guard me. Once you locate Kalugal and I get to him, the whole thing is going to be over in five minutes."

"The problem is that none of the men can go in with you because Kalugal would sense them. They can only guard the exits. If there is more than one, they will need to split up. Also, he is probably not going to be alone. A guy like him doesn't leave the house without a bodyguard or two. I need to add at least two more Guardians to your team."

"You are the boss." She shrugged. "What about Jacki? Is she coming with me?"

"Yes."

Jin pumped her fist in the air. "Awesome." But then her expression turned serious again. "What about Richard and Wendy? They will feel abandoned here. Especially since it could take a long time until Kalugal is spotted somewhere nearby and in a place that I'll have access to him."

"I'm sorry, but you can't take them with you. They would be a liability."

"Not really. Wendy is an empath, and Richard is a touch telepath, and they are both human. They can be part of my backup."

"Does either of them have military training?"

"Only what we were taught in the program. We had firearm training and some hand-to-hand fighting. But that wasn't much. Still, that's all Jacki and I have to work with."

"Let me think about it, but it's probably a no. Jacki is an immune, so she is too valuable not to be used in this situation, but the other two are basically untrained civilians."

Jin nodded. "I understand. I don't like it, but I get it."

"Do you still think you can be ready by Thursday?" Kian asked.

"Nothing has changed about that. I'm ready to be done with this."

"Did you have a chance to tether your friends?"

Jin grimaced. "Not yet."

"Make sure to do it before Thursday."

"I really don't think it's a good idea. It's not like I can follow the tethers all at once. I can do it only one at a time, and when I have several connected to me, it takes a lot of concentration."

"I understand. Like everything else, there is a learning curve, and I'm sure that with practice it will become easier for you to handle."

"Maybe. But it's still uncomfortable. Morally, I mean. I would hate it if anyone did it to me."

"Think of it as a temporary measure."

"Do I have a choice?"

"I'm afraid not."

Jin

Arwel ended the call and dropped the phone on the couch again. "So, where were we?" He palmed the back of her neck and pulled her in for a kiss.

Things were just starting to heat up again when Jin's phone rang.

Arwel groaned. "What now?"

"It's Mey's ringtone." Jin reached into her back pocket. "What's up?"

"Dinner. We are all heading to the kitchen. Kian's butler delivered groceries, and Ingrid brought four extra-large pizzas and a cake for dessert. I say we make a salad to go with the pizzas and leave the cooking for tomorrow."

"Aren't we lucky. I totally forgot that we planned on making dinner for everyone tonight. We need to thank Ingrid for saving us the trouble."

"I already did. So, are you two coming?"

Jin chuckled. "Yeah, in a bit." They were about to, but Mey's phone call had ruined those plans.

"Don't wait too long. The pizzas are getting cold."

Arwel groaned. "I knew that we should have waited with calling Kian."

"It actually worked out better this way. We can eat dinner with everyone, tell them the sad news about us leaving, and then go back and make love for as long as we want. No interruptions."

"Let's get it over with, then." Arwel lifted her off his lap and then adjusted himself. "I'm not going to be comfortable."

"Sweet torture." She winked at him. "I'll make it up to you."

When they got to the kitchen, Mey waved Jin over. "Can you grate the Parmesan? I'm almost done."

"Sure thing." Jin grabbed the thick chunk of cheese and went to work. "Just like old times in Mom's kitchen. It makes me feel nostalgic."

Mey nodded. "I miss Mom and Dad. Maybe after this thing with Kalugal is over, we can go visit them?"

"That's an awesome idea. Except, you forget that I'm a wanted woman. How am I going to fly over there?"

Mey stole a quick glance around to make sure none of the humans were within earshot. "The clan can arrange for fake documents. And if, after you tether Kalugal, Kian feels generous, he might let us use the private jet." She leaned closer to Jin's ear. "Naturally, we won't go until you transition, and then we can take Arwel and Yamanu with us." She smiled. "We can introduce our fiancés to our parents."

"Arwel is not my fiancé. And besides, they are not going to be happy with our choices." Jin leaned closer. "Our guys are pagans who believe in Fates. Mom and Dad are going to have a conniption over us not marrying Jewish boys."

Mey grimaced. "Do you think there is a chance that they will agree to convert?"

Jin arched a brow. "You are an optimist, aren't you?"

From over at the center island, Yamanu cleared his throat. "Not going to happen."

Jin waved a hand. "That's what I thought."

"I think that's enough Parmesan." Mey put a hand on Jin's.

There wasn't much left of the big hunk of cheese. Without paying attention, she'd grated a mountain.

Mey took a plate and emptied half of it into her salad, tossed it, and carried it to the kitchen island that served as their dining table. "Enjoy, everyone."

Sitting between Mey and Arwel, Jin munched on a slice of pizza while watching Ingrid flirting with Richard.

He seemed to be enjoying the attention, and Jin wondered whether the two of them had already had sex. She hoped so, and not only because she felt guilty for moving on so quickly. If things got serious between

Ingrid and Richard, he would be too busy to feel abandoned when Jin and Jacki left for San Francisco.

But that still left Wendy.

Right now, she was talking with Jacki, and the two were laughing about something, but Jacki was leaving too.

Then another thought occurred to her. Mey and Yamanu were staying at the keep only because of her. As soon as she left, they would probably go back to their house in the village.

Damn, she hadn't thought things through. Maybe she should have waited another week?

"You are atypically quiet," Mey said. "What gives?"

"Arwel and I spoke with Kian, and I told him that I'm ready to go after Kalugal. Naturally, he was happy to hear that, and he told us to be ready by Thursday. Jacki is coming with us too, but I didn't tell her yet. I'm worried about leaving Wendy and Richard alone here. You and Yamanu are probably not going to hang around once I'm gone, right?"

Mey glanced at her guy, who shrugged.

"We can stay a little longer, but eventually, everyone has to move on. Richard seems to be in good hands. So that leaves only Wendy."

"I can introduce her to a very nice young man," Yamanu said.

Mey lifted a brow. "Who do you have in mind?"

"You don't know him, but he is Wendy's age."

The girl looked their way. "Are you talking about me?"

Jin nodded. "Yamanu wants to introduce you to a guy he knows."

Wendy blushed. "I don't want a boyfriend."

"Who said anything about a boyfriend? I was thinking about a boy who can be your friend. Vlad is one of the nicest guys I know, he is your age, and he could really use a friend as well."

"Why?" Wendy narrowed her eyes. "What's wrong with him?"

Yamanu shrugged. "He's a bit odd, but he is also very sweet. He attends college in the area, so it's not a problem for him to stop by."

Wendy seemed to warm to the idea. "What's his talent? Is he part of your organization?"

"He's a shrouder like me. Not nearly as powerful, but then he is still young. He might become stronger when he gets older."

That sounded like an awesome solution, provided that the kid wasn't some kind of a freak. For the match to work, Wendy needed to be attracted to him, and if he was odd-looking, or behaved strangely, that might not happen.

Before Yamanu made a big mistake and exposed the poor kid to unnecessary heartache, she needed to ask Arwel what he knew about Vlad.

Arwel

When Jin and he returned to her room, Arwel wanted to pick up where they'd left off before Mey had called, but Jin seemed troubled.

"What do you know about that kid?" she asked.

Arwel pulled her into his arms. "I really don't want to talk about Vlad now." He picked her up and carried her to the bed.

"Just tell me if he is really as nice as Yamanu claims. I worry about Wendy, and Yamanu also said that the kid was odd. In what way? And why is he lonely? Is he socially awkward? And is he good at keeping secrets? Because he will have to keep his immortality from Wendy."

Arwel put a finger on Jin's lips. "Slow down. I can only answer one question at a time. I don't know Vlad well, but those who do say that he has a heart of gold. The thing is, the kid looks like a vampire, and not the sexy

Hollywood kind. For some reason, his fangs are more pronounced in their resting state than those of other immortal males. On top of that, each of his eyes is a different color, he is about six feet four inches tall and skinny like a twig."

Jin's eyes softened. "Poor kid. College must be hell for him. How does he manage?"

"He wears black clothes, covers one eye with his bangs, and fronts the Goth rocker image. People assume that the teeth are glue-on, and the different colored eyes are contact lenses."

"Is he a rocker?"

Arwel nodded. "He plays bass guitar and has a good voice. But right now, he is missing the rest of his band. Jackson, who is the lead guitarist and vocalist, is busy running his sandwich and pastry empire, and Gordon, that's the drummer, is away at college. So that's why he is lonely."

Seeming satisfied with his answer, Jin smiled. "Two lonely hearts. It could work. But I thought that the plan was to bring in Guardians for the girls to choose from."

"It will have to wait. Jacki is coming with us to the Bay Area, and after what Edna said about Wendy, I don't think the girl is ready for a Guardian. None of them are young lads, and I think that Yamanu made a great choice with Vlad. I hope that the kid is not too shy to befriend a girl."

Jin lifted a brow. "Is he a virgin?"

"I don't know for sure, but I suspect that he is. What about Wendy?"

"I don't think so."

"She blushed when you told her about Yamanu's idea."

"So what? A lot of people blush when they are embarrassed. It doesn't mean a thing." Jin sighed. "I just want all three of them to move on, so they can leave this freaking underground and join the living. But I'm still trying to figure out how it's going to work. I understand that inducing Richard is not a problem because he only needs to fight one of your men. Maybe this can be done while Jacki is away? If it doesn't work, his memory of it can be erased, right? But if she is here, we will need to isolate Richard until he either transitions and moves into the village, or gets his memories wiped and you give him a new identity and send him somewhere safe."

"It's not that simple. If he bonds with an immortal female, we can be pretty sure of his loyalty. Without it, he could betray us even if he turns immortal. And after he turns, we won't be able to thrall him at all. That only affects humans."

"Then I really hope Richard and Ingrid fall in love. But if they don't, Kian should send more females down here. They can pretend to volunteer giving classes on this or that like Dalhu did."

"That's smart. We should suggest it to him. But first, let's give Ingrid a chance. She called dibs on Richard, and she'd be majorly pissed if he slipped through her fingers."

"True." Jin plopped back on the bed. "I wish that by the time we come back, Wendy and that kid are in love, and so are Richard and Ingrid. That would leave only Jacki to take care of."

Lying on his side next to Jin, Arwel brushed his fingertips over her cheek. "You are such a mother hen. You want to make sure that everyone is okay before you allow yourself to be happy. They are all adults, Jin, and they knew what they were getting into when they asked to join the escape. You are not responsible for them."

She threw her arm over her eyes. "I can't help it. That's how I'm wired."

He lifted her arm and dipped his head to kiss her lips. "For tonight, none of that matters. It's just you and me. Can you do that? Can you clear your mind of all the noise and concentrate on us?"

A smile tugging on one corner of her mouth, Jin shifted to her side. "I know how you can help me do that. When you make love to me, I can't think of anything at all, especially when I'm orgasming."

"I can definitely help with that."

Jin

All during breakfast, Jin tried to come up with something to say to her friends other than *Kian told me to do it*. To claim that tethering them was for their own safety would insult their intelligence. They were in an underground facility that no outsiders had access to, and they couldn't leave even if they wanted to because the elevator was programmed to prevent them from reaching the exit.

Tethering them was purely a spying device and a terrible invasion of privacy.

When she and Arwel returned to her room, he pulled her into his arms. "You were frowning all throughout breakfast, and you've barely said a word to me. Did I do something wrong last night?"

She chuckled. "You should know better than that. I lost count of the number of times I climaxed." She kissed him lightly. "You were amazing."

"So what's the bad mood about?"

"I don't want to tether my friends." Jin pulled out of his arms and walked over to the mini fridge. "Why can't Kian put trackers on them instead?" She took out a bottle of water.

Taking it out of her hand, he unscrewed the top as if she couldn't handle the task. Usually she didn't mind his over-the-top chivalry, but this morning it annoyed her.

Jin shook her head. She'd known the guy for a total of four days, and she was talking about usual. Except, it felt as if they'd been together for much longer. Maybe it had to do with how intense those four days had been.

Since the first time she'd seen Arwel, they hadn't been apart for more than an hour.

Or maybe it felt right simply because they belonged together, and that was why it seemed so natural, even easy, to be with Arwel. Two pieces of a whole finding each other and sticking together to form something better and stronger than the sum of its parts.

Talk about getting carried away.

"You've tethered them before." Arwel handed her the bottle. "So they shouldn't make too big of a fuss over it."

Jin rolled her eyes. He hadn't seen the resentful looks she'd gotten after tethering the other trainees. And that had been done only as an experiment, not because the director had wanted her to keep tabs on them.

The other problem was holding on to several tethers at once. It was a mental burden, and finding the right tether to follow wasn't easy. She'd had to concentrate hard to figure out which of her friends had been at the end of what string.

"They didn't make a fuss the first time, but it was a big deal." She took a sip from the water bottle. "The stinky eye looks they gave me are still fresh in my mind."

Arwel shook his head, but she didn't give him a chance to respond.

"Why should I have to tether them when they are right here? Especially since Kian wants them to know that they are tethered. I don't get the advantage of my metaphysical spying over that of a physical device attached to them in a way they can't remove. I'm sure your boy-genius William can come up with something."

"Do you want to talk to Kian?"

She wasn't looking forward to it and doubted she could convince him to change his mind, but it was worth a try.

"Can you call him and ask if he is willing to hear me out? I feel odd about calling him directly, especially since I will have to use your phone."

Arwel chuckled. "I get it. Whenever I want to talk to Kian, I prefer to text him first. With everything he has to do, the guy is so busy and short-tempered that it's better to let him answer at his convenience."

Pulling out his phone, Arwel typed up a short message and sent it.

As several long moments passed without a response, Jin concluded that Kian wasn't going to bother acknowledging her request. After all, she was a nobody, not even a member of his clan.

Not yet.

Or was she?

As Arwel's mate, she probably would have been granted membership. According to Mey, no official ceremony was needed to establish them as a couple, so what determined her status? Did Arwel have to make an official announcement?

Jin stifled a chuckle. He could use the one she'd come up with.

When Arwel's phone buzzed, she hoped it was Kian.

"Yeah, she is right here with me." Arwel handed it to her.

Taking a deep breath, Jin closed her eyes for a moment. "Hi, Kian. Thanks for calling back."

"Arwel said that you wanted to talk to me about tethering your friends. I assume that there is a problem?"

"It's not that I can't do it, but I don't think it's the best way to keep tabs on them. It's not like I follow that tether all of the time. That's impossible to do, especially when I have several attached. Besides, if they do something while I'm not watching, I wouldn't know about it. A physical tracker of some sort would do a much better job."

"I see your point. I'll have William put tracking cuffs on Richard and Wendy, but you still need to tether Jacki because she is going with you, and the cuff is not going to do us much good. You can also tell her that it's for her own safety while on the mission."

Jin exhaled a relieved breath. "Thank you. That's going to be much easier to explain and not as creepy. Also, I forgot to mention something about my talent when I was talking to you and Edna. It's really difficult for me to hold several tethers at once, and even more difficult to follow a particular one to the right person. I guess it's a cognitive load that gets heavier the more people I tether. I think it would be best to leave my mind as unencumbered as possible while I'm connected to Kalugal. Keep the connection uncluttered, so to speak."

Which meant that she would have to release Mey's tether. Most of the time, Jin didn't think of it or even feel it, but that was because she wasn't tethering anyone else at the moment, and the load was light.

"Absolutely. I didn't know that it burdens you like that. Did the program director know about it?"

"Yes. That was the purpose of the experiment. I tethered all of my teammates to test how many I could hold at once, and whether I could follow the tethers to the right people. After three, it got messy. The director told me that when I got an assignment, it would be to tether one person only, and that whenever possible, I would get notified when to follow it, like during important meetings."

"I'm starting to get a better picture of how it works," Kian said. "To know what your target is doing, you need to actively follow the string and listen and watch. You need to suspend whatever you are doing at that moment to concentrate on that."

"Correct."

"Then it's not a good tool to keep tabs on someone. It's only good for emergencies and for spying on people at particular times, not on an ongoing basis."

"That about sums it up."

"Let me think about what to do with Jacki. I'm not sure your tether is the right tool for keeping tabs on her either."

"You are right about it not being good for that, but I think I should tether her, especially when we go after Kalugal. If he messes with my mind and makes me see things, my tether to Jacki might help me see what's really there because she is immune to his mind tricks. Or at least we hope that she is. If he is as powerful as you say, he might be able to compel her as well."

Arwel

"You are good." Arwel took the phone from Jin and put it in his pocket. "Kian accepted your explanation without argument."

"I'm just as surprised as you are. Maybe I have some compulsion power too?"

"You just speak in a language he understands. Logic."

Jin sighed dramatically. "You have no idea how hard it is to find people who are fluent in it. Most have no clue."

"How about me?"

She pursed her lips. "You are an empath, so naturally, your thought process is influenced by your emotions and those of others. You are no Spock, that's for sure."

"And neither are you and Kian. You are both motivated by feelings, and doing the right thing is more important to you than doing the smart thing. Turner, on the other hand, is the most Spock-like person I've ever met. I can't remember if I've mentioned it before, but he is the strategic mastermind behind our most daring missions, and he's also Bridget's mate."

"I would like to meet him."

"You'll get your chance when you move into the village. Or maybe even before that. Turner's curiosity might bring him over here sooner."

"Is he curious about me, or is it my spying talent that interests him?

"Neither. I bet he wants to hear every detail about that facility and the people in charge of it."

"I'll tell him everything I know, but I'm afraid it's not much."

"Nevertheless, he'll want to know every little detail and store it in his big brain for later."

Jin finished the last of her water and tossed the empty bottle into the trashcan. "I need to tell Jacki about the tether."

"Do you want me to come with you?"

"Yes, please. You can back me up if she gets snappish."

Since it was no longer Kian who wanted Jacki tethered, Arwel wondered how he was supposed to do that. But if Jin needed him to come with her, he would.

They found Jacki in Mey and Yamanu's place, which had become the central hub for the dungeon inhabitants.

"I need to talk to you." Jin sat next to her friend on the couch.

Arching a brow, Jacki crossed her legs. "About?"

"Tethering you."

Arwel stifled a chuckle. Jin was no diplomat, that was for sure. She rivaled Kian in her no-nonsense, get-straight-to-the-point attitude.

Walking over to the dining table, he pulled out a chair and joined Yamanu. "This should be good," he said in a whisper inaudible to humans.

"I thought that you'd removed the tether." Jacki narrowed her eyes at Jin. "Did you put out a new one without telling me?"

Jin huffed. "Do you always jump to conclusions without hearing the explanation first?"

"Just say yes or no."

"No, I didn't tether you without your knowledge, but I want to explain why I think tethering you is a good idea." She glanced at the open door. "Can you please close it? I don't know how much I'm allowed to say around the others."

"It's better that they don't know too much about your target." Yamanu pulled out his phone and activated the door's mechanism.

When it clicked into place, Jin continued. "I don't have to do it now, but definitely before we go after that guy. Since you are immune to his mind tricks, I might be able to see the real him through your eyes."

Jacki shook her head. "I don't think so. He is not manipulating your eyesight. Your eyes see one thing, but your brain translates it into what he wants you to see. So even though your connection to me doesn't pass through your eyes, it still needs to enter your brain. Your brain will turn what you get from me into whatever Kalugal wants everyone to see."

That sounded logical, and given Yamanu's nodding, he thought so as well.

Mey, on the other hand, seemed to disagree. "Not necessarily. I'm not a neuroscientist, and maybe you should consult Amanda about it, but even as a layperson I know that the brain has many regions and processing centers. It's not straightforward like a computer. Kalugal might be affecting the visual and auditory perceptions, but the feed from the tether may rely on a different mechanism and get processed by a different region in the brain."

That made sense too.

Yamanu nodded proudly. "My lady is smart."

Jacki cast him an amused glance. "And you are not at all biased."

He shrugged. "I am. But I'm also right. You are smart too."

"Thank you." Jacki rewarded him with a happy smile.

It seemed important to her that other people regarded her as smart. Did she feel insecure because of her lack of a college education?

That was nonsense, of course. Should he mention that the formidable Kian had never received any formal education? And that neither he nor Yamanu had gone to school either?

Nah, that would open up a whole can of worms, with a lot of why questions he couldn't answer truthfully.

"So, what do you say? Are you okay with me tethering you?"

"On one condition." Jacki lifted a finger.

"Name it."

"You have to promise to remove it as soon as you tether Kalugal."

"Of course. I don't want to have you tied to me indefinitely. As much as I like you, that's a mental burden I can do without."

Jacki's lips twisted in a half-smile, half-grimace. "That didn't sound very friendly to me, but it will do."

Arwel cleared his throat. "Maybe you shouldn't remove the tether right away. Wait until we get back."

"I don't want Jin in my head for a moment longer than absolutely necessary. It's a creepy feeling. Would you like it if she tethered you?"

He hadn't thought about that before, but Jin having a tether to him might open up very interesting possibilities. When they were making love, she could see herself through his eyes.

Damn. Just thinking about it got him stiff as a baseball bat.

Shifting in his chair, Arwel affected an innocent expression. "I would love it. In fact, I'm going to insist on it."

"Really?" Jin regarded him with a frown. "You don't mind me seeing everything that you do?"

"I have no secrets from you." He pushed to his feet, walked over to her, and offered her a hand up. "Let's go to your place, and I'll explain the benefits."

His lady was smart, getting his meaning right away.

Letting him pull her up, she wrapped her arm around his middle and smiled at the others. "Excuse us, but Arwel and I have some private matters to discuss."

Mey stifled a giggle, Yamanu rubbed a hand over his jaw, and Jacki rolled her eyes.

"Will we see you two at lunch?" Mey asked.

Shrugging, Jin winked. "Maybe."

Kian

"Turner is already here." Anandur pulled into the restaurant's parking lot. "That's his Tesla." He pointed at the car.

"Did you memorize his license plate?" Kian asked. "Turner's black Tesla is a popular model."

Anandur turned the ignition off. "Did you forget that I followed him around after he'd asked you to turn him immortal?"

"I had assumed he'd gotten a new one since then."

"Nah. It's the same one."

Stepping out of the SUV, Kian glanced at his watch. "We are not late. He always gets to the meeting place first."

"That's because his office is less than a five-minute drive away from here. He doesn't have to deal with traffic."

What Anandur had hinted at was that Kian, as the head of the clan, shouldn't have to drive forty minutes to meet Turner. It should be the other way around.

There was something to that, but it wasn't about a power play. He and Turner were both super busy, but since it was Kian who needed a favor from Turner, it was only fair that he meet the guy where it was convenient for him.

"I'm just glad that the place has a good selection of excellent vegan dishes for me. I don't mind the drive."

As usual, they found Turner sitting in the restaurant's most private booth. It was close to the kitchen, which was the main downside, but it was also the farthest from the other tables and booths.

"Good afternoon." Kian slid into the bench across from Turner and offered him his hand. "Thanks for meeting me."

Anandur sat next to him and Brundar next to Turner, which was another habit they'd adopted. Turner didn't like to be crowded, which couldn't be helped with Anandur's bulk, but he was fine with Brundar sitting next to him. It had probably more to do with how quiet the guy was and how still he sat than with his slim build.

"I'm sorry I couldn't make it to the village for a lunch meeting. I'm in the middle of planning a complicated rescue mission, and I want to be done with the initial framework by the end of the day."

Kian unfurled the napkin and put it over his knees. "The downside to meeting here is that I can't smoke my cigarillos. The upside is the food. I need to bring Okidu here to sample them. Perhaps he can figure out what goes into the vegan dishes."

"I'll bring Callie here," Brundar offered. "She can analyze your favorites and write a recipe for Okidu."

"Thanks. That's a better idea." The task might be too complicated for Okidu.

Turner reached for the breadbasket, looked at it, and then pushed it toward Kian without taking anything. "What did you want to talk to me about?"

Kian lifted a slice of bread. "The other recruits. Those we've left behind."

Turner arched a brow. "I thought we decided to leave them be for now."

"My conscience is not letting me do that, especially the kids. I've been thinking about their families, and that they might be at risk too. What if those kids have siblings? Even if they don't manifest special abilities, the program's director might go after them as well. He might even go after the parents and test them to figure out the genetic combination that produced their special children. Given what Jin told me about the super-babies he was pushing for, that's not a farfetched scenario."

Turner leaned back. "They could do that to the families of the adults too. Do you want to rescue them all?"

It was a rhetorical question, but Kian nodded. "If I can."

Turner sighed. "That is not your job, Kian. Shit is happening all around the world that is much worse than this, and you can't do anything about it. You are already going above and beyond by fighting trafficking."

"This is different. These might be my people. The adults, the kids, and their families are all likely Dormants."

When the waitress arrived to take their orders, Turner seemed relieved to hit pause on the conversation. His opinion on the matter was clear, but despite his opposition to taking action, Kian needed the guy's big brain to come up with a creative idea for getting the rest of the recruits out of the program.

Once the waitress left, Turner shook his head. "Give it a rest, Kian. You don't want the government breathing down your neck. You can't ask for a worse enemy. The Doomers will seem like annoying mosquitoes next to the big gorilla that would come after you."

Raking his fingers through his hair, Kian sighed. "I know that. I was hoping that you could come up with a brilliant solution. So far, it seems that they are not making too much of a fuss over the missing talents, right?"

Turner nodded. "There is an APB on Richard. He is accused of kidnapping the three ladies, and photos are included. It's important for all four to stay in hiding or use good disguises when they venture out. Later, those who do not transition should consider either plastic surgery or moving out of the country."

"I've seen the APB. Roni showed it to me. Doesn't it strike you as odd, though, that that is the extent of it? Roni did some snooping around, and apparently there were no airport searches either."

The lack of serious pursuit only reinforced Kian's gut feeling that one of Jin's friends was a mole.

"I know what you're thinking," Turner said. "But there might be another explanation for why their escape didn't get more attention. The program is top secret, and they want to keep it that way. Making too much of a fuss about the four escapees might attract unwanted attention to what they are doing. Especially if some of it is not sanctioned by the higher-ups. I would be very surprised if the program for breeding super-babies had gotten official approval."

Kian snorted. "The government has done much worse in the past. Like exposing soldiers to toxic materials and later covering it up. I wouldn't put it past them to approve a fucking breeding program."

Turner's lips narrowed. "That was a long time ago. Things have changed."

Kian snorted. "Take it from someone who's been around for a very long time. The more things change, the more they stay the same. But if you are right, and the program's director or directors are not interested in anyone finding out what they are doing there, it gives us an advantage. We can snatch people with impunity. They will be more interested in keeping their activities secret than finding out who is stealing the paranormals and their families."

Reaching for a bread roll, Turner tore it in half. "I can assure you of one thing. After the escape, there will be no more outings for the recruits, not without them being implanted with serious tracking devices. And if they do get to go anywhere, it will be with a strong security detail."

That was regrettably true.

"I hoped that we could take them out sooner, but it seems like we will have to wait for the program to end and for the recruits to go home to their families. We can snatch them then."

Turner arched a brow. "What if they don't want to come? And what if they get a tail?"

"We can thrall the tail. I doubt they have immune snoops on staff, other than Eleanor, aka Marisol. And as to willingness, we will need to approach the families first and explain what's going on. If they don't believe us or prefer to ignore what we have to say, we can thrall them to forget about us or compel them to silence. If they agree, we can just compel them to silence to ensure their discretion."

"I see that you already have a plan of action. What do you need me for?"

That was another rhetorical question, but Kian answered it anyway. "I want you to point out all the pitfalls and suggest safeguards."

Turner nodded. "The most important thing is to avoid the government's notice. We need to come up with a decoy, or rather a scapegoat. Someone we can cast suspicion on that would divert attention from us."

"The Chinese," Anandur offered. "They wanted Jin and took whoever was with her."

Kian chuckled. "And then they decided to go back for the others?"

Anandur shrugged. "Why not? They are good at spotting opportunities and even better at stealing ideas from others."

"You might be onto something," Turner said. "The question is how to implicate the Chinese."

Grinning, Anandur spread his arms. "I provided the idea. It's your specialty to turn it into an actionable plan."

Jin

"That's awesome." Mey ended the call and grinned. "Eva is coming to teach you two how to put on your disguises, and she is bringing little Ethan with her." Mey danced a happy dance. "I'm so excited. I can't wait to hold him in my arms and kiss his soft little cheeks."

Jacki smiled. "Someone needs her baby fix."

Jin shook her head. "You and Yamanu should start working on it." She regretted the words as soon as they'd left her mouth. Damn, she really didn't know when to keep it shut.

Way to spoil Mey's good mood.

Her smile melting away, Mey cast Jin a reproachful look. "We need to get married first. You know how Mom and Dad are. They like things to happen in the right order."

The real reason for Mey's sad face was the low fertility rate immortals suffered from. She'd shared the information with Jin on one of the rare occasions that they'd been alone, but she'd also mentioned something about an elixir the other clan doctor had developed that was supposed to help with that. Mey would be miserable if she had to wait centuries to have a baby.

Glad that her sister had brought up wedding plans, Jin jumped at the opportunity to change the subject. "Speaking of nuptials, are you going to design your own wedding dress?"

That brought the smile back to Mey's face. "I have a couple of ideas, but I think I should have a professional work with them instead of doing the whole thing myself. I'm not confident enough in my skills yet."

"If you need someone to sew it, I know how," Jacki offered. "You can get some inexpensive fabric for a trial run or two. I'll need a sewing machine, though."

Jin and Mey exchanged glances. Jacki was full of surprises.

"Where did you learn how to sew, and why?"

Jacki shrugged. "One of my foster moms was creative. She made Halloween costumes for the kids from leftover fabric pieces and altered things that needed fixing."

"That's nice." Jin smirked. "I'm curious to see what Eva has in mind for our disguises. The other time she made me look so different, but I don't think I can pull that off on my own." She waved at Jacki. "You have it easy. A wig and glasses will do the trick."

Jacki shrugged. "The same is true for you. I don't think you should change your ethnicity. There are more than a billion Chinese people in the world. I'm sure many of them are tall. You just need to look a little different, that's all."

"I hear Ethan." Mey jumped up and rushed out into the corridor.

"Your sister must have bat ears," Jacki said. "I didn't hear a thing."

It seemed like Mey's hearing was improving by the day without her realizing it. She should be more careful to hide it from the other humans.

Jin scrambled for an explanation. "I think she has a baby radar."

As the sounds of Mey's baby talk and Ethan's cooing got closer, Jin got up and walked out into the corridor.

"Hi." She offered her hand to the mother, kissed the top of the baby's head, and waved at Bhathian, who was carrying Eva's big trunk.

Holding Ethan, Mey looked in love, and the baby responded with sweet smiles.

Eva shook Jin's hand. "Are you and Jacki ready for your transformation? Kian told me to do my best."

"Your best is not something that Jacki or I can do on our own. We need something just good enough."

"That's what I told Kian. He suggested that I go with you to the Bay Area, but I said that won't be necessary. I can teach you what to do."

"Awesome."

As they walked inside the apartment, Bhathian lowered the trunk to the floor and glanced around. "Where is Yamanu?"

"He is with Arwel in the gym," Mey said.

"I'm going to join them." He kissed his wife's cheek. "Do you want me to take Ethan?"

Mey hugged the baby closer to her chest. "He is perfectly fine with me. Go have fun with the guys."

"Okay." Smiling, he kissed his son's cheek as well. "Be a good boy, Ethan, and don't give Mey any trouble." He leaned closer and pretended to whisper in the baby's ear. "If you behave, she might decide to have a baby of her own, and you'll have someone to play with."

"God willing," Mey said. "I want one just like that. Well, almost. I want my baby to look like his daddy."

"Naturally." Bhathian patted her arm.

"Who goes first?" Eva asked.

"Me." Jacki lifted her hand. "Last time you gave me a makeover but not a changeover. I'm curious to see myself turning into someone else."

Eva pulled out a chair and put it in the middle of the living room. "Take a seat."

"Yes, ma'am."

Popping the lid of her trunk, Eva looked inside, moved a section over, and pulled out four different wigs. "Let's start with the hair. Since your magnificent blond mane is your most striking feature, that is going to be the biggest change."

After pinning Jacki's hair around her head and securing it with a net, Eva fitted her with a shoulder-length brown wig.

"How do I look?" Jacki asked.

She looked plainer and paler. "Twenty percent less sexy." Jin pursed her lips. "Make it twenty-five."

Jacki smiled. "Good. The less attention I attract, the better."

"Put these on." Eva handed her a pair of reading glasses. "Those are the special kind that fool facial recognition software."

"How about now?" Jacki asked.

"Another ten percent reduction in sexiness."

"Does it change me enough, though?" She turned to Mey. "Would you recognize me?"

"Yeah, I would, but only if I looked closely. But if you don't want to attract attention, you should wear a minimizer bra. That cleavage is like a magnet to male eyes."

Jacki looked down at her chest. "Tell me about it. Most guys don't even notice that I have blue eyes."

"About that." Eva pulled out a small box from her trunk. "Have you ever worn contact lenses?"

"Nope."

"These are brown colored. But you might be uncomfortable wearing them."

"I'll give it a try. I'd rather be uncomfortable than get caught."

"Is there anything else Jacki should do?" Jin glanced at the chest. "As drab as the wig makes her look, she is still pretty."

"We don't need to make her look ugly."

"I don't want to attract any attention," Jacki said. "And guys tend to ignore ugly chicks."

"I can do that with makeup." Eva hooked a finger under Jacki's chin and lifted her face. "Put the contacts in first. If you can tolerate them, you'll need less makeup."

Jacki opened the box and looked at the lenses. "What do I do?"

"First, you need to wash your hands. You don't want any dust getting in your eyes."

After several tries the contacts were in, and Jacki looked so different that Jin doubted anything else was needed. "How are you doing? Do you think you can tolerate them for a couple of hours?"

Jacki shrugged. "I can't even feel them. I guess my eyes are not that sensitive."

"That's good." Eva pulled out several jars of foundation from her trunk. "Let's make you look even drabber. I'm going for the grayish, sickly look."

"Awesome." Jacki rubbed her hands. "The uglier I look, the more invisible I become."

Arwel

"Hey, Bhathian, what's doing?" Yamanu called from the bench. "Are you in for some heavy lifting?"

The Guardian grinned. "I'm trying to cut down." He flexed a muscle, straining the seams of his T-shirt. "I keep running out of clothes that fit."

"Show off," Arwel murmured.

Bhathian was a mountain of muscle, and he worked hard for it, but he was also naturally predisposed to gain them faster and with less effort than most immortal males.

"I can spot you guys." He walked over to Yamanu's station.

Arwel could use help with spotting as well. The problem was the ease with which Bhathian could lift what he had to strain for. But those were petty thoughts, unbecoming of a Guardian. They each had their areas of strength, and Arwel had never been on a muscle squad.

"It's good that you came," Yamanu said. "I wanted to talk to you about Vlad. I don't know him well, but you had him in your sex education class together with Jackson and Gordon."

"That was years ago." Bhathian shook his head. "It's hard to believe that Jackson is happily mated and running a successful business of his own. He was such a know-it-all, a real ladies' man, which was what had gotten him in trouble. Someone got jealous of his success with the fairer sex, and that someone was probably Gordon, but he's never admitted it."

"What about Vlad?"

"Vlad is a pure soul. He would have never played such a nasty prank on a friend. Jackson could've been sentenced to whipping."

"Nah." Arwel sat up and reached for a towel. "Not without iron-clad proof. But still, Gordon should have been punished for causing all that brouhaha. Accusing a clan member of thralling a girl into having sex with him is a grave offense."

Bhathian chuckled. "I think Kian decided that suffering through the sex-ed class with me was punishment enough. I scared the living daylights out of those boys. After that, they knew to ask permission for every move they made."

"As it should be," Yamanu said. "But most young guys, whether human or immortal, have no idea how to do that. You should write an instruction manual. It would sell like crazy."

"No one would buy it." Bhathian took the bar from Yamanu and put it on the rack. "The other thing most young guys suffer from is thinking that they know better than their elders. Unless it's coming from the mouth of some idol, or influencer as they call them today, they won't listen to advice."

"We sound like a couple of old farts, bemoaning the shortcomings of a younger generation." Yamanu waved a dismissive hand. "But back to Vlad. I want to introduce him to Wendy. She is lonely. He is lonely. And they are about the same age. What do you think?"

Bhathian rubbed the back of his neck. "Vlad is painfully shy. He wouldn't know how to talk to a girl."

"Wendy seems shy too," Yamanu said.

Arwel dropped the towel on his thighs. "I think that they might work. Usually, I would have advised against putting two timid people together, but you are right about Vlad being the best candidate for Wendy. I can't think of any other male that won't scare her. She's so young."

"Wonder was nineteen when Anandur met her," Bhathian pointed out.

Arwel shook his head. "You can't compare Wonder to Wendy. Wonder entered stasis five thousand years ago. Back then, an eighteen-year-old woman was considered a grownup in every sense of the word. Most had a couple of kids by that age. Nowadays, eighteen is still a child."

Bhathian lifted a weight and started bicep curls. "I assume that you want me to ask the kid?"

Yamanu joined him next to the free weights. "You know him better than I do. He will feel less awkward if you do it."

"I doubt that he will agree, but I can ask."

"Is he that bad?" Yamanu moved the weight to his other hand. "The boy is nineteen, for Fates' sake. At his age, I'd already been active for years." He grimaced. "And had gotten into shitloads of trouble, so maybe Vlad is right about keeping it in his pants."

"I'm sure he is not happy about it," Arwel said. "Show me a nineteen-year-old who wants to be a virgin."

"The boy is a romantic." Bhathian put the weight back on the rack and lifted a heavier one. "He's not the type who would go for a casual hookup."

Yamanu snorted. "I'm a romantic too, but at that age... well, chasing women was a hobby. Hell, it was an obsession. I couldn't think about anything else."

"Is it the same for the lasses?" Bhathian asked. "As an empath, you have the advantage of knowing how they really feel. Do they get boy obsessed?"

"They sure do." Arwel smiled. "When we were setting a trap for Lokan in Georgetown, thoughts of sex were what I was picking up the most, from males and females alike."

"I'm glad I have a boy this time," Bhathian said. "I would have gone nuts if I had been around Nathalie when she was a teenage girl." His face saddened. "Don't get me wrong. My greatest regret is not being there for her when she was growing up. It's just that I know it would have been difficult."

"You didn't mind when Andrew went after her," Arwel pointed out.

"That's because she was a thirty-year-old woman by then, not a teenager. And Andrew is a standup guy. I couldn't have asked for a better son-in-law."

Arwel shrugged. "Same difference. If you trust your daughter and you like the guy she chooses, it shouldn't be a hardship. On the contrary. If I have a daughter, and if she finds a decent guy who is close to her age and who I approve of, I would be happy for her, even if she was still a teenager."

A knowing smirk lifted one corner of Bhathian's lips. "Let's have this talk again when you actually have a daughter, and she is the most precious person in the world to you. No guy will do for your princess. I'm willing to bet on it."

Arwel offered Bhathian his hand. "How much are we betting on it?"

"A hundred bucks." Bhathian clasped his hand. "Adjusted for inflation."

"Deal."

Jin

Undecided about what to take with her, Jin had spent the morning packing and unpacking her few belongings. In the end, she just stuffed everything into the duffle bag Arwel had given her and walked over to Mey's place.

"Are you done packing?" Mey asked.

Jin nodded. "I couldn't decide what to take, so I took everything."

"You're welcome to dive into my closet and take whatever you want."

"Thank you. But I don't need nice things. I need ugly ones, and that's what I'm short on."

Mey pulled her into a hug. "I'm going to miss you. I wish you weren't leaving so soon."

Jin hugged her back. "Thank you for agreeing to stay for a little bit longer. I hope this mission will be over quickly, and I'll return before you have to go back to the village."

Mey smiled. "I wish it was so, but I doubt it. Your target is careful and elusive, and the stakeout will probably be long. They usually are."

"Great." Jin plopped down on the couch. "What am I going to do with myself while the Guardians are trying to locate the *target*?" She smirked. "You sounded like such a pro when you said *target*, like a spy from the movies."

Ignoring her comment, Mey walked over to the media cabinet. "I have a going-away present for you." She opened it and pulled out a flat box.

Jin perked up. "Is that what I think it is?"

"If you think that it's a new laptop, then yes." Mey sat down next to her and handed her the box. "Instead of being bored, you can start working on that business proposal for Kian."

"Thank you." Jin leaned and kissed Mey's cheek. "You are the best. When did you get it? Did you sneak out of here without telling me?"

"I didn't, but Yamanu did."

"Where is he? I want to thank him too." Jin started carefully peeling the cellophane wrapping off. "This is such a nice box."

"He is in the gym, but he said he will be back before it is time for you to leave. He wants to say goodbye."

"What about Vlad? When is he bringing him over?"

"Tomorrow. I hope."

"Why? Doesn't he want to come?"

"He told Yamanu that he has a big project to finish, but Yamanu thinks that Vlad is stalling because he is scared of meeting Wendy."

"Her in particular, or any girl?"

"Any girl."

Jin nodded. "The poor kid has probably never dated before."

"Most likely."

"Maybe they can play William's game together. Wendy gave it another try yesterday, and she's been obsessed with it ever since. She says it's one of the best computer games she's ever played."

"That's a good idea. Maybe Yamanu and I can join them at the beginning, just until they warm to each other, and then leave them to play alone. I can prepare snacks, maybe even dinner."

"Sounds like a plan. Instead of a date, it would be a friendly get-together. That should be less scary for the dude."

Mey chuckled. "I feel like Yamanu and I are the den mother and father."

"Admit it. You are enjoying this." Jin opened the box and pulled out the shiny new laptop. "This is so nice."

"Yamanu also got me a present. But it hasn't arrived yet."

"Oh, yeah? What is it?"

"A tablet and a stylus to draw on it. I'm going to start working on the designs. I haven't done it in so long that I'm out of practice."

Jin hugged the laptop to her chest. "I've been thinking. Since my friends have no job prospects at the moment, maybe we can employ them in our business?"

"We don't have a business yet, and by the time we do, they will probably be doing something else already. Richard is going bonkers from having nothing to do."

"What about him and Ingrid?"

Mey shrugged. "I know just as much or as little as you do. She comes every day, and they hover around each other, but I don't know whether she's stayed the night yet or not."

"I'm sure she has. Ingrid doesn't strike me as the shy type, and I know that Richard is more than ready. The poor guy didn't get any for over a month."

"Right, well." Mey shifted. "That's not the end of the world."

"For us it isn't, but guys are different. I read somewhere that men think about sex constantly."

Mey regarded her with a frown. "Don't you crave Arwel all the time?"

"I do. But that doesn't mean that I'd go crazy if I didn't get him into bed every day."

"Interesting. I was the same way before I met Yamanu, but since then, I crave him quite obsessively. Apparently, it's part of the bond between immortal mates. I wonder why you don't feel the same way."

What was Mey suggesting?

If her sister was wondering whether Arwel was Jin's fated mate, then she wasn't the only one. Jin wasn't sure about it either. In her gut, she felt that he was, but they had just met, and it was too early to make such big decisions.

They liked each other a lot, the sex was phenomenal, and for now, it was enough. Love, commitment, and all that jazz would come later.

Still, it bugged her that Mey doubted their relationship. "Maybe the enhanced libido will come after I transition. Besides, I can talk a big talk, but I might be totally wrong. So far, Arwel and I have been making love at every opportunity, so I didn't have a chance to test my boasting about being able to do without."

Letting out a breath, Mey seemed relieved. "I hope it works out between you two. Arwel is an awesome guy."

"I agree." Tucking the laptop under her arm, Jin pushed to her feet. "I should check on Jacki and see if she needs anything."

"Does she have a suitcase? I can lend her mine," Mey offered.

"Thanks, but Arwel is getting her a bag." Jin leaned and kissed Mey's cheek. "Thank you again for this amazing present. You are the best sister ever."

Mey waved a hand. "Think of it as Yamanu's first investment in our business. That's how he convinced me not to pay him back for the laptop and the tablet."

Smart guy. He might have used it as a persuasion tactic, but Jin was going to take it seriously.

"Ask him for the receipts and write the expense down. That will make it official."

Mey nodded. "Good idea."

Arwel

Jacki's door was open when Arwel walked in with the duffle bag. He'd gotten it from one of the Guardians on rotation in the keep, but it hadn't been given without strings attached. The guy had jokingly conditioned lending it on an introduction to Jacki upon her return, and Arwel had gladly given it.

The sooner Jin's friends found mates, the sooner he could take her to the village and the new home he'd applied for.

He hadn't told Jin about it, first of all because he wanted to surprise her, and secondly, because he didn't want to freak her out by going too fast.

After all, they'd known each other for all of five days, and getting them a house was premature. Jin might think that he was taking her for granted and assuming things he shouldn't.

"Is this big enough?" He handed Jacki the bag.

She put it on the bed next to the small pile of clothes and other stuff. "I don't have much, so that's enough with room to spare."

A minute later, Jin walked in. "Is that all you are taking?" She looked at what Jacki had prepared. "Where is all of Amanda's fabulous stuff?"

"I'm saving it."

"What for?"

Jacki shrugged. "To sell it. I don't know how long I'm going to be stuck in here, or what my prospects are once I can leave. What I'll get for that designer stuff might help me start a new life."

Jin looked at Arwel with sad eyes.

He knew what she wanted, but he couldn't allow it. Until Jacki found an immortal male to bond with, she couldn't know that all of her troubles were most likely over.

"When are we leaving?" Jin asked.

"Kian sent his driver with the limousine. Okidu should be here in about half an hour." Arwel looked at Jacki and rubbed a hand over his jaw. "Once you are done packing and everything is ready, I will need to put you to sleep."

She nodded. "I figured that you would do that."

"Unfortunately, it's necessary," Jin said. "If Kalugal can force you to talk, he can get the location of this hideout from you. But if you don't know where it is, you can't tell him."

Jacki lifted her head and pinned Jin with a hard look. "It's even truer in your case. I'm immune. You are not."

"I'm going to sleep too."

Arwel arched a brow. That wasn't part of the plan. Jin already knew where the keep was.

"I don't understand why blindfolding us is not enough." Jacki started arranging her things in the duffle bag.

"Because we don't want Kalugal to know what city it is in, and since we are flying over to the Bay Area, you might figure it out by the time it takes us to get there."

Jacki looked at him. "Are you that scared of him?"

"He is a dangerous man."

"And yet you are okay with sending your girlfriend after him?"

Arwel pushed his hair back from his forehead. "I'm not okay with her getting anywhere near him, but that's just because I'm overprotective. Kalugal is dangerous to our organization in the sense that he might expose us. But as far as we know, he is not a violent man. He is not going to hurt Jin for just touching him."

"What if he can sense her motives? Maybe in addition to his other powers, he is also an empath?"

Areana hadn't said anything about that, but then the last time she saw her son, he was a little boy. In adulthood, Kalugal might have developed additional powers.

"We will have Guardians securing the perimeter. Worst case scenario, we will muscle Jin and you out."

Jacki snorted. "I was under the impression that Kalugal can compel people. He can tell them to stay away, and they will, including you. Since I'm the only one he can't do it to, I should have a weapon on me. Nonlethal, of course. I don't want to kill him or miss him and kill an innocent bystander. Maybe a taser? Or even mace?"

"That's actually not a bad idea. I'll have to run it by Kian."

That got a smile out of her. "I'm glad that you would trust me with a weapon. I'm sick of being treated like the enemy."

"I'm sorry that you feel that way, but we need to protect ourselves. You should have a pretty good idea about how many people are interested in paranormals and to what lengths they are willing to go to get us."

"I get it. Doesn't mean that I like it." She sat on the bed. "Give me the sleeping pill."

"Are you all done packing?"

She nodded.

"Anything other than the duffle bag that you want to take with you?"

"No, everything is in there, including my purse." She snorted. "That has lipstick and eyeliner in it. I don't have any money or even an identification card."

"Actually, you do." He pulled out an envelope from his back pocket and handed it to her.

Curiosity shining in her eyes, Jacki opened it and pulled out a driver's license. "Charlotte McNamara? Who came up with that name?"

"The guy who made these documents chose it from a list. I think that Charlotte is a nice name."

"I'm Debra Wang," Jin said. "That's not any better."

"It's okay." Jacki looked at the card. "When did you take that picture?"

"Do you remember when Mey was taking photos of your teammates? She took some of you as well. But if you look closely, it's not actually you. The artist created a composite from a stock photo and one of those that Mey snapped."

"Amazing." She reached into the envelope and pulled out a wad of cash and a credit card with the same name. "You guys are thorough. I'll give you that." She riffled through the money. "And generous. Thank you."

There were only three hundred bucks in there, but Jacki regarded the money as if it was a fortune.

Unzipping the duffle bag, she pulled out the purse, put everything he'd given her inside, and then zipped the bag closed. "Now, you can put me to sleep."

Reaching into his shirt pocket, Arwel pulled out a packet with two pills in it. "Julian said these will knock you out for at least six hours."

Jin handed Jacki a bottle of water. "You're gonna have a nice long nap on the plane."

Jin

After saying goodbye to her sister and friends, Jin and Arwel returned to Jacki's room together with Yamanu.

"Come on, sleeping beauty." Yamanu snaked his arms under Jacki and lifted her gently.

Jin appreciated him handling her friend with such care, but she wasn't sure Mey would have approved. "I'm glad Mey stayed in your room. She would have been jealous."

"Nah, my mate knows that I'm hers one hundred percent."

Mey might know it logically, but seeing a beautiful woman in her boyfriend's arms would provoke an instinctive response, especially since he was cradling her like a sleeping princess.

Arwel took Jacki's duffle and added it to the two he was already carrying.

"Give me that." Jin reached for the bag. "You don't have to be such a macho man."

He shook his head. "That's nothing for me. Just make sure that Yamanu doesn't bang Jacki's head into something."

Yamanu cast him a haughty look. "She is perfectly safe in my care. I wouldn't let anything happen to her."

Arwel called the elevator down, and the three of them walked in. "You should at least blindfold me," Jin said. "I feel bad about telling Jacki that I would be asleep too and not doing it."

"What's the point? You already know where the keep is."

"All I know is that it's in Los Angeles. I was half asleep when we got here, and it was dark. I have no idea where in the city we are."

Arwel shook his head. "I trust you. Closing your eyes will have the same effect."

Yamanu's shoulders heaved with suppressed laughter.

"What's so funny?" Arwel asked.

"Your lady asks for a blindfold, and you say no? Shame on you."

Arwel's brows shot up.

Jin shook her head. "You have a dirty mind, Yamanu, but I like the way you think."

The elevator doors opened, and Yamanu walked out first, with Jin and Arwel following several steps behind him.

Arwel leaned close to her ear. "If you want to play kinky games, I'm all for it, just not in company."

It hadn't been Jin's intention, but now that Yamanu had brought it up, the thought excited her. Mindful of the immortals' excellent hearing, Jin brought her mouth close to Arwel's ear and covered it with her hand for good measure. "Jacki is asleep, and she is not going to wake up for a long time. And since we are riding in a limousine, we can raise the partition so the driver can't see what we are doing."

The more Jin talked about it, the more turned on she got. There was something very exciting about the idea of sitting blindfolded in the limo while Arwel did all kinds of naughty things to her.

Where had that come from?

Jin had never played games like that, or even fantasized about them.

"I wish," Arwel whispered back. "But three additional Guardians are waiting for us in the limousine, and if you keep broadcasting pheromones like that, it's going to be a very awkward ride."

Talk about a cold shower.

"I thought they were going to meet us at the airstrip."

"That was the plan. They were supposed to share a ride with Magnus and Vivian, but the guys couldn't wait to see Jacki." He snorted. "All the bachelors wanted to be chosen for the mission. The chief had them draw straws to determine the three lucky ones."

Yamanu stopped in front of a door that was marked as storage and looked over his shoulder at Arwel. "Can you get it?"

Arwel punched in the code, and after they walked in, he closed the door behind them and opened the one on the other side.

A long tunnel stretched in front of them.

"Where is the limo waiting for us?" Jin asked.

"The tunnel leads to the lowest parking level at the building across the street. It's a safety precaution."

"I assume that it also belongs to the clan?"

"Kian built most of the high rises on this street." Arwel glanced at Yamanu. "Are you sure you don't want to use the golf cart? I can jog over and bring it."

"I don't want to wait. It's just a short walk."

The tunnel was wide enough for a car to pass through it, and it had dim lights spaced out every twenty feet or so, but it still made Jin uneasy. The echoes of their footsteps and their conversation, together with the long shadows they were casting on the concrete floor, reminded her of scenes from a horror film.

When they finally got to the end of the tunnel, there was another storage room with doors on both sides, and when Arwel opened the last one, Jin let out a relieved sigh.

"Thank God that's over. I really don't like tunnels."

The limousine was parked right next to the door, and the moment they exited, both the driver and the passenger's door opened at the same time.

A big guy jumped out from the passenger side. "Hello, I'm Duncan." He offered his hand to Jin, shook it briefly, and then turned to Yamanu. "Let me relieve you of your beautiful cargo."

As he took Jacki into his arms and brought her close against his chest, Jin cringed. If her friend was awake, she would not like that.

Very carefully, Duncan folded himself into the limo with Jacki.

Kian's butler bowed to Arwel. "May I take the luggage, sir?"

Arwel handed him the bags and followed Jin into the limousine.

Inside, two more Guardians were looking at Jacki like a pair of hungry wolves, their eyes blazing inner light. Duncan, who was holding her and grinning as if he had just won the lottery, didn't look like he was about to part with his prize anytime soon.

"Hello." Jin leaned forward. "I'm Jin. Mey's sister."

"Nice to meet you. I'm Gregor." The one on the right offered his hand.

The one on the left leaned forward and shook her hand as well. "Ewan. A pleasure to make your acquaintance, ma'am."

"Same here. Duncan, do you mind putting Jacki down on the seat? I don't think she would appreciate being held by a stranger."

The shocked expression on the guy's face was comical. He hugged Jacki even closer to his chest, then sighed and motioned for his two friends to move over. "Jin is right."

Carefully, as if he was handling a Jacki-sized china doll, he put her down and then sat on the floor next to her.

Jin stifled a chuckle. "There is plenty of room. You don't need to sit on the floor."

He shook his head. "It's not safe for her. Jacki is still human, and she could get hurt if we get into an accident. If anything happens, I'll catch her."

Arwel shook his head. "You three better start practicing pretending to be humans. Jacki thinks we are an organization of people with paranormal talents, and it's important that she keep thinking that until she finds a mate."

Duncan smirked. "She doesn't have to look far. I'm right here."

"Hey," Ewan protested. "I'm here too. She's asleep, so it's not like she has chosen you."

"We each get a shot," Gregor said.

"May the best man win," Duncan agreed, but given his grin, he'd already assumed the win.

Oh, boy. Jacki was in for a big surprise when she woke up.

"Goldilocks and the three big bears," Jin murmured.

Arwel

"That's the house?" Jin gawked as Arwel pulled the rented van into the driveway. "It's a freaking mansion." She glanced at her sleeping friend. "Jacki is going to flip out when she sees it."

Julian had been right about the two little pills knocking Jacki out. She hadn't stirred once, not when they put her in the limo, not when Ewan had carried her into the clan's aircraft, and not when Gregor had carried her out and into the van.

The upside of Jacki passing the entire trip sleeping had been that no one needed to pretend to be human, and Vivian had told Jin about her and Ella's adventures and how they had ended up with the clan.

Listening to her tell the story, Arwel couldn't help thinking that Ella and her mother were very gracious about forgiving Lokan for what he had planned for them.

Jin had been appalled, calling him a self-centered jerk with little regard for others. She was convinced that Lokan's selfish interest was the only reason he'd helped Kian get her and her friends out of the program. He wanted to find out what his brother was up to, and Jin was the only one who could do that for him.

Arwel had to agree. Kian and Lokan cooperated because it benefitted them both, not because they liked each other, and not because they were cousins.

"It's easy to get used to luxury," Vivian said. "Magnus and I have been pretending to be rich for a couple of weeks, and I can't say that I didn't enjoy it." She sighed. "I miss my home, though. It was hard to get on the plane and leave my kids behind again. But I owe Kian, and he needs Magnus and me to go on keeping up appearances."

Michael opened the front door. "Do you need help carrying things inside?"

"We've got it covered." Ewan got out of the van.

Without verbally agreeing on it, everyone knew that it was Duncan's turn to carry Jacki again, while the others took care of the luggage.

"Welcome to Chateau Kri." The Guardian spread her arms and turned in a circle. "What do you think?"

"It's impressive." Jin looked at the high ceiling with the exposed wooden beams crisscrossing it. "Are those real?"

Kri shook her head. "It's not structural, if that's what you're asking. It's just a decoration, but the wood is real." She smiled and offered Jin her hand. "I'm Kri." She waved her hand at Michael. "And this is my mate, Michael."

"Nice to meet you." Jin appraised Kri from top to bottom and up again. "You are the perfect customer for the fashion line my sister and I want to launch. Have you ever considered modeling?"

Kri's jaw dropped, and then she started laughing. "Do I look like a model to you?"

"Why not? You are tall and pretty. Our fashion line is going to be for tall women who can't find flattering stuff in department stores."

Kri shrugged her leather jacket off and flexed her biceps. "Do you still think I can model for you?"

"Sure. You'll be perfect for the sports line." Jin didn't sound as sure as she pretended to be, but it was a good save.

"In that case, count me in." Kri smiled happily. "I mean, as much as I can. I work full time as a Guardian, and I volunteer many hours a week teaching girls self-defense."

Jin put her hand over her heart and tipped an invisible hat to Kri. "That's so incredibly admirable."

The Guardian waved a dismissive hand. "It's nothing. I'm good at just one thing, so I make the most of it." She glanced at Duncan, who was still standing with Jacki in his arms. "Let me show you to her bedroom. Follow me." She started walking toward the stairs and then stopped and turned around. "In fact, you can all come, and I'll show you your rooms."

As they all headed for the grand staircase, William walked in. "Hello, everyone. How was your trip?" He looked at Jacki and then lifted his head to Duncan. "Has she been asleep the entire time?"

"Yes," Arwel answered for the Guardian. "Are you done securing the property?"

"I installed the disrupters and they are already working, so everyone can talk freely without fear of being overheard." He looked at Jacki again. "As much as it's possible with our guest."

"Come on," Kri beckoned. "You can go over the security protocol later. Let's get everyone settled first."

When they got to the second-floor hallway, Kri opened the door to what looked like a little girl's room. "You can put Jacki on the bed. Don't blame me for the decor because it was like that when we got here. I tried to make it look more grown up with the bedding."

"Jacki won't mind." Jin walked over to the bed and folded the comforter. "Put her down, Duncan. I'll tuck her in."

Reluctantly, he let go of his cargo.

"Let's keep moving," Kri said once Jin was done taking Jacki's shoes off and covering her with the blanket. "The master bedroom is next."

The Guardian opened the double doors to a big room with a massive king-sized bed. "This is where the three of you are going to stay." She waved at the men.

Jin frowned. "Shouldn't Vivian and Magnus take the master?"

Kri opened the French doors, showing everyone the balcony, and then closed them. "This is the stakeout room. And since it should be accessible at all times, I figured that it would be best for the bachelors to stay in it." She winked at Vivian.

That made sense, but only if there weren't enough bedrooms in the house. They could leave the master unoccupied and use it only for observation.

"How many bedrooms are there?" Arwel asked.

"Six," Vivian said.

The house looked larger. Arwel made a quick calculation in his head. There were three couples and five bachelors. The three Guardians would have to stay in the master bedroom.

Apparently, Gregor had just arrived at the same conclusion. "We can't all sleep in one bed."

"Two in the bed, and one on the couch." Kri chuckled. "Unless one of you prefers to sleep in the bathtub to sharing a bed with a friend. Or, you can run tomorrow to a store and buy an inflatable mattress." She kept on walking. "This is Vivian and Magnus's room. Luckily for us, all the secondary bedrooms have queen-sized beds."

"Lucky indeed." Vivian stepped inside. "This is lovely. And the bedding looks very nice. Thank you, Kri."

"You are welcome."

"When did you and Michael have time to do all this prep work?" Jin asked. "Arwel told me that you got the keys yesterday evening."

"There wasn't that much to be done, and we hustled. We got bedding, towels, food, and some pantry stuff. Whatever is missing, we can get tomorrow."

As Kri assigned the fifth bedroom to Jin and him, Arwel looked out into the corridor, where William was patiently waiting for the tour to be over.

"What about you? Where are you sleeping?"

"The maid's room downstairs. I've set up my command post in the home office, and the maid's room is the closest to it."

Jin

Jin sat on her friend's bed and put her hand on her shoulder. "Come on, Jacki, wake up. It's been five and a half hours since you took the sleeping pills." When that didn't help, she added, "It's dinner time."

Jacki's eyes popped open. "I'm starving."

"I thought so. The last meal you had was breakfast."

Throwing off the comforter, Jacki looked at the room. "Someone likes pink."

"This must have been the daughter's room."

"I don't really mind. I need to use the bathroom."

"It's over there." Jin pointed.

Five minutes later, Jacki was ready, and they headed out.

"This is one hell of a place. It's like a freaking palace." Jacki put her hand on the curving banister. "I've never been in a house like this. This alone was worth the headache." She rubbed her temple. "I don't know how people can take sleeping pills every night. I feel so groggy."

Jin wrapped her arm around Jacki's shoulders. "Did you have nice dreams?"

"If I did, I don't remember. Why are you smiling like that?"

Jin leaned to whisper in her ear. "Three hunky guys were fighting over the right to carry you from place to place, and William is here too. So, from Goldilocks and the three burly bears, the cast expanded to four."

Jacki grimaced. "Yay me. Can you get me a fly swatter? Or better yet, a bear spray?"

"Wait until you see them and then ask me. Come on, I promised Vivian that we will help her make dinner."

"Who is Vivian?"

"Ella's mother. She's very nice."

"Oh, right. She donated some of the clothes for Wendy."

"Yeah, that's the one."

"Where is everyone?" Jacki asked as they passed the family room.

"The three bears are upstairs, setting up the stakeout room. They brought an old-fashioned, non-electronic scope."

"Much good it is going to do them at night."

"Yeah. I don't know what they are going to do about that. Maybe they just want to collect the license plate numbers. Anyway, Arwel and William are in the home office, where William has set up shop. And Kri and Michael are in the home gym."

"Are they nice?"

"I didn't get to talk to Michael much, but Kri is awesome." Jin smiled. "She is as tall as I am, but her shoulders are twice as big as mine. The girl is a serious bodybuilder."

In the kitchen, they found Vivian standing next to a big pot of pasta sauce.

"Hello, Jacki." She smiled. "I'm Vivian. Ella's mom."

Jacki walked up to the petite woman. "You look more like her sister than her mom."

"Thank you. I was eighteen when I had Ella."

"Still, good for you. You must be taking good care of yourself."

"I try." Vivian looked at the pot and grimaced. "I don't know how to cook for so many people. Can you taste this and tell me if it's any good?" She handed Jacki the stirring spoon.

Scooping some on her finger, Jacki tasted the sauce. "It needs some spicing up. I'll tell you what. I'll take over the pasta and you two chop vegetables for the salad."

"Thank you." Looking grateful, Vivian took the mittens off and handed them to Jacki.

Turned out that Jacki knew her way around a kitchen. Bossing them around like a military chef, she managed to produce a big meal with something for everyone.

"Where did you learn to cook like that?" Jin asked as they carried the stuff to the dining room.

"Did you forget that I was a foster kid? Usually, the foster parents took in as many kids as they could get because it was good money. We all had our chores, and that included kitchen duty. I've always cooked for many people."

"Thank you for saving the day," Vivian said. "I'm going to call everyone to the table."

She started walking away.

"Don't go. I'll do that," Jacki said. "Yo! Everyone! Dinner is ready!"

Vivian clapped her hands over her ears. "Did you also serve as a drill sergeant in the military?"

Jacki chuckled. "My skills were honed at the foster homes."

"How many have you been in?" Jin asked.

"A few. It's a common thing to switch homes." Jacki's expression closed up, indicating that the topic was no longer open for discussion.

Grabbing a serving tray, she headed to the dining room. Exchanging glances, Vivian and Jin each grabbed something and followed her out of the kitchen.

William, Magnus, and Arwel were already there, with Gregor and Ewan arriving a moment later. Kri and Michael were the last.

"Where is Duncan?" Jin asked.

"It's his turn on watch." Gregor walked up to Jacki. "I'm Gregor. It's a pleasure to meet you."

"Yeah, same here." She offered him her hand.

He lifted it up to his lips and kissed the back of it.

Jacki pulled it out of his grasp. "Let's do the introductions while we eat. I don't want the food to get cold. Who is bringing a plate for the guy upstairs?"

"I'll do it." Ewan, who looked disappointed at missing his chance to kiss Jacki's hand, lifted a plate and started loading it with food. "I'll need two. One will not be enough for Duncan."

Jacki shook her head. "Take him this one, and once you are done eating, switch places with him so he can eat his second serving with everyone."

"Yes, ma'am." Ewan saluted.

As Jin watched Jacki take over and boss everyone around, it occurred to her that she didn't know her friend as well as she thought she did. This was a whole new facet of her that she hadn't seen before.

Jacki was assertive, but in the program, she had never demonstrated any aspirations towards leadership and had been happy to hang back and watch the others. It seemed, though, that she was a natural at it.

Who knew?

Arwel

"That was excellent." Ewan put his fork down and looked at Jacki. "Thank you to all the cooks."

"You're welcome. Are you going to switch places with Duncan now?"

"Yes, ma'am."

"Thank you." Jacki rewarded him with a smile. "And because you are so nice, I'll bring you coffee and dessert upstairs."

Ewan looked as if he'd just won the lottery. "That would be much appreciated."

Watching the guys compete for Jacki's attention was better than any reality show on the dumb box. So far, the Guardians and William were all acting quite gentlemanly, but that was because she wasn't showing interest in any of them. Once she picked a favorite, the competition could get vicious.

The question was, why wasn't she responding to any of them?

All four men were good-looking, each in his own way. William could still lose some weight and get in shape, but what he lacked in big muscles he compensated for with big brains.

Jacki wasn't into women either. If she were, Amanda and Carol would have gotten some reaction from her, but they hadn't. So that wasn't the issue either.

Perhaps she just wasn't sexual, and what a waste that would be.

Jacki was a knockout, the typical all-American girl, with long blond hair, blue eyes, and a tall, curvy figure that was just right.

Duncan walked into the dining room and sat in the chair that Ewan had vacated. "I saw someone leave the mansion in a fancy-ass car. I got excited, thinking I was going to spot Kalugal, but it was someone else." He turned to Jacki and flashed her his most charming smile. "Hi, I'm Duncan."

"Nice to meet you." She smiled but didn't put her utensils down. Probably to forestall any ideas he might have about kissing her hand. "I don't get how you could see inside the car. Was the light on?"

"It was a Ferrari convertible. I could see the driver perfectly." Duncan started loading a plate. "That's one hell of an expensive car. I wonder if Kalugal lets his men borrow his toys, because I doubt that anyone else has one."

"Maybe they are all loaded," Gregor said. "And since they don't have housing expenses, they can afford fancy-ass cars."

"We don't pay rent either." Duncan scooped up spaghetti on his fork. "Do any of us drive a three-hundred-thousand-dollar car?"

As Arwel nudged his foot under the table, the guy arched a brow. "What?"

Idiot. He shouldn't be talking about having no rent expense. Jacki might ask how come, and then they would have to make up a story.

"We could if we wanted to." Gregor crossed his arms over his chest.

Jacki frowned. "How much are you guys getting paid that you can afford a luxury like that?"

"Not that much," Arwel jumped in before the guys could blurt out more incriminating details. "Gregor is talking hypothetically."

"Did you write down the license plate?" William asked.

"Naturally."

"Text it to me. I want to check something."

Duncan pulled out his phone. "It's done."

"If I ever buy a fancy car, it's going to be a Lamborghini. Those are damn sexy." Duncan looked at Jacki, but she didn't react.

Apparently, fancy cars were not her thing.

While the other Guardians kept the discussion going about which car was best, William got busy texting.

"What is it?" Arwel asked.

"I have a hunch that I want Roni to check up on. I'm having him run the license plate through a program we designed. It's comparing the footage from the parking lots of restaurants, cafés, and bars in the area. Once he gets a match. I want him to look at the feed from inside the place that the car is parked next to."

Several moments and texts later, William grinned. "Bingo. Just as I thought. It was him."

Arwel leaned forward. "Kalugal?"

"The program found the car parked in the valet parking lot of Dorothea's, and Roni identified Kalugal on the feed coming from inside the restaurant."

"Did one of his men drive over to pick him up?" Vivian asked.

"No. He was the dude behind the wheel. Apparently, he doesn't leave the house without shrouding himself, and that was what Duncan saw. Except, his shroud only works on brains, it doesn't work on equipment."

Magnus waved a hand. "Then we should take snapshots of everyone leaving that house."

"That won't be enough," William said. "Apparently, his shroud extends over a large area. It can't fool the camera, but it can fool the observers, unless they are too far away from him to be affected. Because we are within Kalugal's range of mind manipulation, we will see what he wants us to see even when looking at a snapshot. The effect will be lost when he gets far enough, but by then we would have lost his trail anyway. The only thing that will work is sending the picture to Roni right away, and him telling us who's really in the car. Besides, at night, we won't be able to see the driver inside the vehicle, and Roni will need to locate him for us like he did just now.

Jacki rubbed her temples. "This is all so complicated and bizarre that following your logic brought my headache back. Perhaps I should be the one watching the gate. He can't fool me because I am immune to his tricks."

"Right, I forgot about that." William pushed his glasses up his nose. "You can look at the photos taken during daylight."

"What about clubs?" Jacki asked. "He is a young guy, right? Is he single?"

"He is." William put the phone on the table. "But we haven't caught him in a club yet. Actually, this is only the second time that we've gotten him on camera at all, which is odd. He must leave the house more often than that."

"Maybe he has a tunnel leading out somewhere else," Jin suggested.

She was probably thinking about the keep and the tunnel leading to the building across the street.

Arwel took her hand and gave it a little squeeze, reminding her not to say anything about it in front of Jacki. "That's possible, but Kalugal doesn't need it. He is confident that his shrouds are camouflaging his comings and goings."

"Maybe he goes to clubs that you are not monitoring," Jacki suggested. "He might be partying in San Francisco, and if he is, then you are screwed because there are probably hundreds of them."

"Or he takes care of the camera feed." William took his phone and started texting. "I'll ask Roni to watch the feed and see if it disappears at some point. Kalugal might erase it before he leaves the place."

"Why does he go to so much trouble to hide?" Jacki asked. "And why is he so important to your organization?"

Anticipating the questions, Arwel had prepared the answers. "He uses the shrouding to get inside information about stocks. And it's crucial for him to keep his identity hidden or he'd get caught. He also might pose a threat to our organization. We would rather have him as an ally than a foe, but we need to find out the extent of his illegal activity."

Leaning back, Jacki crossed her arms over her chest and narrowed her eyes at Arwel. "I don't buy your explanation, and frankly, I don't care what your real reason is. Just tell me one thing. Are you planning on killing him?"

"No."

"You sure about that?"

"Positive."

"How so? Because you are the good guys?" Her tone was mocking.

"We are, and also because he is Kian's cousin, and Kian's mother would be majorly pissed if we killed her nephew."

Arwel figured the information would be meaningless to Jacki, but because it was the truth, it would sound convincing.

Her eyes widened. "But if he is family, why doesn't Kian just call him and talk to him?"

"Kalugal doesn't know that Kian is his cousin. In fact, he doesn't know anything about his mother's side of the family because he hasn't seen her since he was a boy."

Jacki's eyes softened. "Are his parents divorced?"

"Worse. His father is a dangerous man, and Kalugal is hiding from him." As Jin kicked Arwel under the table, he put his hand over hers and gave it a little squeeze, reassuring her that it was okay before continuing. "That's another reason he is so careful. He probably fears his father more than the authorities and definitely more than us."

Naturally, that answer prompted Jacki to ask more questions. "Why? What would his father do to him if he finds him?"

Jin pulled her hand out of Arwel's clasp. "Force Kalugal to come home and join his crime syndicate," she said. "Or kill him." She pushed to her feet. "I'm ready for coffee and dessert. Are you coming to help me?"

"Yeah." Jacki got up. "Let's divide the chores. The guys can clear the table and load the dishwasher while we take care of the coffee and cake."

"There is a cake?" Kri asked. "Because Michael and I didn't buy any. We only got cookies."

"Cookies will do," Jacki said.

Jin

Jin sat down on the bed and crossed her arms over her chest. "Kian said that this was supposed to be top secret, and yet you just blurted it to Jacki. What's the deal with that? And you also promised to tell me more about Annani and Areana and never did."

She hadn't wanted to ask him in front of Jacki because Arwel would have given her a censored version, and the truth was probably fascinating.

He sat next to her on the bed. "It's a long story, and it doesn't really matter. Kalugal and Kian could be enemies or allies, depending on Kalugal's agenda. Even Lokan doesn't know the guy, and he is his full-blood brother."

After kicking her shoes off, Jin swung her legs onto the bed and pushed up against the headboard. "We have time. Tell me the whole story."

He followed her, wrapping his arm around her middle. "I would rather spend the time doing something else."

Jin wanted that too, but later. Right now, her curiosity had been whetted and she wanted to hear about the two sister goddesses. "Tell me an abbreviated version. Or is it a story I'm not supposed to know?"

"Frankly, I'm not sure." Snaking his hand under her shirt, he drew small circles on her belly. "Kian said that you shouldn't be told too much, not because he didn't trust you, but because there is a slight chance that Kalugal could capture you. He could get any information out of you."

"But he can do that to anyone, right?"

Arwel nodded. "Except for Jacki, but she doesn't know anything. You and she are the only ones who will get close to him, and if he is also a strong empath, he might feel your anxiety or your intention to attach a tether to him. It's very unlikely, but it's always better to err on the side of caution."

"So, tell me only the things that Kalugal already knows."

"I can't. He will wonder how you found out. You already know too much because Kian didn't think it through when he told you Kalugal's background. If he compels you to tell him everything you know, he might realize the clan's weaknesses and how to exploit them."

When the hand that had been drawing lazy circles around her belly button inched higher, it became harder to think.

"You are distracting me."

He smirked. "Do you want me to take my hand away?"

"No. Keep going but keep talking too."

"You think I can?" He cupped her breast over her bra.

"Give it a try. We can call it the focus and endurance test."

"Are you challenging me?" He tweaked her nipple.

"Yes. Let's see who can keep up a coherent conversation longer." She wasn't sure who was going to win that game, but even though it was going to be torturous, it would be fun to try. It was a challenge, and Jin loved pushing herself to the limit.

Besides, she was a spy in training, and spies should be able to extract information from their targets even during sex. Heck, especially then.

Oh, damn. Now she really had to win.

"Any rules?" Arwel pushed her shirt up and the bra cups down, and then dipped his head to lick her nipple.

Jin shut her eyes. He wasn't going to make it easy on her. But then she was planning on doing the same to him.

"No rules. Anything goes."

"Oh, lass, you should never say that to a guy."

He nipped her nipple, sending a zing of pain straight into her core, the tiny current turning the dial on her burner from simmer to high.

"I trust you."

Raking her fingers through Arwel's long hair, Jin was glad that Amanda had only trimmed it a little instead of giving him a full haircut. Fisting his silky hair, she held him to her breast.

He lifted a pair of glowing eyes to her. "That means a lot to me."

The adoration in his gaze was enough to melt her resolve, but she wasn't going to let him distract her. "That look is not going to work. Start talking."

He looked at her breasts with longing. "I can't talk and kiss these at the same time."

"Yes, you can. Alternate."

"Okay." He sucked on her other nipple, then let it go and cupped both breasts. "Annani and Areana are half-sisters. They shared a father but had different mothers. In the gods' culture, that wasn't considered a close blood relation. A half-brother and a half-sister who shared only a father could mate."

"Gross," Jin murmured.

"Yeah, I agree. According to their beliefs, the hereditary material passed through the mother, not the father, but we know it's not entirely true. It seems that the immortality gene passes through the mother, but paranormal talents can pass through the father as well. Lokan and Kalugal are proof of that. They inherited their powers from Navuh."

"Can't you check it? I'm sure that the clan doctor could examine the goddess's blood."

"Even if Annani allowed it, which I don't think she would, we don't have Areana's blood to compare, and we can't get it."

"Do they look alike?"

"Not at all. Annani is a tiny redhead with a strong and fiery personality to match that wild hair of hers. Areana is a tall blonde, who is mellow and timid and so lacking in power that she is supposedly weaker than most immortals."

"So, maybe they were right about the genetics. Heck, one of Kian's single sisters could marry Kalugal and bring peace to the two factions like they used to do in the olden days. They are only second cousins, and that's not a problem genetically even for humans. Second cousins marrying each other is common in many cultures."

Arwel

"Not a bad idea, but I doubt that Sari or Alena would be game for that, and not because Kalugal is a second cousin. He is an ex-Doomer of questionable morality, and even though he is of even purer blood than they are, Annani's daughters would look down on him."

Jin frowned. "What about Amanda? You told me that Dalhu is an ex-Doomer too, and that he was just a lowly commander."

"That's different. The Fates brought those two together. They were destined for each other. No one wanted Dalhu to be Amanda's mate, not even Amanda. She went away for a while, hoping she could get over him, but the pull to come back was too strong. Fated mates can't stay away from each other."

All that talk about the goddesses and their children had distracted them from getting on with the business of making love, and Arwel wasn't happy about it. Apparently, they had both failed at the focus test, but not in the way they'd thought they would.

Instead of necking, they were talking.

Staring into his eyes, Jin caressed his cheek. "Mey says that the pull is very strong. But since we've been together from the moment we met, we haven't had a chance to test it."

"I don't want to test it. I want to be with you always."

"That's sweet, but after this assignment is over, you will have to go back to your everyday work, which I assume is rescuing girls and boys from traffickers, and I'll have to focus on building my business. We will have to be apart."

"We will manage just like the other couples. From what I hear, the first two weeks are the most intense. I guess it's our physiology at work. The insatiable pull lasts until the addiction sets in. Once that happens, it is possible to stretch the rubber band a little further."

Jin's hand on his cheek stilled. "Addiction? What are you talking about?"

Damn. Mey hadn't told Jin about it. Did Mey even know?

"I thought your sister explained."

"She didn't."

"The venom is addictive. The time it takes differs for every couple, but after a while you will crave only me."

"What about you?"

"Same thing. But it takes longer for the males to get addicted to their females."

"Figures. The guys always have it better. Will it work on human males as well?"

"I suppose so. So far, no one has tested it. All the clan couples are happily mated."

"I wonder what came first, the chicken or the egg. That's an awesome way to ensure fidelity."

Arwel groaned. He really didn't want to talk about that while staring at Jin's magnificent, bare breasts. But if he kept the information from her, she would think that he had an ulterior motive for doing so.

"When the mating is fated, the couple doesn't mind the addiction. But in the goddess's times arranged matings were common, and the partners didn't want to limit themselves to the official mate. The way to circumvent it was basically the opposite of fidelity. The more males the female was with, the less chance there was she would get addicted to just one venom. And if she didn't get addicted to her mate, he didn't get addicted to her because her scent didn't change to match his."

Winding a lock of his hair around her finger, Jin smiled. "For an advanced species, immortals have a lot of animalistic traits."

"You don't know the half of it." He climbed up and covered her body with his. "The time for talking is over."

As he took her mouth in a careful kiss, Jin grabbed his T-shirt and pulled it up, bringing them skin to skin. It bunched under his arms and neck, and Arwel wanted to take it off and expose more of his skin to Jin's silky smoothness, but he didn't want to stop kissing her. With the soft mounds of her breasts pressing against his chest, and her hard nipples rubbing against its sparse hairs, it felt too good to interrupt.

Eventually though, he had to let her come up for air.

"What about the others?" Jin whispered in his ear. "You said that they can hear us."

"I don't care. Besides, they are all downstairs watching television. I can hear it blaring from here."

"I'll be quiet. Did you bring condoms?"

"You betcha." They were still in his duffle bag and going for them was a mood killer. "I'll get them." He rolled out of bed.

Well, that was an exaggeration. Nothing short of a fire or some other disaster could kill his mood for sex, but it certainly detracted from the experience.

Taking two packets out, he put them on the nightstand and then pulled his T-shirt over his head.

"I'll never get tired of seeing you like that." Jin pushed her leggings down. "You are made beautifully."

"Thank you." He looked at her long legs. "But you are perfection. When we move into our own house, I want you naked all the time. We will keep the shutters closed so the neighbors won't see anything."

"Same for you." She laughed. "We will live in a nudist colony of two."

Luckily, Jin thought he was joking or talking in the hypothetical. For now, he would leave it at that. There was plenty of time to discuss living arrangements after the mission's completion.

He climbed on the bed and covered her body with his. "I accept your terms."

Kian

As Kian opened the door to his office, his phone buzzed. Glancing at the display, he accepted the call.

"Good morning, William."

"Good morning. I hope it's not too early for our daily update."

Kian put his thermos down. "You have perfect timing. I just walked into my office. What do you have for me?"

"We started watching the mansion shortly before lunch, but Kalugal's gate didn't open until evening. After that, four left the premises and later returned. The first was a Ferrari convertible, so it was relatively easy to see the driver, but Ewan said that it wasn't Kalugal. I had a hunch that only he would be driving a car like that, so I had Roni check surveillance feeds from parking lots of nearby restaurants and clubs. We got lucky, and Roni found it parked outside a restaurant. When he checked the feed from inside the place, Kalugal was there. Apparently, the guy doesn't leave the house without shrouding himself first."

"That complicates things."

"It does. Whenever they can, the guys will snap photos of the driver and show them to Jacki. But the solution might be simpler than that. If Kalugal is into fancy cars, we can narrow it down to just checking those."

"He might have many of them. You'll need more Guardians to follow the vehicles to their destinations. Besides, I wouldn't mind getting snapshots of his men as well. In time, we can collect all of them, provided that they leave the compound during our stakeout."

"That won't solve our Kalugal problem, though. The Guardians won't be able to see past his shroud."

"That's true, but they can report the location to Roni and have him check. That would save him time searching for Kalugal's car in parking lots. Those minutes could make all the difference between Jin getting to him on time or missing the opportunity. And given that not every place has surveillance cameras that Roni can hack into, we won't have that many opportunities to get Kalugal."

"That's true. But managing more Guardians complicates the logistics. We can't fit more people in here unless you want them sleeping on the floor in the living room."

"We'll figure it out. I'll talk with Onegus and let you know."

"What do you want us to do in the meantime?"

"Keep doing it the way you suggested until I get you reinforcements."

After ending the call with William, Kian called the chief. "Good morning, Onegus. Can you come up to my office?"

"I'm on my way."

Less than ten minutes later, the chief knocked on the door.

"Come in."

"Is it about the Bay Area mission?" He took a seat in front of Kian's desk.

"Yes. I just got off the phone with William. We need the cars leaving Kalugal's estate followed. Only four cars have left the gate since they arrived, so that could have been handled by the team already there. But it would have left fewer Guardians in the house to watch over Jin and the gate."

Onegus frowned. "I thought that you didn't want to risk alerting Kalugal to the fact that he's being watched. Following him and his men around would do that. Isn't it better to rely on Roni and William's virtual surveillance?"

"It has limits. Not every place has cameras, and out of those a significant percentage are closed-circuit and not hackable remotely. What can we do to follow him around discreetly?"

"Keep switching cars and drivers, but that requires many more Guardians. We will have to reschedule rescue missions, and I know that you don't want to do that either."

No, he didn't. Every day that passed meant more suffering for the victims, but as Turner had pointed out, the clan could not save all of those who needed saving.

"You are right about that, and I hate postponing even one rescue, but I have a strong gut feeling that the team I've sent after Kalugal is not big enough. It's good for what Jin needs to do, but not if things go wrong." He raked his fingers through his hair. "And we know that nothing ever works as planned."

Onegus nodded. "We don't even know how many men Kalugal has with him. But if we wait patiently, we can get a good estimate. A week of watching that gate will give us that."

"A week is a long time to wait."

Onegus arched a brow. "What's the hurry?"

"Jin has to wait to transition until after this is done. Naturally, she and Arwel are impatient to start."

"Yeah, I can see how that could be a problem. Still, Arwel is a Guardian, so he will understand the importance of good intel. And from what I've heard, Jin is a sensible woman, so she's not going to protest too much either."

"Possibly. But I don't want to wait."

"Aha." Onegus smirked. "So you are the impatient one, not them."

"Nothing new there. Besides, as you pointed out, we need the men to get back to rescuing people. Why waste a week?"

Sighing, Onegus accepted defeat. "How many do you want to send, and where are you going to put them up? Sleeping bags on the living room floor?"

"They've lived through worse. But no. I don't want them coming and going from the rented house. Ideally, they would sit in their cars and wait for the team to give them a signal to follow. The problem is that fucking fancy neighborhood. No one parks on the streets, so it's not like they can wait a couple of streets over and then pull behind the car they are following. That could work once. After that they will get noticed."

"During the day, it shouldn't be a problem. But at night they would have to stay in the house and leave from there. Its front faces another street, so it's not like Kalugal and his men would notice the gate closing and opening." Onegus rubbed his jaw. "We will have to rent high-end cars for them. The more expensive, the less suspicious they will look."

"True. In that city, only the help drives Hondas and Toyotas. But if we put them in the house, we can't send more than four additional Guardians, and I have a feeling that it's not going to be enough."

Onegus arched a brow. "Did you catch the paranoia bug from Turner? Even four additional Guardians is overkill."

"I have a gut feeling, and at my age, I know better than to doubt it. If I could, I would have liked to have a force of at least twenty-five men there."

"Definitely paranoia." Onegus leaned back and crossed his arms over his chest. "I'll tell you what we can do. Since it's Friday, and we have no rescues scheduled for Saturday and Sunday, I can send several later today and a larger group tomorrow and have them return Monday evening. That way, we will lose only one working day."

"Do it. Put them up in a nice hotel and rent them some fancy cars. If I'm just being paranoid and nothing happens, they'll get to enjoy a long weekend off. But I'll feel better knowing that we have enough men on standby if needed."

Onegus smirked. "They can take turns in the house, which will make the guys super eager to go. They all want a shot at the new Dormant."

"Possible Dormant. We won't know for sure until Jacki attempts transition."

Jin

Jin had expected to get some smirking looks at breakfast, but everyone was pretending as if they had heard nothing last night.

The house they were staying in was super fancy, and she was sure it had great insulation, but it had been built with human hearing in mind, not immortal. Those sleeping in the adjoining bedrooms for sure had heard the sounds of lovemaking she and Arwel had made, but they were acting maturely about it.

Besides, the three single Guardians were busy trying to charm Jacki out of her pants, and William was looking at her with longing in his eyes while letting the three hungry bears do the hovering.

Magnus and Vivian probably had been busy last night as well, so they'd made noises of their own.

"Would you like fresh coffee?" Arwel got up. "I'm going to brew some more."

"Sure." She handed him her mug. "I didn't get much sleep last night."

That got a smile out of Vivian. She leaned closer to Jin and whispered in her ear, "There is nothing as magnificent as new love's bloom."

Grinning happily, Magnus took his wife's hand. "There is. The maturing of that love is just as wonderful if not better. When the craziness is over, you can really learn to appreciate your mate."

Jin cast him a polite smile.

She and Arwel were great together, but it wasn't frantic like the other couples were describing. Perhaps the difference was the freaking condoms' fault, and as long as they had to use them, the bond couldn't form.

Or at least that was the explanation she had arrived at.

Arwel wasn't saying anything, but she knew he was bothered by it as well.

"We should get ready," Jacki said. "We need to practice putting the makeup and disguises on."

Jin waved a hand. "It's still morning. It will be hours before Kalugal goes somewhere that I can get to him."

"Maybe. But when he does, we will need to move out right away. There will be no time to get into the disguises."

"You are right." Jin sighed. "Can I at least have my second cup of coffee? I need the energy boost to put all that gunk on."

"Eva said that we don't need much. The wigs, the glasses, and the baggy clothes should do it. Add a little foundation in the wrong color, and we are done."

"Yay, us." Jin waved a pretend flag. "I've never thought I would choose clothes and put on makeup to make myself look worse, not better."

"That's mission impossible." Arwel put the fresh mug in front of her. "No matter what you put on, you will always be beautiful."

"You wanna bet?"

Chuckling, he leaned down and kissed the top of her head. "My girl is a gambling woman."

"That's right. Whoever loses does the lunch dishes."

"Deal."

Mug in hand, Jin pushed to her feet. "Let's go, Jacki. We have a bet to win."

"Your room or mine?"

"Yours."

As Jacki started lifting dishes off the table, Duncan put a hand on her arm. "We will take care of it."

As they climbed the stairs to the second floor, Jin leaned into Jacki's ear. "I don't think you will get to touch the dishes for the rest of this mission. The three burly bears want to pamper their Goldilocks."

Scrunching her nose, Jacki looked over her shoulder down into the dining room. "I don't want to offend any of them, but I wish they'd stop it." She opened the door to her room. "I feel like a prize horse they all want to buy."

Jin patted her arm. "I'll get my stuff and be right back."

There was something to that. Naturally, Jacki didn't know what a rare find she was, and Jin couldn't tell her. Maybe she should ask Arwel to talk to his fellow Guardians and ask them to tone it down. They were making Jacki uncomfortable.

Grabbing the duffle bag with her costume and makeup, she got back to Jacki's room and closed the door behind her.

"What's their deal anyway?" Jacki continued. "They are good-looking guys. Why are they acting so desperate?"

"You are gorgeous. The guys in the program were like that too."

"They weren't as persistent. Those three don't get hints, and I really don't want to be rude, especially since I depend on them to keep me safe."

Jin put the duffle on the dresser and sat next to Jacki on the bed. "Why don't you pick one? If you do, the others will stop."

"I don't feel it for any of them."

"What about William?"

Jacki shrugged. "He is nice and mellow, so I can be nicer to him without him interpreting it as an invitation."

"Talk about picky. What are you waiting for, Prince Charming?"

"Maybe."

For some time now, Jin had been suspecting that Jacki wasn't into men, but she'd been too embarrassed to ask. But heck, they were not only friends, they were also going on a mission together. Perhaps it was time to put their cards on the table.

"Are you into girls? Because it's fine if you are. I won't be offended that you didn't pay me any attention." Jin affected a sniffle.

Jacki laughed. "I'm not into girls. But I'm not too hot for guys either." She grimaced. "Growing up the way I did, and looking the way I do, I had to stave off unwanted advances left, right and center. It got to the point that I feel nauseated when a guy looks at me like I'm a piece of meat."

Jin was taken aback. "The Guardians don't look at you like that. Sure, they want you. But they are not leering."

"Maybe not, but that's what I'm used to."

Jin arched a brow. "You don't like sex?"

"I can do without. I decided a long time ago that I'm not going to do hookups. If a man wants me, he will have to make me fall in love with him first, and of course he will have to love me too. I don't mind waiting for marriage."

"Is it a religious thing?"

Jacki laughed. "No. But I often lie, using it as an excuse. Nothing gets rid of a guy faster than telling him I won't have sex outside of marriage."

As what Jacki was saying sank in, Jin's eyes widened. "Are you a virgin?"

The outspoken, rough around the edges Jacki was a freaking virgin? It was inconceivable.

Jacki snorted. "Of course not. I'm just not hung up on sex. There is more to life than that."

Was she telling the truth?

For some reason, Jin doubted it. Then again, it was hard to believe that Jacki had never been with a man. She could believe it about Wendy, but not Jacki.

Kalugal

"Which car do you want to take?" Rufsur asked.

"The Mercedes. I need to appear rich but not frivolous." Kalugal closed his eyes and imagined the way he wanted the world to see him.

To get the features right, he usually planned ahead, going over magazines and picking several prominent figures. He created a montage by mashing their features together, and after studying the picture he'd created, he would practice the shroud on his men.

There were several advantages to the method he'd developed. First of all, the shroud looked realistic. Secondly, he could pull the montage from memory and reinforce the shroud when it wavered, which happened when he had to maintain it for a prolonged time. Thirdly, he seemed vaguely familiar to whoever he was meeting with, and because his montage was based on well-known businesspeople and politicians, his appearance usually also inspired respect.

"Hello, Mr. Wang Huateng," Rufsur said.

Kalugal inclined his head. "Good morning to you, Rufsur."

"Good accent."

"Of course. I'm fluent in Mandarin."

After English, that was the second most important language to learn, and even though it had been a pain in the rear to do so, Kalugal had made sure to master it, including reading and writing. He was also fluent in most Western languages, as well as Russian, Arabic, and Japanese.

His real passion, though, was the ancient languages: Sumerian, Egyptian, Mayan, Quechua, and several lesser known ones. There was a wealth of knowledge to explore, and doing it without relying on iffy translations was the only way to go.

Regrettably, his hobby wasn't going to bring him closer to his goal of world domination.

Technology would.

As the car lift settled on the ground level, Rufsur opened the gate and drove out. "Who am I supposed to be?"

On rare occasions, Kalugal shrouded his men as well, but today it wasn't required.

"My secretary and translator. From time to time, I'll ask you something in Chinese, and you will lean toward me, pretending to whisper the translation in my ear."

"Can't I just come as your bodyguard?"

"Mr. Wang Huateng is not the caliber of businessman who travels with bodyguards."

Rufsur stopped at a traffic light. "I wish I understood why you are doing things this way. You are just buying startups. Many investors are doing that. Why the elaborate charades?"

"When the time comes, and I put all of these technologies together, it will take everyone by surprise. I don't want Jeff, Larry, and Sergei to know that their empires are at risk. Let them bask in their glass towers and think that they are invincible."

"What about Mark?"

"Facebook is already on its way out. My vision of a social network is one that will emerge from my commerce and internet conglomerates. You know what I have in mind."

"Yes, I do." Rufsur shook his head. "You, my friend, are the most dangerous man in the world, and no one realizes it."

"Which is exactly how I want it. They won't know it even when I control each and every individual on this planet."

That was an exaggeration, but only a slight one.

He was going to control all the humans. The immortals, he was going to leave alone, mainly because they were irrelevant. Except for one. When he was in power, Kalugal was going to get his mother to visit him. Regrettably, Areana loved Navuh, and she had made Kalugal swear never to go after his father, not even when he grew up and became more powerful than Navuh.

He'd only been a little boy when he'd given her his word, but he had no intention of breaking it.

"So, what's the point? Aren't you after the glory?"

"No. That's not my motivation. I don't seek fame. I just want the control." Kalugal smiled. "I'll be a god. Invisible, indescribable, and yet feared and revered."

Rufsur laughed. "No one can accuse you of aiming low. But for now, you can be a god only over half the world's population. China is a whole separate market to conquer. Perhaps you should have started there."

"I have time, and I like it here. After I establish my power base in the West, I'll go after the rest of the world."

His second-in-command didn't say a thing, but Kalugal knew what his friend was thinking.

Rufsur was doubting his sanity, and from his perspective, he wasn't entirely wrong. For a guy of average intelligence, it was difficult to see ten thousand moves ahead and understand how the pieces of the puzzle aligned to form the tapestry of the future.

And that was good.

Only a handful of people around the world could do that, but since there were so many variables, none of them could imagine what Kalugal was planning.

His only real concern was the advancement in artificial intelligence.

At some point, a computer could spit out a picture of the future that Kalugal saw in his imagination.

But even if that happened, no one was going to take it seriously or take steps to prevent it.

Arwel

"The chief is sending more Guardians." Magnus walked into the office, which aside from serving as William's lab had become their command center as well.

Arwel looked up. "What for?"

Hopefully, it wasn't because he wanted more Guardians to meet Jacki. The girl already had more admirers than she could handle. If additional suitors arrived, she might decide to run away, and Arwel wouldn't blame her.

"Kian wants us to follow every car that leaves Kalugal's place," William said. "He told me that when I called him this morning."

That was a one-eighty deviation from the original plan. Not only that, why was the chief calling Magnus and not him? Arwel was a head Guardian. Magnus was not. He was on his way, but the chief hadn't made an official announcement yet.

Besides, Arwel was under the impression that he was heading this operation. It was his mate's safety on the line, and he wasn't about to let anyone else call the shots.

He glared at Magnus. "Turner advised against it, and I agreed with him. Kalugal and his men are too alert and careful not to notice a tail. The whole idea was to keep him unaware that his location was compromised."

Pulling out a chair, Magnus parked it and crossed his legs. "Kian is the boss. I'm only the messenger. Most of the guys are going to stay in a hotel, and only three or four at a time will come over here. In case something goes wrong, Kian wants to have a sizable force on standby."

That sounded better. It was still overkill, but where Jin was concerned, Arwel welcomed any and all safety measures.

"How many are coming?"

"Twenty-five."

Arwel whistled. "That's a lot."

"Onegus said that they were fighting over who gets to come. Kian approved a five-star hotel for their accommodations, as well as fancy car rentals, so they would blend in at this neighborhood."

Arwel had a feeling that the hotel and cars had nothing to do with the guys' enthusiasm.

"Someone is leaving the gate," William said.

Whenever the guys upstairs had something to report, they shot a text message to William. Arwel had suggested mounting one of their phones on a stand and leaving the camera recording function on, but William had shot it down.

Eyes on the gate was the only method that was a hundred percent safe and guaranteed not to get noticed, especially since the men were sitting behind a closed balcony door.

The glass had a reflective coating on it. During the day, it was impossible to see anything inside, even for immortals, and during the night, they kept the lights off. Except, the only information readily accessible was the license plate numbers. It was hard to see who was leaving Kalugal's mansion without either following the car to its destination or checking where it was parked by locating its license plate number.

So far, the method had worked, and Roni had found all four vehicles that had left the place last night. But not all parking lots had hackable surveillance cameras.

"I've alerted Roni," William said. "I just hope that the Mercedes will park somewhere public, and that the parking lot has cameras."

Magnus put his hands on his thighs and leaned forward. "Did the guys see who was inside?"

"The windows were tinted. They saw the driver, but not clearly, and the passenger had his head down, so they couldn't see his face."

That was probably Kalugal. It seemed that the guy had a collection of expensive cars. Last night it had been a Ferrari, and now a Mercedes, which Arwel was willing to bet was the flagship model.

"When are the reinforcements arriving?" he asked.

"Some of them this afternoon and the rest tomorrow." Magnus shifted in his chair. "The good news is that they are not going to be sleeping here. They will work in shifts and return to the hotel to sleep."

William turned around. "Someone needs to tell them not to harass Jacki. The resident Three Stooges are already making her uncomfortable. She doesn't need more admirers."

"I'll do that," Magnus said. "As the father of a young woman, I can speak with authority."

The guy was taking his role as Ella's stepfather very seriously. As a mated woman, she had little need of his parenting, but the girl humored him. Or maybe she liked having him as a father figure in her life.

Magnus was a standup guy, or a mensch as Eva would say, and he loved his stepchildren. Whenever he talked about Parker or Ella, his eyes shone with pride.

Jin

"I hate this makeup." Jin started down the stairs with Jacki right behind her. "It feels like I'm wearing a mask."

Jacki chuckled. "You are. But that's nothing compared to me. I look like a hag."

"No, you don't. Nothing could make you look ugly. Not even this drab getup."

Despite planning for a simple disguise, Jacki had ended up going all out and turning herself into someone else. She either enjoyed it or was really concerned about being discovered.

The brown wig was best described as mousy, the black-rimmed thick glasses were the uglier of the two pairs Eva had given them, and the clothes Jacki had chosen made her look thirty pounds heavier and fifteen years older.

And that was before the makeup.

She'd smeared on a foundation that was two shades darker than her natural, peachy color, and a lipstick that was a shade lighter than her lips. The effect was a sickly-looking woman whom no one was going to spare a second glance. Not ugly, but not attractive either.

"Jacki, can you come to the office for a moment?" William said without looking directly at them.

"Sure. What do you need me for?"

"A..." He stopped and gaped. "What have you done?" He sounded as if she'd run over his favorite pet.

"It's called a disguise."

The guy looked horrified. "For what? The zombie apocalypse?"

Jin laughed. "I told you that you'd gone too far."

"Nah, it's good." Jacki leaned to whisper in Jin's ear. "The three burly bears are not going to drool over Brownilocks."

"Aha, now I get it. This is your version of bear spray."

"Precisely."

Head held high, Jacki sauntered into the office as if she was a participant in a beauty pageant making her grand entry. "What can I help you with, gentlemen?"

Arwel took one look at her and started laughing. "Jacklin, you've outdone yourself." He then looked at Jin. "You too. But at least yours is not as bad as hers."

"You mean as good," Jacki said. "Who is going to recognize me like that, huh?"

"No one."

William cleared his throat. "Can you come over here and look at the screen?"

Jacki got closer and leaned in. "It's him."

"Are you sure?"

"The picture is grainy, but I'm ninety-nine point nine percent sure."

Peeking over Jacki's shoulder, Jin looked at the still photo of two guys sitting at a restaurant table, but neither of the men looked like Kalugal. One was an older Chinese gentleman, and the other a thirty-something geeky-looking guy.

"That's bad news." William pushed his glasses up his nose. "The restaurant is seventeen miles away from here, and Kalugal's shroud is still affecting us. Which one is he?"

Jacki pointed at the Chinese guy. "That's him. Do you see that smirk?"

The guy was indeed smirking, which looked somewhat out of place on the face of a distinguished older gentleman wearing a suit and tie.

"I see it," William said. "What about it?"

"That's Kalugal's signature smirk." Jacki straightened up. "He had the same expression on the picture you showed me. The one the forensic artist sketched. When in doubt, wait for it. I bet that smirk looks the same no matter what face he is shrouding himself in."

"Shouldn't we get going?" Jin asked.

"We are not going to make it in time," Arwel said. "Besides, it's not the right environment. We need a crowded place, like a bar or a club."

Jin leaned against the desk and crossed her arms over her minimizer-bra-flattened chest. "I don't think we will get another chance today. I put all of this on for nothing." She waved a hand at her face.

"Not for nothing," Jacki said. "We needed practice, and I also wanted to ask the guys if it's obvious that we are wearing ugly-looking makeup."

William, who up until now had been doing his damnedest not to look at Jacki, lifted his head from the computer screen and then got up and walked closer to her. "I can see that you are wearing makeup, but I would have assumed that you look even worse without it, and that it's meant to make you look good."

She smiled, and the radiance of those pearly whites obliterated the ugliness in a flash. "That's awesome. Thank you."

"You are welcome." William pushed his glasses up his nose and returned to his seat.

"When we are out, try not to smile," Jin said. "Even with all this gunk you look gorgeous when you do that."

"Right." Jacki nodded. "I wish there was makeup for teeth. Some yellow tint could have been useful."

"I heard there was a sighting." Kri walked into the office and then stopped. "Damn. That's one hell of a transformation. Both of you. But Jacki, wow." She shook her head. "It takes guts to make yourself look that bad."

"Thank you." Jacki smiled. "Whenever you want to look ugly, I'm your girl."

Kri nodded. "I wanted to show you two some self-defense moves. But I guess that's out of the question with all the makeup you have on. You don't want to sweat it off."

"I don't," Jacki said. "It took over an hour to put on."

Jin pushed away from the desk. "I need something to distract me from feeling this gunk on my face. I'm going upstairs to start working on my business plan."

"Can I help?" Jacki asked.

"Sure."

"I have a few ideas," Kri said. "If you are interested in hearing them."

"Of course." Jin threaded one arm through Kri's and the other through Jacki's. "Three brains are better than one."

"For what?" Vivian walked in.

"We are going upstairs to create a business plan. Do you want to join us?"

Vivian chuckled. "What would I know about clothing for tall women? I have the opposite problem." She leaned closer and whispered. "Don't tell anyone, but sometimes I shop for clothes in the teen department."

"I have an idea," Jacki said. "Perhaps you should design two fashion lines. One for tall women and the other for short ones."

Mey

"How are we going to fit everyone into this small living room?" Yamanu dropped the groceries on the kitchen counter. "Maybe we should have the party here."

Mey glanced around the commercial kitchen with its stainless-steel appliances and counters, white cabinets, and concrete floor. They had gotten used to having meals around that long central island, but the place definitely didn't have the right atmosphere for romance to flourish.

Which was the entire point of arranging the get-together.

"There won't be that many people. Bhathian and Eva are going to bring Vlad. And Ingrid is coming. We can squeeze eight people in there."

Regrettably, Eva was going to leave Ethan with her daughter. A couples get-together was not the place for a baby, but Mey would have loved to cuddle him some more.

That was another reason for getting out of the keep as soon as possible. In the village, she would have plenty of opportunities to hold Ethan, and maybe Eva would even let her babysit him from time to time.

"I don't know what to do about the Guardians that Kian sent over." Mey leaned against the counter. "The evening is supposed to be about Wendy and Vlad getting to know each other, and Ingrid and Richard to come out and admit that they are a couple. Bringing two bachelors into the mix is going to be counterproductive to what we are trying to achieve."

Smiling, Yamanu leaned against the counter next to her and wrapped his arm around her shoulders. "And what is that exactly?"

She rolled her eyes. "Getting those two out of our hair so we can go home. I'm tired of living here. I need sunshine, and I want to hang out with my new friends in the village café and go out for walks and have some privacy in my own home."

"You are an optimist. Wendy and Vlad haven't even met yet, and they might not click. And as for Ingrid and Richard, in my opinion, they are just scratching each other's itch."

Regrettably, that was Mey's impression as well. Ingrid was showing up every day, and the two were spending a lot of time in Richard's room, but there had been no public displays of affection other than fond glances.

"They seem to like each other, but it's not like it was for us."

Yamanu arched a brow. "Was?"

Mey chuckled. "Is. But I'm talking about the falling in love part. That was so fast and intense. A whirlwind romance."

He pulled her around, so she was wedged between his thighs. "I'm still falling in love with you. As impossible as it seems, I love you more with every passing day."

Richard walked into the kitchen. "Should I come back later?"

Reluctantly, Mey pushed away from Yamanu's hard chest. "We need to start working on dinner."

"That's why I'm here." Richard peeked inside one of the grocery bags. "What are we making?" He moved to the next.

"Nothing fancy." Mey walked over to the center island and started pulling things out. "Dips, cheeses, crackers, salads and finger food. Unless we want to dine here, we can't have a proper sit-down dinner. Our place is too small."

Richard lifted a head of lettuce. "What's wrong with eating here? This counter is big enough for twenty people to dine comfortably, and there will be only ten of us."

"Eight. I'm not inviting the Guardians." She looked at Yamanu. "Can you come up with a good excuse? I feel bad about excluding them."

Yamanu shrugged. "I could tell them the truth."

Mey tensed. Had he forgotten about keeping Richard and Wendy in the dark about the matchmaking and the reasons for it?

"You can't just tell them that it's a couples' evening. They'll feel offended."

She cast Richard a sidelong glance, checking to see if he would react. He and Ingrid had made no official announcement, and in public they acted more like friends than lovers.

But all he did was take the lettuce to the sink. "It's their job to guard us, right?" He opened the faucet and started rinsing the lettuce leaves one at a time.

Yamanu shook his head. "What I'm going to tell them is that we are introducing Wendy to a nice young man. And since she seems intimidated by big guys with lots of muscles, with them around she might not open up to Vlad."

"That's good," Richard said. "And it's also true. I usually don't notice things like that, but you are right. Wendy shies away from big men. It took her a long time to get comfortable around me, and I'm not nearly as big as those two." He snorted. "They look like they live in the gym."

"It's part of their job." Yamanu flexed. "You want the people guarding you to have muscles."

"Absolutely." Richard pulled out a chopping board and a knife. "But it's not just about the muscles. You are a big guy, and yet Wendy is not intimidated by you."

Mey put her hand on Yamanu's arm. "That's because Yamanu is a sweetheart. Everyone can see how kind he is."

Richard paused with the chopping knife. "What about me? Do I look kind?"

Mey chuckled. "To me, you seem harmless. But you are not overflowing with kindness."

"Hey, I'm chopping lettuce for the get-together. That's nice of me."

Vlad

Vlad stood next to Bhathian's car, his hand hesitating on the handle of the back passenger door. "I don't know about this."

"Just get in." Bhathian opened the door for Eva. "You know how the saying goes. No guts, no glory."

There wasn't going to be any glory regardless of him having the guts to talk to the girl or not.

Girls didn't like him. They didn't look at him, and they didn't talk to him. He was invisible.

"Wendy is a nice girl," Eva said before getting in. "You'll like her."

That wasn't the problem, but it was too late to back down now.

Stupidly, he'd let Bhathian convince him to meet the girl. The Guardian had played on all of his strings, saying that Wendy was lonely and that she was shy, and the other village males were all too old for her. Maybe even intimidating. And then he'd pulled the trump card of her possibly being a Dormant and perhaps even Vlad's fated love.

As if that was ever going to happen for him.

He wasn't lucky like Jackson, and his mate was not waiting for him in the old keep. But he wanted to believe in the fairytale Bhathian had sold him on.

The truth was that he was lonely too.

It was difficult to make friends with humans, especially for someone who looked like him, and his immortal friends were busy living their lives.

Chase had moved to Scotland more than two years ago, Jackson had Tessa and a business to run, and Gordon was away at college.

With a sigh, Vlad opened the door and slid into the back seat.

Eva turned around and smiled at him. "You are not going to be alone with Wendy. Bhathian and I are going to be there, Mey and Yamanu, and Richard and Ingrid. So, if you don't like her, you don't even have to talk to her."

He nodded.

That was good. Not because he expected not to like Wendy, but because he never knew what to talk about with girls.

As Bhathian pulled out of the parking garage, he glanced at him through the rearview mirror. "Do you still remember what I taught you and your buddies in my sex-ed class?"

Vlad felt his ears heat up. Luckily, his long black hair was covering them, as well as half of his face, so no one would notice. "How could I forget? But why do you bring it up now?"

Hopefully, Bhathian didn't think that Vlad still needed instruction in that area.

He was twenty, for Fates' sakes. Most guys his age had been sexually active for years. But then they didn't look like lanky vampires. He was six foot five, but most people thought he was shorter because he walked hunched over, he weighed a hundred and forty-two pounds, had paper-white skin, fangs that were elongated even when he wasn't excited, and eyes that were different colors.

Bhathian chuckled. "I don't mean the sexual stuff, which is obviously what you were thinking about. Do you remember the relationship advice I gave you and your three clueless buddies?"

Vlad frowned.

The emphasis of the class had been on consent and how important it was not to make assumptions. He'd internalized that, and not because of the horrifying consequences Bhathian had threatened them with. There had been a lot of advice on how to approach kissing a girl, which he had hoped to put into practice.

Regrettably, he hadn't had a chance to try it out yet.

"Well?" Bhathian prompted.

"I remember the stuff about kissing a girl, and how I was supposed to stop an inch away from her lips and wait for her to close the rest of the distance. That was good advice. It was all about consent, and making sure to get it, not assume it."

"True. But I also spoke about the importance of communication and respect. As long as you communicate clearly and show Wendy that you respect her, everything is going to be fine. Provided of course that she does the same. If she doesn't, just walk away."

Vlad nodded. "Now, I remember. You also said that confidence makes a man seem more attractive to women. Especially when he also has a job because no girl wants a penniless loser."

He was good on the job front. Jackson was paying him well for the part-time baking gig he did at nights, but his confidence was still nonexistent.

Bhathian grinned. "Good memory. So, let's see what you've got. You are a nice guy, so I know you will treat Wendy with respect, you have a job, and you are attending college. You have most of the requirements covered. Now all that's left is confidence and communication skills."

"Yeah. Tell me something I don't know. I don't have either."

Eva turned around. "You can fake confidence. Most guys do."

Bhathian nodded. "It takes courage to approach a girl, and no one likes rejection. Just remember that you are not the only one feeling like that."

"Did you?" Vlad asked. "I mean before you met Eva?"

Bhathian shook his head. "It was different for me than it is for you. I wasn't expecting to find my mate, so I didn't care about rejection."

Vlad stifled a snort.

Looking like he did, Bhathian had probably never encountered that problem unless the lady was taken. And perhaps not even then.

Looking at him as if she could read his mind, Eva smiled reassuringly. "Don't build up too many expectations and try to relax. Pretend that Wendy is just a girl who needs a friend, and don't expect anything romantic. That will make the entire thing less stressful for you. Probably for Wendy as well, since she is also shy."

"Just remember," Bhathian said. "Wendy, Richard, and Jacki think that we are an organization of humans with paranormal talents, who try to stay under the government's radar and watch each other's backs. Don't mention anything about immortals, the clan, or the village. They don't even know where the keep is, so don't say anything about Los Angeles or the college you attend. If you have to, make up some name she won't recognize and say that it's a private institution."

"Got it. What talent am I supposed to have?"

"Yamanu told her that you are a shrouder like him."

Vlad chuckled. "I'm nothing like him. I can shroud a room, not an entire city."

Bhathian shrugged. "It's still better than most of us can do. I can only shroud myself for several minutes. You have a unique talent, which is another point in your favor."

Eva turned around. "You are a real catch, Vlad. Try to remember that."

Wendy

As the last episode of her anime ended, Wendy glanced at the open door and switched to another one, hoping that the loud Japanese voices would keep visitors away.

That was why she preferred to watch anime in its native language and read the subtitles instead of watching those with English dubbing.

In the Japanese original, there was always one obnoxiously excitable character who screamed a lot.

It gave her a headache, but it was worth it. The screaming was her shield.

Since everyone left their doors open during the day, Wendy couldn't close hers without getting looks and questions, but she didn't want anyone coming in either.

They were all so freakishly nice.

Even Richard, who'd been somewhat of a jerk in the program, was acting all goodie two-shoes. He'd even volunteered to help Mey in the kitchen, which he would have never done back in the program.

Was he falling in love with that interior designer? Was love making him suddenly soft? Or was he trying to win over their hosts?

Probably the last one.

If he loved Ingrid, Wendy would have felt it. He liked the woman and lusted after her, but Richard was too self-absorbed to love anyone other than himself.

Oh well, it wasn't as if she cared one way or another.

Flicking through the offerings, Wendy searched for something new to watch. She was all caught up on her favorite shows, but she needed to fill the time with something, and it wasn't with the guy Yamanu had invited to meet her.

Why the hell were they playing matchmakers?

Wendy didn't want to meet anyone, or date, or even to go through the torture of making small talk. Guys only did that to get into her pants, and she had no intention of allowing anyone in there.

She was perfectly fine with staying celibate for the rest of her life. If she believed in God, joining a convent would have been a perfect solution.

But she didn't.

If there was a God, Wendy was majorly pissed at Him. So, it was better to believe that her life didn't suck because God was punishing her for something and wanted her to suffer. Life was just unfair, and shit happened to good people for no good reason.

What could she possibly have done as a baby to deserve abandonment by her mother?

Had she pooped and cried too much?

Her father had claimed that it had been all her fault, and he'd used it as an excuse to torment her. Countless times he had called her a curse, a plague, a good-for-nothing worthless shit, blaming her for driving her mother into drug addiction and into leaving and never coming back.

Wendy suspected that he had abused her mother as well, and that was what had driven her away. But after hearing that same crap for most of her life, she sometimes wondered whether there was something to it.

Maybe she'd been a hellish baby, one of those who never slept and who had cried all the time?

Nah. That was no reason to leave a child behind. Her father was full of shit, a jerk, an abuser, and a liar.

The thing was, everyone thought that he was a charming guy, and people admired him for raising his daughter on his own. No one knew the monster he'd become when there was no one there to watch.

He'd always been careful not to hit her face or her arms, and he'd never beaten her up badly enough for her to miss school or need medical attention.

On the face of things, he'd looked like a great dad. She had nice clothes, a good laptop, two gaming systems, and a room kitted out for a princess.

It had been a great cover for the constant abuse.

Wendy had kept quiet because she'd been ashamed to admit that her life had been hell. She still was. Part of it was because she knew he would have convinced people that she was making it up, that she was a disturbed teenager, and that her bruises had been self-inflicted.

They would have believed him too, because how could a charming guy like that abuse his own daughter?

Besides, even if anyone had listened to her, she had nowhere to go. She would have been sent to a foster home, and that might have been even worse.

The lesson had been learned, though.

No men for Wendy.

No matter how nice and charming they appeared on the outside, some had monsters living inside of them that even her empathic ability couldn't detect. A guy could seem and feel perfectly normal, until some trigger awakened the sleeping beast lurking below the surface, and he lashed out.

She wasn't going to become anyone's punching bag ever again.

"Wendy? Can I come in?" Mey poked her head into her room. "Everyone is here already."

With a sigh, Wendy swung her legs over the side of the bed. "I'm coming. But don't expect me to be nice to that guy. I told you that I didn't want to meet anyone."

Shaking her head, Mey walked up to her. "Don't think of Vlad as a potential boyfriend. Think of him as a possible friend who happens to be a boy."

That, she could do.

"Fine. I'll try to act friendly."

Mey smiled. "That's all I'm asking."

Vlad

As soon as Vlad walked in with Bhathian and Eva, Yamanu got up and wrapped his huge arm around his shoulders.

"Vlad, let me introduce you to Wendy." He turned him around to face the couch, where a girl sat huddled between Mey and Ingrid, looking as if she was trying to hide.

"Wendy, this is Vlad."

She lifted a pair of eyes that were sad and annoyed at the same time.

Great, her response was exactly like that of all the other girls he'd met in college. No one wanted to get to know the freak boy.

Vlad tried to take a step back, but Yamanu's arm around his shoulders kept him from moving an inch.

Wendy's eyes softened. "Hi," she murmured. "Nice to meet you, Vlad." She extended her hand.

For a moment, he just stared at it, but then Yamanu squeezed his shoulder, reminding him to move.

"Yes, nice to meet you too." He took her hand gently, mindful of his strength.

On top of his weird appearance, he was also freakishly strong and had to remember to be careful when interacting with humans.

Mey rose to her feet. "Come sit next to Wendy, Vlad. I'm going to check on the food in the kitchen."

"I'll help you." Ingrid got up as well.

Damn, why wasn't he a telepath? He could have projected a *no way* straight into Mey and Ingrid's heads. But since he wasn't, he had to sit next to the girl who was obviously not interested in him.

Richard and Yamanu pushed to their feet as well and followed the ladies out.

Now he was stuck alone with Wendy.

There was one good thing about being built like a twig, though, his butt didn't take up much space, and if he squeezed all the way to the left, he could leave at least three feet between him and Wendy.

She smiled. "I don't bite, you know."

Yeah, but I do. Hell. Where did that thought come from? He'd never bitten anyone in his life. Not in a fight and definitely not sexually.

Frowning, she narrowed her eyes at him. "Did I offend you? I'm sorry if I did. I'm just not good at talking with people."

Her admission helped him ease up a bit. "I'm not good at it either. Usually, I just don't say anything."

"Same here. The best way not to put a foot in your mouth is not to open it in the first place, right?"

He nodded. "That's my philosophy as well."

Well, at least they had that in common but nothing else.

Wendy was pretty, soft, and feminine, and there was nothing strange about her. He wondered why she felt awkward around people.

She glanced at him from under lowered lashes. "Yamanu told me that you are a shrouder like him."

"Not like him, but yeah. I can shroud a small place for a short time."

"That's awesome. No one in the program had an ability like that. I didn't even know that it existed."

Wanting to change the subject, he asked, "What's yours?"

"I'm an empath, like Arwel. Not as strong as he is, though. Not even close."

Great, she was a freaking empath, and no one had bothered to tell him?

Most likely intentionally.

So, that's why Wendy was suddenly being nice to him. She'd felt how hurt he'd been by the look she'd given him.

"What's wrong?" She leaned to try to see his eyes under his bangs. "Why did you get upset?"

Remembering what Bhathian had told him about the importance of open communication, Vlad decided to go with the truth. "Girls usually don't talk to me. And the only reason you are doing it is that you felt me getting upset when you gave me the look."

She arched a brow. "What look?"

"Annoyance. Like you really didn't want to be where you were, and you were mad at the others for inviting me and introducing us."

As the guilty look in Wendy's eyes confirmed his suspicion, Vlad started to get up, but she put her hand on his arm to stop him.

"It's not what you think."

Goosebumps popping all over his arms, he sat back down. "How so?"

"You are right about me being annoyed at Mey and Yamanu for doing this, but it had nothing to do with you personally. I just didn't want to meet any guys. But they were right about you. You are really nice."

He couldn't help the blush that heated his skin. "You don't know me well enough to know whether I'm nice or not."

Smiling, she tapped her temple with two fingers. "Empath, remember? I can feel you, and you feel safe. I don't often get that from people."

It was an odd thing to say. "Everyone here is safe. I don't know Richard, but I know Yamanu and Bhathian. Both are awesome men, and superb Guardians. With them around, you are as safe as a baby bird under its mother's wing."

She laughed. "That's a cute analogy. I didn't mean to say that they are not safe. And Richard, with all his faults, is not a bad guy either. But you are different."

"You think? Different is my middle name."

Shaking her head, Wendy put a hand over her heart. "I didn't mean your Goth getup or your multicolored eyes, which I think are super cool." She took in a deep breath. "I don't know how to describe it, so I'll use your mother bird analogy, but with a twist. You are like a hawk, with huge wings that you want to spread over others to protect them, but because you look different, they run away instead of getting under those wings and seeking shelter." She chuckled. "Maybe you should become a Guardian like Yamanu and Bhathian. It's in your blood."

Embarrassed, Vlad laughed. She'd nailed it about him wanting to shield others, but he wasn't Guardian material.

"You think anyone is going to accept my application for Guardian training with these sticks?" He waved his spindly arms.

"Hey, you might fill out. You are still young. How old are you? They told me that you are nineteen, but you look younger."

"I've recently turned twenty."

She shrugged. "It's good to look younger than you really are. When you are in your thirties or even forties, you are going to look like you are in your twenties."

"True."

He was probably stuck with looking like a walking twig for eternity, but it wasn't as if he could or wanted to tell her that. Maybe if she thought that one day he would look like a man, she would take a chance on him.

Wendy

Vlad was indeed a sweet guy, just as Yamanu had described him.

Even though he was reserved and anxious and generally uncomfortable in his own skin, his emotional makeup was beautiful, and it was as clear to her as if she was able to see his aura, which of course she couldn't.

She wondered what Spencer would have said about Vlad.

There was a fierceness in him, but it was warm and kind and completely nonaggressive. She doubted he could swat a fly.

It was rare to meet someone who was an open book like that. Only to an empath like her, though. Regular people couldn't even see his eyes, which he was hiding under long bangs. She wondered if he colored his hair, which was raven black, glossy and smooth.

And those teeth, they must have been filed to look that sharp. He was rocking the vampire look, and even had the name to match. Was it his real name, though?

And why would a nice guy like him put so much effort into looking menacing? Was it to protect himself from bullies?

Probably.

Kids were mean, especially to those who were different in some way. Maybe by putting on the vampire costume, Vlad was making himself look more dangerous so no one would mess with him.

"What are you studying?" she asked. "Yamanu said that you are going to college."

"Graphic design."

She smiled. "With that getup, I figured that you must be the creative type."

He looked down at his black jeans and his black boots with the metal buckles, then back up at her. Except, it was only with one eye because the other was covered by his bangs. "I play bass guitar in a band. It's part of the image."

He wasn't telling her the truth, and she could tell that he felt bad about it. That was probably the answer he gave everybody who asked about his fashion choices.

Poor guy. It wasn't easy to be different.

Wendy had been different her entire life, in part because of her empathic ability, and in part because of her home situation. But at least she looked normal to strangers.

Vlad probably got stinky looks from everyone.

Not from her, though.

For some reason, Wendy wanted him to feel comfortable with her. She wanted to be his friend, for real, not just pretend it so the others would leave her alone.

It was a shame that their friendship had to be temporary, though. She wasn't going to stay any longer than she absolutely had to. The first opportunity that presented itself, Wendy was going to run.

But maybe in the meantime, she could boost Vlad's confidence a little.

One small good deed to compensate for the betrayal of these kind people who had taken her in and were trying to help her.

"You can tell me the truth, Vlad. It's okay to like dressing in black. It simplifies life. When you get up in the morning, you don't have to think about what pants go with what shirt because everything matches. And if impersonating a vampire makes you look tough, so other guys don't mess with you, then go for it."

"That's not why I do it."

"Oh yeah? Then why?"

He shrugged. "This is the only look that works for me. Can you imagine me in blue jeans and a white T-shirt? Talk about a dorky geek. Like this, I at least look cool."

It was a legitimate answer, and this time Vlad wasn't covering up the real reason. He believed it to be true, and perhaps he was right.

Looking weird but cool certainly beat looking weird and dorky.

Except, he was going too far with it.

Tilting her head, she tried to see under his bangs, then reached with her hand and pushed them back. "You have beautiful eyes. Don't hide them."

He pulled the bangs back down. "They freak people out."

"Only the idiots. I think they are beautiful, and I'm sure that I'm not the only one." She pushed his bangs back again. "You also have amazing lashes. They are so long that they look fake."

Taking her seriously, he frowned. "They are not."

"I know that. But anyway, don't hide your eyes. At least not from me."

He nodded, and the bangs fell back down, but this time he pushed them back himself, tucking the long strands behind his ears.

Wendy smiled. "You have a handsome face."

"Thank you."

"You're welcome."

As he looked down at his hands, she noticed how long and elegant his fingers were, like a pianist's. Except, his nails were long and painted black. Another detail to add to the vampire look. Or maybe to the rocker image?

"I've never gotten so many compliments. It feels strange."

"But you believe me, right? I'm not just saying it to make you feel good. You really have a handsome face and beautiful eyes and gorgeous eyelashes."

Vlad's pale cheeks reddened, and he looked away. "I wonder what's keeping the others. Do you think they decided to eat in the kitchen?"

"I think they wanted to give us privacy."

The blush deepened. "I'm sorry about that."

"Don't be. They must have roped you into coming just as they roped me. But now I'm glad that they did."

"Yeah, me too."

Arwel

"Are you clear on what you need to do?" Arwel looked at the four new arrivals.

Douglas nodded. "We wait in the cars until we get the go signal from William."

"We are going to do it in four-hour shifts." Arwel clapped the Guardian on the back. "I know that's a long time to sit on your ass, but since you don't have to be alert until the signal arrives, you can take a nap or watch something while you wait."

"No worries. We are on it."

After the Guardians left, Arwel headed back to William's office. Jin was upstairs, working on her business plan, the new team members had been assigned their tasks, and Arwel had nothing to do but wait for a fancy car to exit Kalugal's gate.

"I have them on the screen." William pointed. "Do you see those four dots moving? Those are our guys."

Arwel watched them until they stopped in various spots next to the major streets crossing the neighborhood.

Whenever a car left Kalugal's mansion, they would get the model and license plate, and once it passed by one of the Guardians, he was going to follow it while the others remained in place for the next one.

It was risky, but hopefully with enough cars to switch around, Kalugal and his men would not notice the tails.

"And now we wait." He pulled out a chair, sat down, and fired an update text to Onegus.

"We should give the girls earpieces," William said. "I don't like the idea of them going in with nothing."

"Kian doesn't want anything about them to arouse Kalugal's suspicions, and even a small earpiece might get noticed from up close."

"Not if it's covered by hair. They could braid the wigs over their ears to hide the devices."

Arwel chuckled. "True. It will match the dorky look they are going for."

William leaned down and pulled two devices from a box he had stashed under the desk. "Do you want to call them?"

"Not yet. They are brainstorming Jin's business plan."

William put the earpieces next to his keyboard. "I would feel better knowing that they have them and know how to use them before we next spot Kalugal."

"You are right." With a sigh, Arwel pulled out his phone and texted Jin.

She replied a moment later. *Give us five minutes.*

"They'll be down shortly." He put his phone down.

Not surprisingly, Arwel could feel William's excitement rising, and it wasn't because of the earpieces.

"You like Jacki."

William shrugged. "She's beautiful, and I like her assertiveness, but she is not interested in me."

"She is nicer to you than she is to the other guys."

"That's because she doesn't view me as a threat." He grimaced. "I'm the cuddly teddy bear, not one of the wolves."

Arwel chuckled. "Jin calls Jacki Goldilocks, and the Guardians the three burly bears."

William smiled. "Good one."

"I think that Jacki is not interested in anyone. Jin says that she was the same way in the program. She might be asexual."

"Or she might be waiting for the right guy. It's uncommon these days, and especially for a knockout like her, but it's possible."

They both fell silent at the sounds of footsteps coming down the stairs.

"You wanted to show us something?" Jin asked.

William held out the two earpieces. "I know that we agreed on no communication devices, but I feel uneasy about it. I want you to try hiding it under your hair. I mean the wig's hair. Maybe braid it over it to hide the earpieces."

Jacki took one and pushed it into her ear. "I don't think it's a big deal even if he notices the thing. People wear earplugs to clubs, and many have earphones on. I thought you were concerned about him somehow picking up on the transmissions."

William shook his head. "If he can do that, it's another talent I've never heard of. To monitor transmissions the conventional way, he would have to travel with a van full of equipment, and we didn't see one following him the few times that he left the compound."

Jin took the other piece and put it in her ear. "Can you see it? It's really small."

Arwel nodded. "But that's because your ear is showing. Try pulling your hair over it."

She shook her head, letting the wig's thick waves cover her ears and half of her face. "Better?"

"It's invisible."

"Good." William walked up to her. "I'll show you how to work them."

When he was done, Jacki tried it first. "How come there is no wire coming out of it? I thought it was needed to talk back."

"These are special," William said. "Tap once to connect just to me and tap twice to connect to everyone in the loop."

Jin took the piece out and examined it closely. "So, the moment I tap it once, you hear everything that's going on around me?"

William nodded. "That's correct."

"And I hear what you are saying?"

"Only if I open a talking channel to you. I can talk to everyone in the loop at once, or I can select one or more people at the same time."

"But I have only two options, right? I can talk either to you or to everyone. I can't choose just Arwel if I want to."

"Correct. But I can do that for you. I'm like a switchboard."

"Who do I hear? Do I hear everyone, or just you?"

"Normally, just me. But if, for example, Arwel wants to talk to you, he can tell me, and I can connect the two of you."

Jin nodded. "Got it. So basically, the moment I walk into wherever Kalugal is, I tap the earpiece once and leave it open."

"That's right."

"Shouldn't Jacki and I be connected?"

"Of course."

"What about Arwel?"

"You'll have to ask me. Arwel needs to communicate with the other Guardians, so he can't be connected to you the entire time."

Kalugal

Kalugal peered over the crumbling fragments of an ancient tablet and snapped a photo. Piecing the puzzle together was his favorite part, and the best way to do that was to upload the pictures to a large-screen computer and move them around until things started to make sense.

A lot of guesswork went into filling in the blanks, and sometimes he would go to bed frustrated with the results because he knew he hadn't done it right. Oddly, the answer would often come to him in a dream.

The mind was a curious thing, and little was known about its functioning. Should he invest in research in the field? Doing so would not provide any immediate benefits for him, or even long-term ones, and it would cost a lot of money. But then Kalugal didn't have to justify his actions to anyone, and not everything he did was motivated by financial gain.

He was spending most of his free time deciphering ancient texts and piecing together fragments of the past, and he could hardly claim that it was good for anything other than stimulating his intellect and satisfying his curiosity. Even if he discovered more clues about the gods, those probably weren't going to give him anything tangible either.

"We were supposed to leave by now," Rufsur said as he walked into the room.

"I know." Kalugal straightened up. "I needed to take more photos of the tablet I'm working on." He walked past Rufsur and put the camera on his desk. "I'm ready."

Rufsur looked him up and down. "You've got dust on your pants."

"No one is going to see them anyway."

"You are, and it's going to bother the hell out of you."

His number two knew him well. Kalugal slapped his thighs, clearing some of it.

"Phinas is coming with us," Rufsur said.

That was a surprise. The guy liked to go hunting alone.

"I'm glad. The more, the merrier."

They were going out to celebrate the successful acquisition from that morning. No documents had been signed yet, but he'd shook on it with the human. If for some reason the guy went back on his word, Kalugal could compel him to go through with it.

As a rule, he didn't use compulsion or thralling to convince people to sell their businesses to him. It wasn't because he was such a straight-up guy, but because it tended to backfire.

He needed the owners to keep working on the new technologies he was acquiring, and if they'd been coerced, their reluctant subconscious would sabotage progress.

In the bunker's sprawling car garage, they found Phinas leaning on the wall next to the door.

"I didn't know which car you wanted to take."

Kalugal glanced at the rows of cars, and as always, his eyes were drawn to the Ferrari.

It was a forty-five-minute drive to San Francisco, long enough to enjoy his favorite toy.

"The Ferrari, and I'm driving."

Jin

"Take a look, is that Kalugal?" Arwel handed Jacki his phone.

She nodded. "That's him. He's wearing aviator glasses, but I recognize that mustache. What does he look like to you?"

"A handsome young dude in his mid to late twenties. His shroud is wearing aviators as well."

"Does yours also have a small mustache?"

Arwel shook his head. "No. He's clean-shaven."

While they were talking about glasses and mustaches, Kalugal was getting farther away. Jin put her hand on Arwel's shoulder. "So, do we go after him?"

"Let's see where he is going first."

"He is going out to party," Jacki said.

Arwel looked up at her. "How do you know that?"

"He is shrouding himself as a young, handsome guy. When he goes out to business meetings, he put on an older man's shroud. We should get in the car and drive in whatever direction he is going, so when he gets there, it won't take us long to reach him. And if he is not going anywhere public, we'll go home."

"Let's do it." Jin pulled out the earpiece from her pocket and put it in. "I just need to get my purse."

"Yeah, me too." Jacki rushed after her. "I wish I could see what he looks like while he's shrouding himself. I can't even tell you it's the guy in the white button-down because he can project whatever clothes he fancies. I can only describe whoever he is standing next to."

"It's still possible that I could see the real him through the tether. Which reminds me that I need to do that."

"You can tether me on the way," Jacki said. "You can't do it while rushing out. It requires concentration."

"Yeah, you're right." Jin slung the strap of her purse across her body. "I'm so nervous that my hands are shaking. I'm actually going to do this."

Jacki looked her over. "Take your puffer coat. It's freezing outside."

"Right. I forgot about that."

Jacki shook her head. "You need to relax, girl."

Easier said than done. Up until now Jin had thought of herself as such a badass. She was going to attach a tether to a very dangerous man and spy on him. But when it was actually time to do it, she was scared like a little mouse.

Down in the house's garage, Arwel was waiting for them next to one of the cars, while two of the three burly bears were sitting inside another.

"Who's driving?" Arwel asked.

Jacki lifted her hand. "I am."

He tossed her the keys. "Tap the earpieces open as soon as you get into the car and test them."

Jin nodded.

Arwel pulled her into a quick hug. "We will be right behind you. You have nothing to worry about." He kissed her hard before letting her go.

Planting a smile on her face, Jin waved goodbye before getting in the car with Jacki.

"Arwel said to tap the earpieces open."

"I heard him. Mine is on."

Jin tapped hers. "Testing. Can you hear me, William?"

"Loud and clear."

Letting out a breath, Jin leaned back and closed her eyes.

"Don't forget to tether me."

"Right. Let's do it now."

She put her hand on Jacki's arm and imagined attaching a hook to her mind and tying a string of her consciousness around it.

"Is it done?" Jacki asked.

"Yup."

The whole thing had taken no longer than a couple of seconds, but Jin wondered whether it was too long for the brief contact she would have with Kalugal. The way she envisioned the encounter, she would bump into him and then clutch his arm as if to stabilize herself.

She would have to buy time by apologizing. The thing was, she'd never tried tethering anyone while talking. Hopefully, it wouldn't be a problem.

It hadn't occurred to her to test it before, and now she considered releasing the tether from Jacki and then reattaching it while talking.

Yeah, she should definitely test it.

"I want to release the tether and reattach it while talking to you. I need to find out if I can do that."

Jacki shrugged. "Go for it."

"Okay." Jin put her hand on Jacki's arm. "I'm releasing it now." She checked the connection. "It's done. That wasn't hard to do while talking."

"Talk about something else while you are tethering me again. You need to find out if you can concentrate on two separate things."

"Good idea. So, what do you think about dyeing my wig red? I think I would look good as a redhead."

"Horrible. But I'm willing to do it." She cast Jin a sidelong glance. "Did it work?"

"Yup. You are tethered."

That was a relief. "My plan is to fall onto Kalugal and apologize while holding on to him. I need about two seconds to latch on to his mind."

"Good plan. I can push you."

"Yeah, that will look more natural."

Kalugal

"There's no selection here." Kalugal emptied the whiskey down his throat and signaled for the waitress to bring him another.

Rufsur frowned. "What are you talking about? They have the best whiskeys from all around the world. That's why we come here. And for the Cuban cigars."

The Cubans were illegal, but for the right price the owner was willing to sell them, sans the label, of course. He only sold them to regulars he knew well, and the transactions took place inside the humidor. Cash only.

It was a good place to celebrate successful business deals, but it was probably the worst for hunting. After a good drink and a great cigar, the only thing missing was good sex.

Kalugal waved a hand at the mostly male clientele. "No gazelles."

Phinas arched a brow. "Did you expect to find any here?"

"So far, it's been a lucky day. I hoped my luck would hold, and we would find a trio of hotties here. I had this image of slender fingers with long nails holding on to thick cigars, red lips curling around them as my imaginary seductresses puffed out smoke, cloaking themselves in mystery."

Rufsur laughed. "I didn't know you had such an active imagination."

"How do you think I come up with all my world domination schemes?"

"I guess that requires a creative mind."

"Of course it does." He leaned back in his chair and contemplated buying another Cuban.

Rufsur puffed on his cigar. "We can go after I finish this." He looked at Kalugal. "Unless you'll allow me to smoke in your precious Ferrari. Then we can leave right now."

"You know the rules. No one smokes in my cars. Not even me."

They were more than vehicles of transportation. They were a collection, and Kalugal took good care of the things he collected.

When the door opened and two lovelies walked in, he smiled. "Perhaps I'll get another cigar."

"They are not going to stay," Rufsur said. "And besides, there are only two of them and they are nothing special."

Kalugal shrugged. "Up to you, gentlemen. But I think they have potential." He pushed to his feet. "I'm going to get another thick one and see if either of them would like to take a puff."

It was true that the young women were plain-looking, and they were brunettes, which wasn't his favorite. But the one with the long hair had a very nice butt, and the other one had lush lips that would look amazing wrapped around a thick cigar.

As the owner opened the door to the humidor, and the two went in, Kalugal followed them inside.

"Are you ladies buying for yourselves or for someone else?" he asked, to start a conversation.

The one with the lush lips smiled seductively and flipped her hair back. "We are getting a birthday present for our father." She leaned closer to him. "Cubans are his favorite. But I hear that they are quite pricey."

Sisters.

That could have been fun if his men weren't there and he didn't have to share.

"They are," the owner said. "For a present, I would suggest a box of superb Dominicans. They are almost as good, and you can get the entire box for the price of one Cuban."

Apparently, they were new to the store, and he didn't trust them with his illegal stuff.

Smart man.

He'd offered Kalugal the first Cuban only after they had become pals.

"I agree with John." He clapped the owner on the back. "You can trust his recommendations." He offered his hand to the one who was doing all the talking. "I'm Kenny."

She put her hand in his. "Nice to meet you, Kenny. I'm Bella, and this is my sister Victoria, but everyone calls her Vicky."

Vicky smiled shyly. "Hi." She offered him her hand as well.

As the owner went to retrieve the box for the sisters, Kalugal affected a hesitant smile. "My friends and I are heading to a club later. Would you ladies care to join us?"

"Which club?" Bella asked.

Vicky shook her head. "We need to get up early tomorrow. Did you forget?"

Bella rolled her eyes. "We are driving home to Arizona, but we can leave whenever we want."

"Have you ever been to the Magnet?"

It wasn't one of Kalugal's favorites, but it was trendy and incredibly hard to get into, which would whet the sisters' appetites.

Bella snorted. "It's impossible to get into. Especially on a Friday night."

"The owner is a good friend of mine. I can get us in."

That was no problem for Kalugal and his men. A little thrall could get them in anywhere they pleased.

"Fine," Vicky relented. "But we are taking our own car."

He dipped his head. "Of course. It's the prudent thing to do. But it's also a shame. I could have offered you a ride in my Ferrari."

Bella's eyes widened. "No way? You drive a Ferrari?"

"Here is your box, ladies." John came back and opened it for them. "It's two-hundred and ninety-nine dollars before tax, which is a bargain for these."

Bella looked at Kalugal for confirmation.

He nodded. "It's a good price. I've seen those sell for double at an airport duty-free shop."

"We'll take it," Vicky said.

"Excellent choice." John smiled and opened the humidor's door.

While the owner rang up the sale, Kalugal motioned for his men to get up and join them at the counter. "These are my friends, Rufus and Phillip. Guys, meet Bella and Victoria."

After the handshakes and small talk were done, the five of them headed out.

"Can we at least see your Ferrari?" Bella asked.

"You can even sit in the driver's seat. I paid the valet to keep it close."

"Smart move." Bella zipped up her puffer jacket. "A car like that is a magnet for thieves."

Jin

"Should we leave the car with the valet?" Jacki asked.

Jin glanced at the street stretching out in front of them. Cars were parked on both sides, and there was no vacant spot in sight. "We don't have time to look for parking. Kalugal might leave the bar before we get there."

There had been an accident on the freeway, and they had been stuck in stop-and-go traffic for an hour. What should have taken forty-five minutes had ended up taking twice as long.

Jin's earpiece crackled a moment before William came through. "Park in the valet. The Guardians are going to watch the entrance from across the street."

"Did you hear that?" she asked.

Jacki nodded and pulled into the bar's long driveway.

When she saw a guy outside puffing on a thick cigar, her confidence took another nosedive. "It's not a bar. It's a freaking cigar lounge with a bar. How are we going to stage it? I bet there are no women inside, or just a few."

Jacki stopped in front of the valet booth. "Do you want to turn around? This is definitely not the optimal environment for what you need to do."

The truth was that Jin wanted nothing more than to grab on to the out that Jacki had given her and go home.

She was scared.

On the other hand, if she succeeded tonight, the mission would be over, and she could start her transition process. Putting an end to the limbo she and Arwel were hanging in was worth the risk.

"I want to be done with it. We can pretend to be buying a gift for someone. You know, like a box of fancy cigars. During the holidays, I bet a lot of women come in to buy presents for their husbands and fathers, right?"

Jacki shrugged. "Maybe. Besides, some women might be into cigars." She snorted. "There is something erotic about sucking on a thick one."

The naughty comment managed to ease some of Jin's anxiety, and she laughed. "You're so bad."

As the valet opened the door for her, a blast of cold air hit her face, and she hurried to zip up her puffer jacket before getting out of the car. San Francisco was at least ten degrees colder than where they'd come from, and the humidity made it feel even colder.

"I should have worn a scarf." Jacki threaded her arm through Jin's, and they huddled closer. "Let's get inside before we freeze."

They took two steps toward the door when it opened, and a group of people spilled out.

Jacki jerked on Jin's arm, pulling her back. "It's him," she whispered in her ear.

There could be only one *him*, but Jin didn't know which one of the three men was Kalugal.

Jin could've followed the string of consciousness to Jacki and seen him through her eyes, but she was too terrified to move. Like a deer caught in the headlights of an oncoming semitrailer, she could do nothing other than stare.

"The one talking to the girl," Jacki whispered.

He must've have heard her and turned to look at them. Appraising them with his intense eyes, he frowned. "Do I know you, ladies?"

"Aren't you Barry's brother?" Jacki asked.

It was a good save, and even though the arm holding on to Jin's was shaking, Jacki's voice didn't waver.

He smiled, or rather smirked. It was what Jacki had called his signature smirk, which gave him away no matter who he shrouded himself as.

"I'm sorry to disappoint you, but I don't have a brother named Barry."

"My bad," Jacki said. "You look just like him."

She gave Jin a little push, but Jin's legs refused to move.

"I must have a generic-looking face because I get that a lot." He took the elbow of the girl standing next to him. "Good night, ladies." He walked toward the valet, who was waiting with the Ferrari's door open.

"Go," Jacki urged in a whisper.

Jin shook her head. "I can't."

Her feet felt like they were embedded in the pavement, and she couldn't force them to move.

Trying to save the situation, Jacki turned and waved at the group.

As one of the girls got behind the wheel and sat in the luxury car for a few moments, all Jin could do was keep on staring.

Jacki, bless her heart, pretended to admire the Ferrari so Jin's imitation of a statue wouldn't look strange.

Once the men drove off, leaving the two girls behind, the shorter one turned to her friend. "You are insane. Going to a club with three guys we just met in a bar? How stupid can you be? I'm going home."

The other one put her hands on her hips. "He can get us into the Magnet, Vicky. And besides, what are you so scared of? Serial killers don't drive Ferraris."

"Maybe not. But rapists might. And I don't care about the club. I want to go home."

"I could skip the club, but not the opportunity to hang out with three super-hot guys. Come on, Vicky, don't be such a scaredy-cat."

As the two kept arguing, the valet pulled up with their car. They got in, drove away, and only then did Jin manage to move her shaky legs.

"Fuck!" Jacki cursed. "He was right there. If you had followed my lead, we could've introduced ourselves, and you could have shaken his hand while I talked about going with them to that club."

"I'm so sorry. I froze."

Arwel

"Do you want me to follow the Ferrari?" Douglas said in Arwel's earpiece.

"There is no need. We know where he is going."

For some reason Jin had hesitated, but maybe it wasn't a total loss, and they could follow Kalugal to the club the girl had mentioned.

But first, he had to check up on Jin.

She was still rooted to the same spot, distraught despite Jacki's attempts to console her.

Arwel could feel her distress all the way from across the street.

Turning the earpiece off, he got out of the car and walked over to her. "Let's get inside. It's freezing out here."

The valet was watching them, and Arwel didn't want the guy to get suspicious. The incident might prompt

Kalugal to come back and ask the valet about the two women.

No empathic ability was required to see how agitated they both still were, especially Jin, who seemed badly shaken.

He found them a table in the back and signaled for the waitress. They all could use a drink. After ordering, he leaned closer to Jin. "What happened?"

"I froze. I just couldn't move a muscle."

"Kalugal must have done something to you," Jacki whispered. "He might have given you a subliminal command or something."

"I wish it was so." Jin closed her eyes and took in a deep breath. "I got scared. That's all. And then he looked right at me, and I couldn't move. I'm not ready for this."

Jacki groaned. "We are screwed. He's seen us up close and he is going to recognize us. We need to come up with new, more elaborate disguises, and we don't have Eva to do it for us."

It seemed like following Kalugal to the club was a no-go, and that was a pity. After overhearing the conversation between Vicky and the other one, Jin and Jacki could have shown up there with the perfect excuse. They could have pretended to want to get into that club as well.

But Jin was too distraught for that.

When the drinks arrived, she finished hers in two gulps.

His heart going out to her, Arwel wrapped his arm around her shoulders. "Don't beat yourself up over it.

You are a newbie, and it's perfectly understandable for you to freeze on your first go."

Her badass attitude and assertive character had blinded everyone to the fact that Jin was a twenty-four-year-old girl who had just graduated from college. The month of training she'd gotten at the government program was not enough to teach her any real skills, and she had no field experience.

She shook her head. "I was so sure that I was ready." She cast an accusing look at Jacki. "Where is your precognition when I need it? How come you didn't see this coming?"

Jacki shrugged. "As I've said many times before, it's a useless talent. I didn't get any glimpses lately, not even the random stuff I occasionally get. It's like there is a power outage up there." She tapped her temple.

"Is there a way to jump-start it?" Jin asked.

Jacki leaned back and crossed her arms over her chest. "I'm not going on drugs again, if that's what you are suggesting."

Jin gaped at her. "I would never do such a thing. How can you even think that?"

"That's what they did in the program to jump-start my visions."

"I'm not them. I was thinking about things like meditation. It helps Mey when she does her thing."

"Even if that helped, my visions are about random things. I'm surprised they showed me your sister coming for you."

Jin rolled her eyes. "That's why I thought that they might tell us something about Kalugal and when it is best for me to approach him."

"I'm sorry to disappoint you."

"It's not Jacki's fault," Arwel said. "If you are looking for someone to blame, Kian and I are guilty of thinking that an inexperienced girl could pull off such a difficult task on her first go. Before going on this assignment, you should have had months of practice on easier targets."

Jin sighed. "Should have, could have. It's water under the bridge. What do we do now? Follow him to that club?"

"You are in no shape to go after him tonight. We will have to wait for the next opportunity."

"I still think that he compelled you," Jacki said. "You are not the type who crumbles under pressure. I've never seen you act like that."

"I wish that was true." Jin slumped in her chair. "I would feel like less of a failure."

"You are not a failure." He squeezed her shoulder. "I think you were terrified of him compelling you, and that was why you froze."

"Maybe subconsciously."

"I have an idea that I should have thought of before. Lokan could compel you to resist Kalugal's compulsion."

If nothing else, it would boost her confidence.

She turned hopeful eyes to him. "You think it will work?"

"It's worth a try."

Kalugal

"Even with the damn shroud you are a chick magnet," Rufsur grumbled. "Did you see how those girls gaped at you like you were a movie star?"

That had been an odd experience on several levels.

The shroud Kalugal used was of a handsome young man, but not a striking one. He'd purposely chosen a composite of features that made him look like the average American guy. Brown hair, brown eyes, a strong chin. He'd kept the height and physique the same as his because it was easier to maintain, especially when getting naked with a woman. But at six foot two he wasn't overly tall, neither was he overly muscled, so that didn't stand out either.

"They stared at me because they thought I was someone else. Barry's brother. That composite I use as a shroud makes me look like a lot of guys."

"Yeah, maybe." Rufsur shifted in his chair. "If they were better looking, we could've invited them to the club. I have a feeling that the sisters are not going to show up."

"They weren't ugly," Phinas said. "And both had decent figures under those puffy jackets and loose pants. The Asian was too tall, but the other one was just right."

Rufsur shook his head. "You have low standards, my friend."

For a change, Kalugal agreed with Phinas. At first glance, both girls had been nothing special, and yet something in him responded to them.

What was it, though?

He didn't recognize the feeling. It was as if he knew them from somewhere, but he was pretty sure he'd never met them before.

Except, they could be students at Stanford, and since it was his favorite hunting ground, he might have bumped into them but not committed them to memory. Neither was his type, and Rufsur was right about them being nothing special.

He liked tall blonds with kind, smart eyes, and from those he chose the ones who were prettier than average.

Kalugal could afford to be picky. With so many to choose from, he didn't have to compromise his preferences unless there was a good reason to do so.

A particularly bright mind could compensate for less than average looks, and not only in terms of exchanging ideas and interesting conversations. Experience had taught him that smart females were also better sex partners. It probably had something to do with having thriving imaginations and being open to new experiences.

Or maybe it was about having someone to talk to that was interested in the same things they were. Stimulating conversations stirred more than just the mind. If he got excited by just talking, it was reasonable to assume that his partners experienced the same.

Still, Kalugal was sure that he had never engaged with those two, sexually or otherwise. He would have remembered them.

The likeliest explanation was that he'd passed them by, or that they had been around someone he had engaged with.

That could also explain why the girls had stared at him as if they knew him.

"No response?" Rufsur asked.

"What do you want me to say?"

"Would you have taken either of them to bed?"

"I don't know. I didn't get the chance to talk to them."

Rufsur shook his head. "Sex and talking are two separate things. If you want to talk, you can make appointments with top professors in the university that you admire so much. That way you'll know for sure that they are smart. No guesswork involved."

"And where's the fun in that?" Kalugal cast him an amused glance. "Sex and talk go together like cheese and wine. Both are good on their own but even better when put together."

Phinas nodded. "The problem is finding women who want to talk about interesting stuff. You know, like politics, or economics, or philosophy, or even books. But most girls today want to talk about this or that blogger and this or that celebrity. I have no patience for that, so I prefer to go straight to the business of getting them naked and shutting them up."

"That's why I like hunting at Stanford."

Except, it seemed that Kalugal hadn't been changing his shrouds as often as he should. The problem was keeping track of which ones he'd used where. That was why he had them organized by activities.

Going for more than the five or six that he usually employed would require keeping a log, and that was a hassle. Unless Rufsur did that for him.

After all, his job was to assist Kalugal in any way he could.

He turned to his deputy. "Since being recognized is becoming an issue, I need you to start a log of which disguise I use when and with whom. I'll give each shroud a different name, which you will notate next to the activity."

Rufsur smirked. "Does that mean that you won't be sneaking out alone anymore? Because if you do, you'll have to keep the damn log yourself."

"Not really. When I travel abroad for my archeological digs, it's always as Professor Gunter. And when I venture out alone while I'm here, I'll let you know who I am going as."

"That's good enough. At least you'll let me know, so I won't have to find out that you have left the compound from whoever is in charge of monitoring the gate on that day."

"I don't need a babysitter, Rufsur. I've told you that often enough."

Phinas shook his head. "I'm with Rufsur on that. You are too valuable to lose. If something happens to you, none of us would be able to continue your work. You keep those world domination plans of yours all in your head."

"Unless disaster strikes and a plane explodes while I'm on it, you have nothing to worry about. With my compulsion, shrouding, and thralling abilities, I'm invincible."

Rufsur cast him a sidelong glance. "So why are you still worried about your father finding you?"

"I'd rather avoid conflict if I can. My plans don't involve any outward struggle. One day, I'll just be the one pulling all the strings with no one any the wiser. A peaceful, non-hostile takeover."

Phinas let out a long-suffering sigh. "If no one will know, why bother?"

Kalugal chuckled. "Because I'll be a god."

Kian

"Fuck!" Kian pushed to his feet and started pacing. "What do you mean, she froze?" he barked into the phone.

Syssi looked up at him. "Calm down. It's not Jin's fault. She wasn't ready."

Taking a deep breath, he tried to do as his wife suggested while listening to Arwel explain.

"Jacki thinks that Kalugal compelled Jin, but Jin says that she just got scared. We didn't prepare her well enough."

If the Guardian was implying that Kian had sent Jin after Kalugal without proper training, he wasn't wrong.

Except, it was supposed to be simple. How hard could it be to bump into a guy and touch him?

Girls sometimes did that just to get a guy's attention, and Jin wasn't the shy type. She'd projected a badass attitude, but apparently, it had been all bluster.

Kian raked his fingers through his hair. "Now Kalugal knows what she looks like."

"He does, but that isn't really a problem. So what if he sees her in another club or bar and recognizes her? It's not like San Francisco is a huge metropolitan area with thousands of places for young people to party. She could go up to him and say hi, and he wouldn't suspect a thing unless she panics again."

"How do we ensure that it doesn't happen again?"

"We get Lokan to help. He can compel her not to respond to Kalugal's compulsion. I think that was the main source of her fear. If that's no longer an issue, she will regard him as just any other guy and won't be afraid to approach him."

"I'm not sure Lokan can do that. In fact, I'm pretty sure that he can't. His compulsion works only on humans, not on immortals. Kalugal can manipulate both."

"True, and there is no doubt that Kalugal is more powerful, but since Jin is still human, Lokan might be just as effective in compelling her as Kalugal."

Kian stopped in front of the sliding door to the back yard. "I assume that Jin is not within earshot."

"No. I'm in the car by myself. I was sent to get ice cream. Apparently, that's what women medicate with when they are upset."

"I can call Lokan and arrange a conference call with Jin."

"Please. Even if it ends up not working, it's worthwhile just as a confidence booster. She needs it."

Kian opened the slider and stepped out. "I should send Parker to join his parents. Having a compeller in the house would make her feel even safer."

"Vivian and Magnus would never agree to that. We are about two hundred feet away from the lion's den, so to speak. It's too dangerous to bring a kid in here."

They were all overestimating how dangerous Kalugal was, including him. True, the guy was a powerful immortal, but he didn't seem inclined to commit acts of violence.

Then again, when cornered, even a peaceful gorilla could tear a human to shreds.

"I've already suggested it, and they've already declined. But I thought that under the circumstances they might relent."

"They won't, and I agree with them." Arwel sighed. "Putting Jin in danger is killing me, especially since I have to pretend that it's not a big deal for her sake. Is there a chance I could convince you to call the whole thing off? We can tell Areana that we found her son but that it's too dangerous for us to approach him."

"I'm not doing it just for her." Kian lifted the box of cigarillos from the side table and pulled one out. "Kalugal might be a threat to us, and now that he is in our neighborhood, we need to safeguard ourselves. Jin's tethering ability could give us the only advantage over him to be had."

"That's not the only advantage. We also have more people. From what we have seen so far, he has about a dozen men with him. Maybe even less."

"Our numbers are meaningless when Kalugal can blanket compel everyone other than Turner and Jacki. And we are not even sure about that. If he can compel immortals, he might be able to compel even the immunes."

It was a scary thought, but Kian was right. Which meant that they couldn't afford to cancel the mission.

"When are you going to call Lokan?"

"Right after I hang up with you."

"I'll be back in the house in about ten minutes. I'll tell Jin to get ready."

Syssi shook her head. "The girl needs to rest and unwind. It can wait until tomorrow."

As usual, his wife was the voice of reason.

"I'll call him tonight, but I'll have him do it tomorrow, and not only to Jin. I want him to compel each of the Guardians as well. I'm pretty sure that's a futile exercise, but what do we have to lose?"

"True. As you said, we need every advantage we can think of."

When he ended the call, Kian lit up his cigarillo and called Lokan.

"Hello, Kian. If you are calling me this late, there is trouble. Bad news from the Bay?"

"You might say so. I need your help."

Jin

"Don't sweat it," Kri said. "You'll get him next time."

Everyone was being so freaking nice, and it was annoying the hell out of Jin.

She wished someone other than herself would berate her and tell her that she couldn't do it, so she could get mad, double down, and stubbornly prove that she could.

That had always worked for her. Whenever a teacher had told her that she wasn't good at this or that and should choose another subject, she had studied her ass off and had proven them wrong.

That was how she'd ended as a business major. Math had been a struggle in middle school, and not her favorite subject, but after a teacher had made a disparaging comment about her inability to keep up, Jin had asked her parents to hire her a tutor.

Unlike her schoolteacher, the retired professor had been excellent at explaining and simplifying all those concepts she'd had trouble with, and after two months with him she'd gotten her first perfect score on a math test and had never looked back.

Jin needed someone to challenge her now, to tell her that she wasn't good enough and make her so angry that she would forget about her fears.

But even Jacki, who she'd expected to be tough on her, was being uncharacteristically quiet.

Maybe she was shaken up as well?

Probably.

Except, Jacki was putting up a calm façade, while Jin was letting it all out. "Where is Arwel? I need that freaking ice cream."

She didn't like keeping things boiling up inside. It was better to let it go and move on.

"Do you need to spar?" Kri asked. "When I'm frustrated or angry, that usually helps."

Michael nodded. "All that negative energy needs an outlet. If you are not into sparring, you can run on the treadmill."

"Thank you, but that's not how it works for me. I need the anger to fuel my resolve. I operate best when I have something to prove."

"You do have something to prove," Jacki said. "Next time we go after Kalugal, don't freeze. Imagine that he is a big ice cream cone and that you need to get it."

Vivian laughed. "I don't think Arwel would appreciate that imagery."

Jacki waved a hand. "I didn't mean it like that. It's just that Jin is so desperate for Arwel to come back with that ice cream. She needs to feel just as strongly about tethering Kalugal."

Kri snorted. "Hey, he could shroud himself as an ice cream cone. That could be fun for his lover."

As Jacki's expression turned dreamy, Jin wondered whether it had anything to do with Kalugal. After all, she'd gotten to see what he looked like without the shroud.

"How hot is he?" Jin blurted.

"Hot." Jacki fanned herself. "He has that bad boy vibe that women find irresistible. I wonder why he shrouds himself as a less attractive guy."

Jin cast a quick glance at William. As she'd expected, he had a pained look on his face.

Damn, Jacki was so obtuse.

"Maybe he doesn't want to attract too much attention," Vivian said.

"Then he shouldn't drive a Ferrari." Jacki rose to her feet and stretched. "I'm beat. I think I'm going to skip the ice cream and hit the sack."

"Me too." Vivian got up. "Doing nothing is very tiring."

Naturally, Magnus followed. "Good night, everyone." He looked at Jin. "Don't agonize over what happened.

We've all been rookies and have made our share of mistakes. Tomorrow is a new day."

"Thanks. I'll try."

When they were gone, she turned to the three burly bears. "Did you make mistakes when you were newbies?"

Ewan chuckled. "I was fifteen the first time I had to fight off invaders. I didn't only freeze, I pissed myself."

Jin's eyes widened. "Fifteen? You were just a kid!"

"Back then, fifteen was old enough. I wasn't even the youngest."

Shaking her head, she crossed her arms over her chest. "I can't believe that. Who sends kids into battle?"

"It's obvious that you are not a history buff," Gregor said. "When needed, anyone who could swing a sword joined the defending force. Don't forget that we were post transition immortals, and we were much stronger than the human males we fought."

"Yeah, I forgot about that. Still, mentally you were boys."

"They still are." Kri chuckled. "I'm the youngest Guardian, and when they start goofing around, I feel like I'm their mother."

Michael wrapped his arm around his mate's broad shoulders. "You are not the youngest, I am."

"You are not a Guardian yet. You are a Guardian in training."

"Semantics."

"How old are you, Michael? If it's okay to ask. I don't know what the immortal etiquette on age questions is."

"It's okay to ask, but not everyone will answer. I'm twenty-two."

Jin looked at Kri, who looked about the same age as Michael, but that didn't mean that she was.

"If you are wondering about me, I'm fifty." Kri flipped her long braid back. "But just for your information, I'm considered a very young immortal. Gregor here is over three hundred years old, Ewan is pushing five centuries, and Duncan is a youngling at two hundred and something."

"Wow. Is there a way to tell?"

Kri smiled. "Nope. Unless you are told, there is no way you can guess. We just don't age physically, and the men don't age mentally either. I think their brains stop developing at fourteen." She cast Michael a fond look. "Except for my mate, who is incredibly mature at twenty-two."

It occurred to Jin that she didn't know how old Kalugal was, and whether it had anything to do with how powerful he was.

"How old is Kalugal?"

"He is young," Kri said. "I don't know his exact age, but I know that he is less than a hundred."

"Does age have anything to do with an increase in power?"

Kri nodded. "It's scary to think that he is already so powerful. He is going to surpass his father as the strongest immortal ever born."

Jin lifted a brow. "Stronger than Kian?"

"Definitely."

Damn. And that was who they were sending her up against?

"Suddenly, I feel like a sacrificial lamb. What chance do I have against him?"

Kri leaned forward and braced her arms on her thighs. "None. But you are not going up against him. Your only job is to touch him briefly. Try to think of it as touching a fully armed jet fighter. It's much bigger and stronger than you, but you are not fighting it. You are just walking up to it and putting a hand on the metal. That's it."

Arwel

"I have a stomachache." Jin walked into the bedroom with a towel wrapped around her head and another one around her body. "But at least I washed the gunk off my face, and that feels wonderful."

Sitting on the bed, Arwel spread his legs. "Come here, gorgeous."

She sauntered toward him, sat on his thigh, and wound her arms around his neck. "I like hearing you say that. I know you mean it, and it makes me feel sexy." She dipped her head and kissed him softly.

Delving into her mouth, he could still taste the ice cream even though she'd brushed her teeth. "Sweet," he murmured.

"I should be after all that sugar."

"You are sweet no matter what you eat."

"And a little prickly."

"That's what makes you so exciting." He put his hand on her belly. "How is that stomach ache?"

"If you rub my tummy, it will go away."

"I can do that. I can also rub you all over and massage the bad tension away while arousing the good kind."

"I could go for that."

He lifted her off his lap and put her on the bed. "I'll get the lotion."

Just imagining Arwel's big hands all over her body made Jin purr like a kitten. "I'll be waiting right here."

She pulled the towel off and lay on her tummy.

"Now I can't go. I have to kiss that beautiful ass first."

She wiggled it. "Be my guest."

Cupping both cheeks, he kissed one and then the other. Then went back for another round. It was a struggle to tear himself away, but he'd promised her a massage.

"Don't move."

Grabbing the lotion from the bathroom counter, Arwel rushed back into the bedroom.

He found Jin in the exact position he'd left her, which was what he had hoped for. That gorgeous ass of hers needed a lot more attention.

"That was fast," she murmured.

"I didn't want you to fall asleep before I got back."

"No chance of that. I'm still buzzing with nervous energy, and I'd rather spend it playing with you than sparring with Kri." She chuckled. "If she were standing next to Kalugal, I would have been less afraid of him than her. Kri's shoulders are broader than his."

"She's a helluva fighter. Excellent instincts and the muscle power to back them up."

Arwel squeezed a generous amount of lotion into his palm and then rubbed his hands together to warm them up.

"I like her. But her offer to spar with me wasn't smart. Even if she does her best not to hurt me, she's going to."

Arwel put his hands on the small of Jin's back and fanned out from there.

"She won't. Kri teaches self-defense at the sanctuary and also at the halfway house. She knows how to handle fragile human girls."

"I'm not fragile."

Arwel smiled. Jin still thought of herself as a badass, which was good. It meant that her confidence had been shaken but not broken.

"Of course not. I meant the rescued girls."

Her hair was still wrapped in the towel, which gave him free access to her shoulders and neck. "Your muscles are all knotted up here." He applied gentle pressure.

As Jin moaned in pleasure, the sound sent a bolt straight to his shaft.

"That feels so good. You have magic hands."

Suddenly, Jin lifted her head. "Crap, I forgot to untether Jacki."

He gently pushed her head back down. "Good. Then we don't have to worry about her running off on William."

"No, wait. I did untether her. I did it in the car on the way back. I just forgot." She put her head down. "They are probably back already. Jacki only needed to buy dye for the wigs."

"I didn't hear them coming in. But I'm sure William would have called me if she gave him the slip."

"Jacki is not going to run. But I wish she'd give William a chance. He's such a nice man, and so smart."

"Maybe the outing is his chance, and this day isn't going to be a total loss." Arwel regretted the words as soon as they'd left his mouth.

Jin groaned. "Now that you mention it, I remembered what my mom used to say. Bad things come in threes. Maybe I shouldn't have untethered Jacki."

He'd heard about that superstition. "Only one bad thing happened, not two. So, you have nothing to worry about."

"Not true. Two bad things happened. I froze and didn't tether Kalugal, and then I ate too much ice cream and got a stomachache."

"I don't think the stomachache counts. Just relax. Jacki isn't going anywhere. I would have sensed if she was planning something."

"I'm not worried. I was speaking hypothetically." Jin turned her head and looked at him. "Can you sense how I feel when we make love?"

Arwel nodded. "I know when you get impatient and want to rush forward but don't say anything because you trust me to bring you pleasure." He leaned forward and took her lips in a gentle kiss. "And I know when you are about to come."

"That's not fair. You have insider information. No wonder you are such an exceptional lover." She smirked. "But there is a downside. I can't fake orgasms with you."

Even though he knew she was teasing, Arwel arched a brow. "Did you ever do that?"

"No. There was no need."

He paused with his hands on her shoulder blades. "Do you always climax?"

"With you, yes."

That was a smart answer to a question he shouldn't have asked. The past and other partners were inconsequential.

"Good to know. But then I knew that already." He cupped her ass cheeks and gave them a squeeze.

"I wish I could feel you the way you can feel me."

"You can if you tether me."

Jin flipped around, her perky breasts mesmerizing him for a moment.

"That would be amazing. I could actually see myself through your eyes, and experience what you are experiencing. That's going to be surreal. Are you sure you don't mind?"

"Mind? I think it's sexy as hell."

Jin

What a surreal trip that could be. She could actually experience sex as a man. Or rather as both a man and a woman.

Double the pleasure. Or double the confusion.

For a woman, climaxing required a certain level of mental focus. It wasn't a purely physical thing like it was for a man. Seeing herself through Arwel's eyes might be distracting.

Still, the intimacy would be at a whole different level, and she just had to give it a try.

As Arwel's hands traveled up her torso and cupped the undersides of her breasts, Jin clasped his wrists and closed her eyes.

Attaching her tether had never been easier. The string of consciousness floated toward Arwel's mind without her having to direct it, as if it belonged there.

The moment she switched to watching through his eyes, Jin gasped. "Is that how you see me?" She opened hers to look at him.

His answer was a fanged smile.

As she'd expected, the experience was confusing. She couldn't look at Arwel and at herself at the same time, and since she was fascinated by what she saw through his eyes, Jin closed hers.

The face she saw wasn't the same one that stared back at her from the mirror. Arwel's perception colored her in a much more flattering light. If only she could look like that for real—radiant, sexy, every feature perfectly chiseled, skin smooth like silk.

Jin was stunned to discover that she could actually feel the texture of it under Arwel's hands. That had never happened before with the other tethers, which had been limited to transferring only visual and auditory signals.

But that wasn't the half of it.

Through the tether, she could also feel Arwel's emotions, desires, needs, which was no less shocking. She wasn't an empath, and thoughts and emotions normally didn't travel along the strings of consciousness she'd attached to others before.

It was an entirely different experience with Arwel.

Jin felt his desire for her as if it was her own, and she was stunned by the level of aggression he was keeping in check because he was afraid of hurting her.

Arwel's need to possess her was so overwhelming that it was scary.

Damn, she hadn't expected that.

Arwel seemed so mellow, so accommodating. Where was that intensity coming from?

She'd tasted some of it the other times they had sex, but he'd been holding back more than she'd realized.

Surprisingly, Jin didn't feel threatened by Arwel's caveman urges, or offended. All of the feminist objections that she should have felt were overshadowed by a resounding *Hell yeah! Bring it on*!

The primitive female in her responded to the primitive male in him, and letting her cave-girl out felt liberating.

What a curious contradiction it was.

Jin could never have imagined submission could feel so liberating.

But then she'd never been with anyone whom she trusted as completely as she trusted Arwel. The direct mind connection he'd allowed her to form proved what she'd already known. Arwel was her safe haven, and as much as he yearned to possess her, he also yearned to be possessed by her.

"The intensity is electrifying. The overwhelming need. I don't know how you are holding back and taking your time with me." She opened her eyes and smiled. "Actually, I do know. You care for me, and I'm precious to you. You are fighting your urges in order to protect me."

As he dipped his head and kissed her, she tasted him and herself at the same time, got excited and sensed his arousal flare as well, much hotter than hers.

Was it because he was male and his higher testosterone level made him more sexed up? Or was it the difference between a human and an immortal?

She felt dizzy with the wealth of emotions ricocheting between them. Her feelings sensed by him and then transmitted back to her, augmented by his.

It was too much.

She had to let go of the string, leaving it in place but not following it to Arwel's mind.

Somehow, he felt it. "Why did you stop?"

"It was too much. Too intense. The feelings, I mean. Your need is so savage."

"It doesn't frighten you?"

"No. I welcome it."

Lacing his fingers with hers, he pulled her arms over her head. "I can't wait for you to transition."

She knew what he meant. There was no way he could let go while she was still human.

"Me neither. I want all of your unleashed ferocity, and I want to be just as ferocious back."

He smiled, his fangs gleaming white in the dim light. "I have a feeling that you will be."

"I think I am pretty wild already."

Was it Arwel's aggression that was spurring hers on?

Because suddenly she felt like fighting him, not because she didn't want him, but because she wanted him to prove that he could subdue her.

Since she had no fighting chance, it was an utterly stupid reflex, but the instinct was so strong that she couldn't help the urge to scratch, to bite...

Damn. It must be coming from him.

"I like it when you get feisty."

His hands still clasping hers over her head, he slid down her body and licked her nipple before sucking it into his mouth.

Jin ground. "Arwel." His name left her mouth on a breath.

He lifted his head, his elongated fangs gleaming like twin daggers. "What do you need, love? Tell me."

"I need you to take your pants off."

His tongue curled out and he licked his fangs, looking more predatory than she'd ever seen him.

"With pleasure."

Arwel

The self-feeding loop Jin had created with her tether had been a revelation.

His mate was a fighter, and she craved his dominance. Which in turn, had spurred on his aggression.

He wanted to take her savagely while she fought him, thrust into her and keep on pounding until they both climaxed and he sank his fangs into her long neck.

Regrettably, for now he could only give her a symbolic taste of it, which would leave them both unsatisfied.

Getting rid of his pants in one fluid move, he tossed them on the floor and gripped Jin's legs.

She tried to close them. But he pulled them apart, spreading her wide for his hungry eyes.

Panting, she fought his grip, but his unrelenting hold only added to her rapidly rising arousal.

As the sight and scent of the moisture coating her folds wrested a hungry growl from deep in his throat, Arwel tasted venom on his tongue.

He was dangerously close to losing control.

First, though, he was going to make sure that Jin could take the pounding he was about to treat her to.

Lifting her legs over his shoulders, he went after that sweet nectar like a man possessed. He latched his mouth onto her silky folds, sucking, licking, nipping...

The urge to turn his head slightly to the right and bite her inner thigh was so strong that he had to summon all of his willpower to keep his touch gentle.

As Jin's breathing became labored and her legs started trembling, she lifted her head to look at what he was doing. "Even without following the tether to you, I can feel the echoes of your thoughts. I know that you want to bite me."

"I'm not going to. Not yet."

As he licked into her, she let her head drop back on the pillows.

Her petals were swollen, like ripe peaches for him to lick and suck on, and as he did just that, her hands clutched his shoulders, her fingernails digging into his skin.

The little pain Jin was causing was like pouring gasoline on an already raging fire.

He had to be in her, but first, he was going to make her come.

Pushing two fingers inside her, he closed his lips around her clit and sucked.

It was like detonating an explosion, and the sound Jin made as her body arched up was probably heard all the way to Kalugal's complex.

In a heartbeat, Arwel was on top of her.

His mouth latching on to Jin's to muffle her screams, his shaft breached her entrance, and he surged inside her.

Glorious.

Gripping her hips, he pulled back and shoved in again, then ducked his head and sucked on a nipple.

But when his shafting became too frenzied, he had to let go.

As Jin's arms closed around him, she lifted her long legs and wrapped them around the back of his thighs. Holding on to him as he pounded into her, her fingers were clutching his back muscles, and her nails were digging into his skin.

Then she bit his shoulder, and he nearly came.

She moaned. Arching up and sliding her hands down to grip his ass, she was meeting him thrust for thrust.

Their lovemaking was beautifully synchronized.

Was Jin following the tether to his mind? Was she feeling what he was?

Arwel was too far gone to differentiate between his feelings and Jin's, his need and hers, his desire and hers.

They were one entity, moving, pulsing, throbbing.

The connection was phenomenal.

"Please," she whispered. "I need to come."

Arwel needed that too, but he didn't want this to end yet. It was too good to cut short.

Shifting sideways, he drove into her in a corkscrew motion, rubbing against the center of her desire with every stroke.

As Jin's second orgasm blasted out, shaking her body violently, he shook along with her, and when her spasming sheath tightened around his shaft, he could no longer hold back.

Latching his lips on to her neck, he licked the sweet spot and then hissed before striking with his fangs.

Jin screamed, but it wasn't in pain. She was coming again, milking him as he shot into her.

Only when he was spent, and she lay limp under him, did he remember that they had forgotten to use a condom.

"Fuck," he murmured into Jin's neck.

When she didn't respond, he lifted his head and looked at her beautiful face and the blissed-out expression that he'd helped put on it.

What a pity that bliss was going to dissipate once she floated back down and realized what they had done.

Jin

"Oh, my God." Jin draped her arms over her eyes. "We are in so much trouble. Kian is going to excommunicate us."

Arwel groaned. "He just might."

Pulling her arm over her head, she smiled at him. "I'm not sorry, though. First of all, this was the best sex ever, and I mean in the entire history of humans and immortals alike. And secondly, I want to transition." She lifted on her elbows. "Worst case scenario, we will leave the clan and establish a new community. You and me and the ten kids we are going to have together."

She was just teasing, trying to bring a smile to Arwel's worried face. Having a bunch of kids was Mey's dream, not hers. Jin was in no hurry to start a family, and when she was ready, two or three would do.

Arwel arched a brow. "Is that a proposal? Because I heard you telling Mey that she and Yamanu should get married before having kids."

Winding her arms around his neck, she pulled him over her. "You are mine, Arwel. And I am yours. I'm taking it for granted that we are getting married."

He kissed the tip of her nose. "Don't you think something is missing?"

She frowned. "Like what? The bond you keep obsessing about? I don't care about that."

His expression turned serious. "That too, but there is another, more crucial component missing. Do you love me?"

Jin's eyes widened.

They had never said the love word. There hadn't been time for mushy feelings. Since her escape, things had been moving fast, and stress levels were high. It wasn't the most conducive environment for love.

Did she love Arwel?

What was love?

With a sigh, he rolled off her and lay on his back. "That's what I thought."

"Don't do that." She turned on her side and faced him. "I've never been in love, so I don't know if what I feel is that. I was trying to think, but you immediately jumped to conclusions." She huffed. "Talk about insecurity."

He turned to look at her, his turquoise eyes still glowing from the lovemaking. "What were you thinking?"

"That I want to be with you, like all of the time. I can't imagine being separated from you for more than a few hours. I need you in my bed, and I don't ever want to go to sleep without you right next to me. Is that love?"

His eyes softening, he put an arm around her and pulled her closer to him. "Sounds like love to me."

"What about you? Do you love me?"

"I'm in the same situation that you are. I've never been in love either. My reaction to seeing just your picture was so powerful that it confused the hell out of me. Rationally, I realized that a photo is not enough to fall in love with someone, and yet the moment I saw you, I knew you were destined for me. My problem is that I'm not a believer in the Fates or some other power like Yamanu is. I'm still trying to analyze and rationalize how I feel and why."

Jin nodded. "We just met a week ago. Can people fall in love so quickly? Or is it just lust and like? It is so confusing." She scrunched her nose. "Mey told me that it happened just as fast for her and Yamanu. So maybe it is the Fates' work."

He caressed her cheek with two fingers. "That's how it happened for all the couples I know. Or at least those who shared their experiences with me." He chuckled. "Lokan and Carol bonded their first night together. I was right there on the other side of the wall, feeling what they felt, and it was phenomenal."

So that was why Arwel was obsessing about the bond. He'd felt it form between Lokan and Carol and he was expecting the same to happen between them.

"Lokan and Carol were both immortal when they bonded, correct?"

He nodded.

"So that's why it happened so fast for them. And they probably didn't use freaking condoms either because they had no need for them. You can't compare us to them. I'm still human, and this is only the second time we've made love without protection."

He grimaced. "We've messed up. You could enter transition tomorrow and Kian would probably fire me."

"So let him. You can help me with my business." She clapped her hand on her forehead. "I'm so stupid. If we fail Kian, he is not going to invest clan money in us. Both of us are going to be out of a job."

Arwel smiled. "I've known Kian my entire life. He is going to be majorly pissed, and he will berate us both for our carelessness. He might even put me on suspension, but eventually he will get over it."

Jin plopped onto her back and draped her arm over her eyes again. "He needs you, so he will reinstate you. But he doesn't need a fashion line. I can kiss that idea goodbye."

"You might still get Kalugal before you enter transition. It took Mey two weeks, and that was while she and Yamanu were going for it full speed ahead. As much as I don't want to, I'll make sure that we use protection until this mission is over."

Letting out a relieved breath, Jin turned toward him. "You are right. There is no way my transition has started on an unlucky day like this."

He gathered her into his arms. "We don't know whether it was a lucky or unlucky day. Perhaps by not tethering Kalugal today, you saved yourself and Jacki. And maybe our lovemaking was fruitful, and we've created a child." Arwel put his hand on her belly.

He looked so wistful that Jin felt bad about delivering a dose of reality. "Did you forget that I'm on the pill?"

"Yeah, I did. And anyway, that was just wishful thinking."

Yamanu

"Anyone want more coffee?" Mey asked.

Wendy shook her head. "No thanks. I'm going back to my room." She picked up her plate and took it to the sink to rinse. "Thanks for breakfast. Call me when you are ready to make lunch. I want to help."

"Sure thing."

Yamanu and Mey exchanged glances. The girl was a recluse, preferring to spend her time alone rather than interact with them and Richard.

Not that they were such great company for a young woman.

The truth was that since Jin, Arwel, and Jacki had left, it was damn boring in the keep.

Yamanu was spending most of his time with Mey, which was great. But since she was busy working on her fashion designs, he was also putting in many hours in the gym and the swimming pool, getting back into the shape he'd been in before leaving for New York.

But other than that, there was nothing to do.

He used to spend a lot of time meditating every day, but the main purpose of that had been managing his celibacy. Thankfully, that stage of his life was over, and his meditation routine had shrunk to twenty minutes a day.

Yamanu was very happy to substitute all those hours of solitude with making love to his incredible mate.

Instead of the cravings subsiding over time, they were only getting stronger, and they were making love for breakfast, lunch, dinner, and a midnight snack.

Nevertheless, it still left many hours of nothing.

"I'll have some." Richard lifted his mug for Mey to refill, and then turned to Yamanu. "When are you heading to the gym?"

"In an hour. Are you joining?"

Richard shrugged. "It's not like I have anything better to do. By the time Kian lets me out of this hole in the ground, I'll be in fantastic shape."

The trouble with the guy using the gym was that Yamanu couldn't train with the Guardians on rotation in the keep or use his full strength. They were too strong and too fast, and watching them spar, Richard would have figured out that something was up.

Yamanu had toyed with the idea of telling him that they were all on some experimental steroids, but Richard was just the type who would ask to have some of that for himself.

"Are you sure? Yesterday you said that you were going to take a break today. You whined about being sore all over."

"Ingrid brought me Motrin from the clinic."

It was still unclear whether there was more than just sex going on between the two, and Yamanu decided to just come out and ask.

"What's the deal with you and Ingrid? Are you dating?"

Richard snorted. "Dating? Where am I going to take her out on a date? To the kitchen? Or the home theater? No, we are not dating. And even if I could take Ingrid out of here, I don't have any money. I'm a pauper with nothing to offer a woman other than my fabulous body." He flexed his arms.

Could that be the problem?

"I meant, are you serious about her, or is it just sex?"

"I don't know." Richard ran a hand over the back of his neck. "She is a fine woman, but we don't have a lot in common."

Lifting both brows, Mey gave Yamanu a barely perceptible shrug.

It seemed like Ingrid and Richard were not a fated match. The question was how to introduce the guy to some other clan females while Ingrid was still spending every night with him.

A conundrum.

It wasn't the kind of talk Yamanu was comfortable having with Ingrid, and Mey wasn't a good candidate for that either. Perhaps he should ask Amanda to intervene?

Things couldn't go on like this forever. He and Mey needed to go home, which meant finding potential mates for Richard and Wendy.

Yesterday's get-together had been a success in that regard. Vlad and Wendy had warmed to each other, but because they were both shy, things hadn't progressed beyond a friendly conversation.

It was a good start, though. Given the rebellious expression she'd had on her face prior to Vlad's arrival, Yamanu had been afraid that Wendy wouldn't give the kid a chance.

The question was how to move things along.

As his phone rang, he lifted it and looked at the display but didn't recognize the number.

"This is Yamanu," he answered.

"Hi, it's Vlad. I was wondering if it's okay for me to come over. I have a bunch of video games for Wendy."

Yamanu grinned. "When should I tell her you are coming?"

"Are you sure it's okay? Maybe she doesn't want to see me."

"I'm sure she does."

"Then I'll be there in an hour."

"Good deal. See you here."

Yamanu lifted his face to the ceiling and offered his thanks to the Fates. They must have been tuning into his thought stream.

Mey rose to her feet. "I'd better tell Wendy to get ready. I just hope that you are right, and she wants to see him."

"Who is coming?" Richard asked.

They'd forgotten that he couldn't hear the person on the other end of Yamanu's phone.

"Vlad. He has some video games and books for Wendy."

Richard nodded. "That's good. He is a nice kid, and she needs to get out of that room. This must be really hard on her."

"Wasn't she like that in the program as well?"

"I have no idea what Wendy did after hours, but during the class sessions, she was much friendlier than she is here. She must be stressing over what's in store for her."

Jin

Jin opened her eyes to find Arwel staring at her.

His handsome face and those kissable lips of his was the best view to wake up to.

"Good morning, love." He kissed her cheek. "How are you feeling?"

Hearing Arwel calling her his love warmed Jin from the inside. Their love was just in its infancy, they still had so much to learn about each other, and so much was happening that had nothing to do with them as a couple.

But Jin had no doubt that their love would grow and flourish and that its roots would thicken, wrapping around their souls and connecting them at the very essence of their being.

That was what she imagined the bond that Arwel was so desperately hoping for would feel like. The seeds were already there, but it needed time to grow.

It was morning, though, and much too early for sharing her philosophical musings with him. Maybe he wouldn't like her tree analogy, thinking that it was too simplistic.

For now, exploring their physical connection was enough. After only one week together, it would be premature to talk about them being soulmates or fated mates.

Stretching her arms over her head, Jin smiled. "I feel fabulous. Sex with you is like an injection of vitality. I'm ready to conquer the world."

He seemed relieved. "That's good. It means that your transition didn't start yet."

"Does it usually start in the morning?"

"I'm not sure. I'll have to ask Bridget, but then I'll have to admit to our mess up, and I'd rather not say anything unless I have to."

Jin nodded. Them using or not using protection should be nobody's business. "It's bad enough that Kian butted into our sex life and told you to use condoms."

"Yeah." Arwel grimaced. "That wasn't a comfortable conversation. I should've realized it first and saved him the trouble."

"I can't wait to be done with this stupid mission. If I weren't so damn chicken, it could have been over and done with, and we wouldn't be having this conversation."

She flung the comforter off and slung her legs over the side of the bed. "I'm starving." Her stomach rumbled in agreement. "What time is it?"

"Ten-twenty." Arwel sounded slurred.

She glanced at him over her shoulder and smiled. His gorgeous eyes were glowing, and his fangs were showing.

"Are you randy again, my love?"

It felt just as nice to say it as it did to hear it.

"You can't expect me to remain indifferent when you reveal your beautiful nude body to me."

He'd only seen her back, and that was enough to excite him?

Sweet.

"You've only gotten a glimpse." Pushing up to her feet, she turned around and struck a pose. "How about now?"

"Dangerous. If you don't hurry into the bathroom, you might not make it there for another hour or two."

With the hunger in his eyes and his husky tone awakening her desire, Jin decided that breakfast could wait. But she really needed to use the bathroom first. "Would you like to join me in the shower?"

His fangs punched down even lower. "I would never refuse such an invitation."

It was a full hour later when they finally made their way to the kitchen.

"Good morning." Vivian looked up from her book. "You're late, but I managed to save some eggs and hash browns for you. Just stick the plates into the microwave."

"Thank you."

While Arwel took care of the food, Jin walked over to the coffeemaker and put two cups under the twin nozzles. She put a new packet in, pressed the button, and leaned against the counter.

"Where is everyone?" she asked.

Vivian turned sideways in her chair. "Douglas is upstairs watching Kalugal's gate, and the other Guardians are waiting in their cars for a signal from him. William is in his office with Magnus."

"What about Kri and Michael?" Arwel put two plates on the table.

"In the gym."

"And Jacki?" Jin asked.

"I think she is still sleeping. I haven't seen her this morning."

Jin and Arwel exchanged glances. Had Jacki and William gotten busy last night?

That would be awesome.

"I'd better check on her." Jin pushed away from the counter.

Arwel waved her over. "Eat your breakfast first. You said you were starving an hour ago."

That was true, but her curiosity was stronger than her hunger.

"I guess I can let Jacki sleep a few more minutes."

Stifling a smirk, Jin pulled out the coffee mugs from the device and brought them over to the table. What she'd really wanted to say was that Arwel hadn't been all that concerned about her empty belly when they'd been making love in the shower.

Vivian closed her book and got up. "I'll leave you two alone to enjoy your breakfast."

After they were done eating, Jin took their plates to the sink. "I'm going to check on Jacki." Holding a plate under running water, she looked over her shoulder at Arwel. "Your job is to coax information out of William."

He handed her the coffee mugs to rinse. "Guys don't talk about things like that."

"Right." Jin rolled her eyes. "I don't mean getting him to reveal details. Just general stuff. Does he like her? Does she like him back?"

"I'm just going to join him in the office. It's up to him if he wants to talk about it."

"Fair enough." Jin dried her hands on the dish towel. "But I'm crossing my fingers."

Vlad

Vlad stuffed his entire collection of video games into a duffle bag, added several fantasy books that he had read and enjoyed, and some romance novels that he'd borrowed from his mother.

Was it too much?

Maybe he should leave some of it behind so he would have more excuses to visit Wendy?

Yeah, that was a better plan.

He pulled out all of the romance novels except for one. Perhaps she wasn't into that genre. He knew she liked fantasy, though, so he took out only two of his books. They were part of a series, so once she was done reading the first three, she would want the other two and would have no choice but to invite him over.

Except, he wanted her to do it because she liked him and wanted to see him, not because she needed the books.

Then again, if she was as shy as he was, Wendy would need an excuse as well.

Vlad smiled.

It was a good plan.

Zipping up the duffle bag, he wondered whether he should buy some chocolates on the way. Everyone knew that girls loved them. Then again, it would imply that he had romantic expectations, while Wendy hadn't given him any indication that she was interested in him that way.

With a sigh, he slung the strap over his shoulder and headed out of the house.

It wasn't a big surprise that she wasn't attracted to him. But at least she'd been friendly, and that was more than he'd gotten from other girls, or guys for that matter.

Even if all he gained was a new friend, it was worth the effort.

On the way to the pavilion, he stopped by the café and bought coffee and several pastries. That wasn't the same as chocolates, and he was bringing enough for everyone, so it couldn't be construed as a romantic gesture.

"Good morning, Vlad." Anandur clapped him on the back. "Heading out for a study session with friends?"

For a moment, he was tempted to lie. It would have been so simple to just nod in agreement and keep on walking. Not a biggie.

And then there was Anandur's proclivity for gossip. If he told him about Wendy, the entire village would know about it in less than an hour.

Except, Anandur could learn the truth from Yamanu or Bhathian or from the Guardians on rotation in the keep.

Maybe he could get away with partial truth.

"Bhathian asked me to befriend one of the newcomers. She is about my age, and she has no one to talk to. I'm bringing her books and video games."

"That's kind of you." Anandur smirked. "Is she pretty?"

"She is okay." *Beautiful*. "But we are just friends. Or rather acquaintances at this point. I've only met her once, and today is going to be the second time."

"Good luck." Anandur clapped him on the back again. "Friendship is a good start for a relationship. Just don't let her put you in the friend zone. Keep your options open."

Vlad didn't want to ask, but he couldn't help it. "How am I supposed to do that?"

Wrapping his massive arm around Vlad's slim shoulders, Anandur led him to a table. "Sit."

"I don't have time. I told Yamanu that I'd be there in an hour, and that was fifteen minutes ago."

"It's Saturday, so the traffic isn't bad, and this will only take a minute or two."

Perhaps Anandur's advice was worth a short delay. If he was late, he could always blame traffic.

"Okay." Vlad planted his ass in the chair.

The Guardian pulled one out for himself and sat down. "I'm not an expert on dating, but I know a thing or two about women. The thing they find most desirable in a guy is confidence. That's why assholes have such great success with them. Contrary to popular belief, women are not attracted to the jerkiness, they are attracted to the confidence those guys exude."

Vlad grimaced. "It's easy for good-looking dudes to be confident. I'm a walking scarecrow with fangs and mismatched eyes."

Anandur leaned closer. "That's where you are wrong. I've seen ugly dudes score with the hottest girls just because they were confident or faked it well. And you are not ugly, Vlad. You are not ordinary looking, and you can use that to your advantage. You are an awesome guitarist and vocalist, I hear that you are also a talented graphic artist, and you make good money working for Jackson. Don't be shy; tell her about your passions and your accomplishments."

"I don't want to boast."

"It's not boasting when it's true, and if you don't tell her, how will she know?"

"Maybe I can show her instead?"

"Even better. Show her your art, sing for her, bake her some goodies. You have a lot to offer, my friend."

"Thanks, Anandur." Vlad rose to his feet and offered the Guardian his hand. "That was good advice."

"Any time."

Jin

Jin knocked on Jacki's door. "Can I come in?"

When there was no answer, she tried the handle. It wasn't locked, and the door opened.

Jacki's bed was made, and through the open bathroom door, Jin could see that she wasn't there either.

Smelling a strong chemical scent, she went inside and followed her nose to the shower, where the two wigs were draped over clothes hangers, still dripping.

It was hard to tell their color while wet, but it looked like one got a deep reddish hue, while the other was light brown.

Maybe the strong smell had chased Jacki out of her room, and she went out to the back yard for some fresh air?

Why hadn't she come into the kitchen, though?

Feeling a little apprehensive, Jin walked over to the window and looked out into the yard. There was no one there, but with the screen preventing her sticking her head out, she could only see a part of the area.

Wait, maybe Jacki went straight to William's office? If the two had spent a night of passion together, she would want to give him a good morning kiss.

Or better yet, what if she'd spent the night in his bedroom downstairs?

The wigs were wet, though, which meant that she'd dyed them this morning. Still, she could've come upstairs to do that, and then gone back down to cuddle with William in bed.

Not a likely scenario, but it was worth checking out.

After rushing down the stairs, Jin slowed down before entering the office. "Good morning, William. Have either of you seen Jacki? She is not in her room."

William shook his head. "The last time I saw her was yesterday."

Arwel frowned. "Did you come home straight from the store? I didn't hear her door open."

"We did some grocery shopping, so it took longer than we originally planned, but not by much. We were back before midnight, unloaded the stuff in the kitchen, and said our goodnights."

That was disappointing and a little worrisome.

"Where could she be?"

"Let's check the gym." Arwel pushed to his feet. "Maybe she took Kri up on her offer to teach her self-defense moves."

Jacki wasn't in the gym, and Kri and Michael hadn't seen her that morning. Checking the back yard didn't produce her either.

"Maybe she is in the master bedroom with the guys." Jin started up the stairs. "It would be odd if she is, though. She tries to stay away from them as much as possible."

"The outing with William might have changed her mind." Arwel followed her up. "Perhaps she realized that he wasn't who she wanted, and she decided to give the others a try."

Again, that wasn't likely, but they had run out of places to check.

Jacki wasn't in the master bedroom either.

"Have any of you seen her this morning?" Arwel asked.

Ewan shook his head. "No. I thought she was still sleeping."

"I assume that you didn't see or hear her leave the house either?"

"How is this possible?" Jin put a hand on her hip. "You guys are supposed to have superior hearing, and as far as I know, Jacki can't fly or levitate. You would have heard her open the door and go down the stairs."

"There are a lot of people in the house." Duncan ran an agitated hand through his short hair. "Our job is to watch Kalugal's gate. We don't pay attention to doors opening or closing or check who is going down or up the stairs."

The Guardian's nervousness and slight blush had finally clued Jin in.

Freaking hell. They had been too busy listening to her and Arwel making love to notice Jacki giving them the slip.

Embarrassed, Jin turned toward the door. "We need to go look for her."

"Wait." Arwel stopped her with a hand on her shoulder. "Let's check her bedroom first. I need to know if she slept in her bed at all, or if she snuck out last night after she and William returned from the store."

"Her bed is made, but she didn't leave last night. I know that she dyed the wigs this morning because they are still wet."

If she could get Arwel alone, Jin could tell him what she suspected about the Guardians listening in on their lovemaking instead of paying attention to Jacki's comings and goings.

"Let's check the garage." Arwel turned to the three men. "Duncan, you stay here. Ewan and Gregor, you come with us. If she's on foot, we still have a chance to find her."

Arwel

Arwel scanned the garage. "All the cars are here, which means that she's walking. She couldn't have gotten far."

He turned to the Guardians. "Ewan, you go west. Gregor, you head north. Magnus, you are going south. I'm going to take the east."

"I'm coming with you," Jin said.

"Of course." He opened the passenger door for her.

"I don't think Jacki ran away." Jin buckled up. "She wouldn't have bothered dyeing the wigs if that was her plan. She's probably out jogging."

Arwel arched a brow. "Is she a jogger?"

"Not as far as I know. But it's a nice day, and her room is stinky from the hair dye, so she might have decided to go out for some fresh air."

"She could have waited for the right opportunity." He cast Jin a sidelong glance. "We gave her the perfect cover this morning."

"So you figured it out, huh? The perverts were too busy listening to us making love to hear Jacki leave the house."

"It's not like they could help it. This house has standard insulation, and we didn't bother to keep quiet."

Jin had been loud, thinking that the running water would mask the sounds she'd been making. On his part, Arwel was just as guilty for not saying anything. He'd enjoyed hearing her sounds of pleasure too much to do anything to stop them.

"It's so damn embarrassing. Maybe the noises we made were the reason Jacki left. She doesn't have immortal hearing, but she's in the room right next to ours. It's not fun listening to other people making love." She grimaced. "Although it seems like your fellow Guardians enjoyed it very much."

"Don't let it bother you."

"I can't help it." Jin crossed her arms over her chest. "I think your freaking Fates are messing with us. Do they want us to abstain? Because it seems that our sex life is endangering the mission."

"At least we were good and used a condom this morning."

Jin huffed. "Yeah, like it's a good thing."

Arwel decided not to respond. It seemed like Jin needed to vent her frustration, so it didn't matter what he said.

"Look." She pointed at a woman walking stooped over with her hands stuffed in the pockets of her hoodie. "That's her. I recognize those sweatpants."

As Arwel pulled up to the woman, she turned to look at them. "What are you doing here?"

Jin lowered the window. "Looking for you. Everyone is worried sick about you. Get in the car."

"I'm just taking a walk. What's the big deal?"

Arwel threw the gearshift in park and got out of the car. "You are not supposed to be alone on the street." He opened the back passenger door for her. "Did you forget that you are a wanted woman?"

Letting out an indignant huff, Jacki got in the car. "I have the hoodie up, and I'm wearing the special glasses. That's good enough to fool surveillance cameras if there were any out here. But there are none. Do you see any? Because I don't."

Jin turned around to look at her friend. "Still. You should have at least told someone that you were going out."

"Why? So they could tell me that I can't? I'm sick of being treated like a freaking prisoner and at the same time being expected to help your organization."

Arwel looked at her through the rearview mirror. "You are not a prisoner. Do you think that you would have been allowed more freedom in a witness protection program?"

Shrugging, she looked out the window. "I've never been in one, so I don't know."

"Next time tell someone. There is also the issue of Kalugal and his men. It's not smart for you to be walking around his neighborhood, and especially not after last night. What if you were recognized? It's not like there are many people out on the streets for you to go unnoticed. In fact, we haven't seen anyone else walking around."

Jin nodded. "You should have taken one of the guys with you."

It wouldn't have helped Jacki if she was discovered by Kalugal or his men, but the immortals were not the only threat to a woman walking alone on a deserted street. Human males were dangerous too, even in broad daylight.

Jacki ignored Jin. Looking out the window, she appeared just as pissed as Arwel felt she was. Usually, he didn't pick up on her emotions, either because they weren't strong or because she was good at erecting walls around them.

Still, Jacki knew that he was an empath, and anger was a strong emotion that easily overshadowed other, more subtle ones like anxiety over plotting an escape.

This whole episode could have been designed to test the waters and see if she could get away with sneaking out of the house unnoticed. Even dyeing the wigs and leaving them to dry could have been part of the setup.

Was he giving her too much credit?

On the contrary. He probably wasn't giving her enough.

Arwel had a feeling that the girl was much smarter than she appeared and way more devious.

Wendy

Wendy checked the time on the television screen. She still had a few minutes until Vlad got there.

She'd hoped he wouldn't come over again. He was such a nice guy and leading him on was wrong.

Not that she had done it intentionally, it just happened. Yesterday, she'd planned to act indifferent so he would get the hint and not bother coming back. But she'd found it impossible to be mean to Vlad. He was so sensitive, so unsure of himself, that she'd felt compelled to help him out.

No, not compelled. She shouldn't use that nasty word when she knew what it really meant.

How could the director have allowed Marisol to use it on her?

Eh, who was she kidding? He probably told the bitch to do it. The guy didn't trust anyone, not even his own niece.

Still, she owed him. If not for Director Edgar Simmons, she would have still been in her father's grip.

Literally.

Wendy hadn't known anyone on her mother's side of the family until one day the director had knocked on her father's door, introduced himself, and offered her a lifeline.

Her father had been more than happy to get rid of her, but only after negotiating with her uncle that half of her pay would go to him, supposedly to compensate for the expenses he'd incurred raising her alone.

There hadn't been any warm fuzzies between Wendy and her uncle. He'd claimed that he hadn't known about her existence and that as soon as he'd found out, he'd come for her. Not because he'd wanted to get to know his niece, but because as his blood relative, she was likely to possess some paranormal talent. And if not talent, then at least an immunity to mind manipulation like his.

Hopefully, he knew that she'd joined the escape group only to gather intel for him.

That had been the task he'd assigned her to. She'd been his ears, eyes, and sensor to anything out of the ordinary going on in the trainee group.

She'd failed to detect Jin and Jacki's plotting an escape, but she had salvaged the situation by going with them.

Except, she was stuck with no means of communication, and she couldn't leave. Perhaps she could use Vlad to do that.

He was so sweet and naive that it shouldn't be difficult. First of all, she could find out from him where she was. He'd been told to keep quiet about it, but she could trick him by asking him the name of the college he attended or to tell her about his favorite hangout places.

Maybe she could even get him to sneak her out.

The worst part was that she really liked Jacki and Jin, and Mey and Yamanu and Arwel and everyone else. Betraying them wasn't easy.

She even liked Edna, whom she'd been terrified of but had managed to fool just like everyone else, despite her probing ability.

There were advantages to having been so well-practiced in disassociation. Only this time, she'd done it in reverse, stepping back into her real life instead of the one she'd created as a substitute and was living so comfortably in.

First, Wendy had swamped her mind with memories of the abuse she'd suffered throughout the years. With that filling every brain cell and nerve in her body, there had been little else for Edna to latch onto. But then Wendy had added a twist, imagining the director making advances towards her.

It wasn't hard to do since there was some truth to it. He had never actually done anything, but she'd felt his perverted desire for her.

Having an empathic ability was both a gift and a curse. Without it, she probably would never have known her uncle had the hots for her because he wouldn't have acted on it.

At least she hoped he wouldn't have.

Men could never be trusted.

Nevertheless, she owed him and was dependent on him for her future. The lifeline he'd offered her had been the first stroke of luck she'd had in her entire life. It got her out of the house and provided her with a great income for skills she'd been born with and didn't have to work on acquiring.

It was a chance of a lifetime. Heck, it was her only chance.

Hopefully, Edna had forgotten all about her promise of cupcakes and girl talk and wasn't going to show up anytime soon. Wendy wasn't sure she could pull off the same trick again, and if possible, she would rather avoid immersing herself in memories of pain and insults.

It had been hard enough when she'd forced herself back into her real life. In fact, she was still reeling from the aftershocks. Usually, the catalyst for entering her alternate reality had been her father's abuse. Without it, she was struggling to go back to the better place she'd created for herself.

 Jin

The drive back to the house lasted less than five minutes, but those minutes were tense. As soon as Arwel parked the car in the garage, Jacki opened the back passenger door, got out, and then slammed it behind her.

"Someone is in a bad mood," Jin muttered. "I'd better go talk to her."

She got out of the car and followed Jacki inside.

"Wait up," she called after her. "Are you hungry? You left the house without eating breakfast."

"I'm going to my room." Jacki continued up the stairs.

Arwel put a hand on Jin's shoulder. "I'm going to the office."

"Coward."

"She is your friend. You deal with her tantrum."

Jacki was already at the top of the stairs, and Jin had no intention of going up after her.

"Don't be an idiot, Jacki. Are you punishing me by going hungry?"

Jacki stopped and turned around. "I did nothing wrong, and yet you and your boyfriend treated me like a criminal."

Rolling her eyes, Jin beckoned with her hand. "Come on. You can yell at me over eggs and toast. I'll even make them for you. Together with hot chocolate." That was an offer her friend couldn't refuse.

One corner of Jacki's mouth twitched with a ghost of a smile, and then it bloomed into a full one. "How can I stay mad at you when you offer to make me food and hot cocoa?"

"That's the idea."

In the kitchen, they found Vivian waiting for them with fresh coffee.

"I heard you coming in and made two cups. Would you like some?"

"Yes, please." Jacki sat at the table. "Aren't you going to berate me as well?"

Vivian shook her head. "I'm sure you've gotten an earful already. We were worried about you. That's all."

Jacki took the mug Vivian handed her. "I'm a grown woman, and I wasn't abducted by humans or aliens through my second-floor bedroom window. The logical assumption should have been that I'd gone for a walk."

The fact that they'd thought she had run away hung in the air unspoken.

"I actually considered the alien theory," Jin said to break the silence. "They'd taken you during the night but were nice enough to make your bed and dye the wigs."

She pulled a tray of eggs out of the fridge and cracked three into the pan.

"The stinky hair dye was the reason I went out for a walk. How did they come out?"

"I don't know." Jin popped four slices of bread into the toaster. "They were still wet when I saw them. You should have blow-dried them."

"I thought about doing that, but then I figured that we should ask Eva if that was okay. It didn't occur to me until after I'd applied the color that maybe the wigs were not meant to be dyed."

"I'd better call her while you eat your breakfast. We need to ask her how to change our appearance with what we have. We might have to buy some new stuff."

When the eggs were ready and the toast popped up, Jin put everything on a plate and brought it to the table. "Enjoy."

"Thank you."

As Jacki dove in, she placed the call.

"Jin. I was waiting for your call."

"Why? Have you already heard about what happened?"

"Kian called me and asked me to design a new disguise for you. I'm waiting for Ella to come over so I can demonstrate on her. We can do a Skype session, and you can do Jacki's makeup while following what I'm demonstrating on Ella, and then you can switch."

"Awesome. By the way, Jacki dyed the wigs. I hope that's okay."

"That's fine. What colors did she use?"

"Let me put you on speaker." She turned to Jacki. "Eva is asking what colors you used for the wigs."

Jacki wiped her mouth with a napkin. "I used L'Oréal. One was cayenne red and the other deep golden brown. After I washed the color off, I left them to air dry. Any styling ideas?"

"We will do the makeup first, and then check on the wigs. You didn't alter the colors by much."

"I was afraid to go with something too bold. We are supposed to blend in, not stand out."

"True. Most of the work will have to be done with makeup and hairstyles rather than color. I'll call you as soon as Ella is here."

"Thank you, Eva." Jin took the call off the speaker. "And I'm sorry for bothering you on the weekend."

"No problem. As a stay-at-home mom, weekdays or weekends makes no difference to me."

"Nevertheless, I'm sure you would rather have spent the day with your family."

"I'm glad to help, Jin. In any way I can. Besides, nowadays, that's the only excitement I get. I'm living vicariously through your and Jacki's adventure."

Jin chuckled. "I could have done with much less excitement. I don't think that the spy lifestyle is for me."

Vlad

"Hello, Vlad." Mey welcomed him with a hug.

When she let go, Yamanu clapped him on the back. "I'm glad you came." He slung a towel around his neck. "I'm heading to the gym. You don't need me here, right?"

Vlad glanced at the couch where Wendy was patiently waiting for her turn to say hello.

"I hope you are not leaving because of me."

Yamanu laughed. "It's not you. It's me." He winked. "I have a date with Richard at the weights station." He looked Vlad over. "You should come with me sometime. I'll show you the proper way to build up muscle."

From the corner of his eye, Vlad saw Mey glaring at Yamanu.

She probably thought that Vlad had been offended by the suggestion, but the truth was that he didn't need the training. He was already freakishly strong. To develop muscles, he would probably need to push up semitrailers.

"I'll take you up on your offer once you and Mey go back to the village."

Now it was Yamanu's turn to glare. "You mean the neighborhood gym."

"Yeah, that's what I meant."

"Good deal." Yamanu clapped him on the back again. "Have fun, kids."

Vlad rolled his eyes. Yamanu looked to be in his late twenties or early thirties. Calling Vlad and Wendy kids was telling.

When he left, Mey ducked into the bedroom but left the door open as if they needed a chaperone.

"What's all that?" Wendy pointed at the duffle bag slung over one shoulder and the guitar case slung over the other.

He dropped the bag on the floor and put the case on a chair. "You said you were bored, so I brought you video games and books…"

"Thanks. And what's that?" She pointed at the case.

"I brought my guitar, thinking that you might want to hear some of the songs my band used to play. We wrote them ourselves."

"I would love that."

He clicked the fasteners open. "I play the bass and Jackson plays the lead guitar, but for a solo performance, I figured an acoustic would be best." He pulled it out.

Wendy sat up straight. "I've always wanted to play an instrument."

"Why didn't you?"

She grimaced. "My father didn't think it was necessary."

"I can teach you if you want."

"That would be nice. Although I would have preferred to play the piano."

"I can teach you that as well, but we don't have one down here."

Her eyes brightened with admiration. "You play three instruments? That's amazing."

Remembering Anandur's advice, Vlad decided to boast a little. "Six. I can also play the flute, the clarinet, and the saxophone."

"Wow. That's impressive."

He strummed a chord. "Ready?"

"Yes."

He chose one of the quieter songs, and when the first notes left his throat, Wendy gaped a little.

Mey came out of the bedroom and joined Wendy on the couch.

Feeling shy, he watched his fingers on the guitar even though he didn't need to. But looking at Wendy while he was playing would have been too nerve-racking.

He was a good singer, but she might not like his style, or the lyrics, or whatever.

Once he was done, Wendy and Mey started clapping, and Vlad took a bow. "Thank you."

"You are an amazing vocalist, Vlad," Mey said. "Your voice is unique, and you have perfect pitch."

"It was beautiful." Wendy crossed her arms over her chest.

Was she suddenly feeling shy? Had he gone overboard showing off?

"Did you go to music school?" Wendy asked.

"I had tutors that I went to."

"That's nice."

She sounded sad, maybe a little envious, which was a first for him. What he got most from people was either pity or wariness.

Perhaps showing Wendy his artwork could wait for another time.

He lifted the duffle bag, put it on the coffee table, and unzipped it. "Check out the games I brought for you. If you find one that you like, we can take it to the theater. Playing a video game on the big screen is an experience. You have to try it."

She pulled out several and looked them over. "I like them all, but I'm not in the mood for playing. Maybe we can just watch a movie?"

That was even better. Perhaps while watching, he'd gather the nerve to put his arm around her shoulders.

"Sure. We have all the latest movies on the server."

Wendy rose to her feet and turned to Mey. "Would you like to join us?"

Mey waved a hand. "You two go and enjoy yourselves. I could use the time to work on my designs."

Vlad held his breath. Was Wendy going to find an excuse not to go?

He wanted to be alone with her again, but what if she'd asked Mey to hang around because she didn't want that?

"We even have an antique movie popcorn machine," he murmured.

"I know. And it's the best ever."

"So you've been there already?" He started for the door.

Thankfully, she followed. "There is not much to do here."

As Wendy walked next to him, Vlad was very aware of the difference in their heights. She was so small, and he had an intense urge to protect her, to wrap his arm around her shoulders and bring her close to him so he could shield her.

It was a silly thought because, despite his freakish strength, he wasn't a fighter. Not in skill and not in inclination. The only times he'd felt violent was when witnessing injustices, the strong preying on the weak. But he'd never acted on those impulses, and he wasn't sure that he could.

"I get a weird vibe from you." Wendy looked up at him. "What's going on?"

He'd forgotten about her empathic ability. But wasn't she supposed to touch someone to get a read on them?

"I was thinking about Yamanu's invitation to train with him in the gym. He is a Guardian, so I assume that some hand-to-hand combat training would be part of it. The thing is, I'm not sure I can strike someone even in self-defense. But I probably could do that to defend someone else."

She smiled. "You are really a nice guy, Vlad. Too nice. Training could be good for you. If someone attacks you, your training will take over, and you'll defend yourself without even thinking."

"Did you experience that?"

She shrugged. "We had a self-defense class in the program, and that was what the instructor said. She said that it was important to practice a lot so the response would be instinctive. If you have to think about your next move, you are already too late."

"That sounds reasonable. Maybe you can come with me and Yamanu can train us together?"

She looked up at him, examining his skinny arms and probably thinking that he was a weakling.

"Is Yamanu a good teacher?"

"I don't know. I've never attended any of his self-defense classes. I guess we will have to find out."

Wendy

"Which movie would you like to watch?" Vlad scrolled through the selection on the tablet that served as the remote for the theater.

"Have you seen *Ready Player One*?"

She'd watched it on Netflix in her room, but she wanted to watch it again. Living inside a virtual game world appealed to her on so many levels. She could choose an avatar that was beautiful and strong, and she could do things that were impossible in the real world.

The possibilities were endless.

"I did. But I don't mind watching it again." Vlad selected the movie. "Would you like some popcorn?"

"Yes, please."

"I'll be right back."

Vlad had surprised her today. It seemed like her pep talk from the day before had done him good. He was less timid, and he'd even sung for her.

His voice was as beautiful as his soul.

She sighed, wondering whether growing up in a loving home had made him a good person, or was it genetic? Did children of decent, loving people inherit their parents' genes, which made them good as well?

What did it say about her, though? Was she destined to be bad?

Neither of her parents were good. Her father was a nasty man with a drinking problem who had taken out his frustrations on his daughter, and her mother was a drug addict who'd left her baby to be raised by a monster.

That was probably another good reason to never get into a relationship. With the example she had, what kind of a mother could she possibly be?

Perhaps people with her genetic makeup should never have children.

"Here you go." Vlad handed her a paper bag filled to the brim with popcorn.

"Is it all for me?" she teased.

"I'm going to help." He took a fistful. "And we can always make more."

"I don't think we will be able to finish this one."

Vlad shrugged and pretended to drape his arm nonchalantly over the back of her seat.

It was cute for a twenty-year-old guy to make a middle-schooler move, and she was glad that he was so reserved. If he had put his arm on her shoulders, she would have removed it. They weren't on a date, and she shouldn't encourage him.

Except, if she wanted to get out of this basement prison, perhaps she should pretend that she wanted to be more than friends. Using Vlad like that would be a nasty thing to do, but then she wasn't a good person, so why would she care?

Her objective was to stay in her uncle's good graces, and giving him a cache of paranormal talents would earn her a permanent position as his favorite person. She could have a good future in the program, helping her uncle run the secret paranormal division.

She would just have to make it clear that making babies, normal or super, was not part of the deal. She was never going to get married or become a mother. Her life would be about her work and nothing else.

Wendy grimaced.

She'd just described Marisol.

Did she want to be like that heartless bitch?

Thankfully, Vlad hadn't gathered the courage to move his arm from the back of her chair to her shoulders. But he was thinking about it while nervously shoving popcorn into his mouth until it was all gone long before the movie was over.

Wendy felt the battle he was waging with himself and was glad that the timid side was winning.

When the movie ended, she lifted the empty paper bag and shook it. "I think I would like some more after all."

"Do you want to watch another movie?"

"No, I just want more popcorn. We can take it to my room and play one of your video games."

Vlad's eyes sparkled with excitement, or rather the one she could see. The other one was covered by his long bangs.

Wendy reached up and swiped it aside. "You will ruin your eyesight like that."

"Not much chance of that." He climbed the stairs to the back of the theater.

"Yeah, right. You think that you are invincible because you are still young, but it's all downhill from here."

He smiled, his long canines gleaming white in the dark theater. "Not for me."

Wendy rolled her eyes. "Pretending to be a vampire doesn't make you one."

That seemed to amuse him, but he didn't respond. Instead, he loaded the machine with more corn kernels and pressed a button.

Nothing happened.

"Is there a power outage?" She looked at the dim lights illuminating the back of the theater. Those could be powered by backup batteries.

Vlad shook his head. "We have generators that come online automatically when it happens. Something must be wrong with the machine."

"Usually, it's as simple as the plug getting loose."

Wendy crouched and looked under the antique popcorn maker. She could see the cord and part of the socket. If she flattened herself on the floor, she could reach it.

"What are you doing?" Vlad sounded alarmed.

"I can see part of the plug, and it looks loose. I think I can reach it." She pushed herself forward on her tummy, but her arm was still too short.

"Let me do it. I have longer arms."

"I almost got it."

She pushed a little further, stretching her arm as far as it would go, and made contact with the socket, as well as something furry that moved.

"Yikes!" Jerking back, Wendy bumped her head against the underside of the machine, and the whole thing started listing.

Closing her eyes, she expected to get crushed under its weight, but it never happened. Instead, she felt the whole thing vanish.

A split second later, Vlad was crouching next to her. "Are you okay? What happened?"

Turning around, she wondered where the popcorn machine had gone. She saw it behind Vlad, resting innocently on its spindly legs as if nothing had happened.

"I bumped my head on the underside of that thing. How did it get there? Did I black out or something?"

"I hope not. I caught it before it fell on top of you and moved it there."

Wendy looked at the machine again. It was about five feet tall, two feet wide, and four feet long, and it looked heavy.

"How did you manage that? That thing must weigh a ton."

"It doesn't. It just looks heavy. How is your head?"

She rubbed the spot. "It's okay." Then remembering what had caused the incident, she jumped to her feet and shook out her hands.

"What are you doing?"

"There was a spider on the socket. That's what freaked me out."

Vlad shook his head. "You could've been killed because of a harmless spider."

"Hey, you just said that the machine wasn't that heavy, so it couldn't have killed me."

Curious, she put her hands on it and tried to push it. "It doesn't even budge."

"That's because its legs are wedged in the carpet."

"Okay, then I'll try to lift it."

She grabbed a bar on one side and tried to just tip it, but barely managed to lift it an inch before letting it drop back.

Narrowing her eyes at Vlad, she put her hands on her hips. "Is telekinesis one of your talents?"

He laughed. "No. I lifted it with my arms, not my mind. I was so scared for you, and the adrenaline rush must have added strength to my muscles."

What muscles? He didn't have any.

Then again, she'd heard about impossible feats that had been fueled by adrenaline, so maybe Vlad was right.

"I think I'll skip another serving of popcorn. Let's grab a beer from the kitchen instead."

He frowned. "You're nineteen. You are not supposed to drink."

"Who is going to tell me no? Come on. I'm sure that after all this excitement, you can use one yourself."

Kian

Syssi walked into Kian's home office with a guilty expression on her beautiful face. "I'm heading out to the café to have lunch with Amanda. Are you going to be okay here by yourself?"

He knew that the guilt was not over leaving him in the house to eat his lunch alone. It was over keeping secrets from him. Syssi and Amanda were planning a surprise birthday party for him, and that's what the lunch was about.

"I'll miss you, of course. But don't worry about me. I still have a lot of work to do, and I also need to call Lokan and arrange a conference call between him and the Bay Area team."

"Should I tell Okidu to bring your lunch in here?"

Kian nodded.

Rounding the desk, Syssi leaned over to give him a kiss, but he wasn't satisfied with the quick peck on the lips and pulled her onto his lap for a proper one.

When she came up for air, they were both panting and ready for more.

"Do you have time for a quickie?"

Her eyes were glazed with desire, but she shook her head. "I wish I did. But Amanda is waiting for me." She pushed up.

"That's a shame."

She smiled coyly. "I'll be back in about two hours. Try to be done by then, and I'll take you up on your offer."

"Deal. Only it's not going to be a quickie then. I'm going to take my time with you." He adjusted himself.

As always, the mention of sexual play made his wife blush, her pale cheeks flushing with the most beautiful pink hue. Which had him thinking about turning her other pale cheeks pink.

No doubt the same thought, or something along those lines, had caused the blush and the sudden flare in the scent of her arousal.

Syssi loved their kinky games.

"I'd better get out of here while I still can." She blew him an air kiss and walked out the door.

For a long moment, Kian stared at the open file on his desk, trying to read but comprehending none of it. With images of what he and Syssi would do in a couple of hours dancing in front of his eyes, it was impossible to get his mind back on track.

It could wait for later.

He had phone calls to make, and those could be done outside the house in the back yard while enjoying a cigarillo. Maybe a shot of whiskey as well? Or was it too early for that?

Beer would be better.

Pulling the sliding door open, he stepped out, closed it behind him, and sat down on one of the easy chairs right outside of his home office.

After lighting up, he called Lokan first. "Are you ready for the conference call?"

"Give me five minutes. Carol and I are just about done with lunch."

"No problem. I'll get everyone ready for you and call you back."

"Good deal."

Arwel was next. "How are things going, is everyone ready for Lokan?"

"I have everyone here in the living room, and the others are waiting for his call in the hotel. Three of the guys are on watch duty, but he can do them last."

"Good plan. Anything else?"

"Yeah." He heard Arwel get up and start walking. "We had an incident this morning that might be nothing or might be something. Jacki gave everyone the slip and went out for a walk around the neighborhood."

Kian frowned. "How could that have happened? Did no one hear her leave?"

"It's a big house, and people go in and out of rooms and the front door all of the time. Besides, the Guardians on duty were not aware that they were supposed to keep an eye on Jacki."

"I assume that you found her, and everything is okay?"

"We drove around the neighborhood and found her walking several streets over. She had her hood up and was wearing the special glasses."

"Do you think she was planning to escape?"

"It crossed my mind that it might have been a test run to see if she could get away."

"Keep an eye on her."

"Of course. I told the Guardians to do the same and report to me if she leaves again. I don't want them to stop her because we are trying to maintain the illusion that she's not a prisoner."

"Technically, she is not. If she really wants to leave, we will have to let her go. But unless she is very clever and knows how to stay under the radar, that would mean an immediate capture for her."

"Unless we give her fake documents and drop her off in another country."

"That would increase her chances of evading capture, but not eliminate them. The government is investing a lot of resources into finding paranormal talents. They want them back."

"Any new developments on that front?"

Kian took a puff of his cigarillo. "Surprisingly, very little is being done. Which reinforces my suspicion that one of the three is an informant."

"Who's at the top of your suspect list, Jacki?"

Kian chuckled. "That position keeps rotating every few hours. Each of them has something to gain or lose, and they all passed Edna and Andrew's tests."

"That's what makes Jacki the most likely suspect. She has the strongest protective walls, and as far as she knows, she has a lot to lose and little to gain by staying with us."

"True. On the other hand, she was the one who convinced Jin to run."

"Jacki is a seer. She might have seen more in her vision than what she told Jin. She could have realized that it was a great opportunity for bringing a bunch of new talents into the program."

Jin

"Jin, is that you?" Lokan leaned closer to the screen. "If I saw you on the street, I wouldn't have recognized you."

Eva's online tutorial had worked out great. With tons of makeup and new-colored and styled wigs, Jin and Jacki were hardly recognizable. They were also wearing layers of clothing to make themselves look fatter.

Luckily for them, it was cold outside. Unluckily for the rest of the house's occupants, they had to go without heating.

"That's because you can see only my face and it's a small screen. I can't hide my height, and that's what people notice first about me."

"You look fifteen years older. Can I see Jacki?"

Her friend popped her head next to Jin's. "What do you think?"

"Same for you. Fantastic job."

Jacki grinned. "I never thought that I would be so happy about looking old and ugly."

"You're not ugly. Not even with that on."

Jacki waved a dismissive hand. "You're such a charmer, Lokan. But let's get down to business. Tell Jin not to listen to anything Kalugal tells her to do, and just in case I'm not immune to him, do the same for me."

He chuckled. "Compulsion needs more precise wording. If I do what you suggest, neither of you would hear a word he says."

"Yes, master." Jacki mock bowed. "Whatever you say."

"Refuse to obey Kalugal's commands. It's as simple as that."

Jin frowned. "That's it? What if he asks nicely?"

"Jin, you must refuse Kalugal's commands and requests no matter how politely he phrases them."

"That's better. Is that all?"

"Yes. You can give the tablet to Jacki."

As Jin listened to Lokan give each of them the same command, she wondered whether it would do any good.

Logically, the answer was no. Given that Kalugal was much more powerful than his brother, he could most likely override Lokan's compulsion.

And yet, combined with the new disguise, it helped her feel a little more confident and a little less scared.

When he was done with the last Guardian in the room, Arwel took the tablet, thanked him, and ended the call.

"How are you feeling?" he asked.

"Even though it's probably a placebo effect, I feel more confident."

Kri walked over and put her hand on Jin's shoulder. "Your problem is not enough practice. When you saw Kalugal, you started to think about how you were going to touch him and about everything that could go wrong. The trick is to just do it. Move forward without thinking, and that can be achieved only with a lot of training."

"Who am I going to practice on?"

Kri waved a hand around the room. "Everyone here. We will put music on and pretend the living room is a club. All of us will dance while you walk around with a drink in your hand, bump into people and tether them. Then you are going to release the tethers and start all over again."

Arwel shook his head. "If Jin expends all of her mental energy on practice, she will have nothing left by the end of the day. And since it's Saturday, there is a good chance Kalugal will go out hunting tonight."

Jacki grimaced. "Why do you call clubbing hunting? It sounds like a safari."

Kri snorted. "Because that's exactly what it is. But back to Jin. She has to practice no matter what. Worst case, she will get Kalugal some other day or even next Saturday. It's better than blowing another disguise."

"I agree with Kri," Jin said. "The draining part is not attaching the mental hook or removing it, it's holding on to several strings at once."

"Then let's party." Vivian clapped her hands. "Guys, start moving furniture. We need to clear an area for a dance floor."

When the living room was ready, Arwel put on music, and everyone other than Jin started dancing. It was fun to watch, especially William, who had surprising moves.

Even Jacki looked impressed.

Two of the three burly bears just swayed in place, holding their beers and pretending to be scanning for girls.

Hunting, as Arwel called it.

Wine glass in hand, Jin concentrated on the loud music instead of looking at the people she knew well. Letting her vision blur, she started a meandering path.

She bumped into one person and then another and caught the arm of the third as if to steady herself.

"I'm so sorry." She wiped nonexistent wine drops from Ewan's sleeve while tethering him. "I spilled some on you."

"That's okay," the Guardian said. "No harm done."

And so it went on.

After she'd tethered and released everyone twice, Arwel turned the music off. "I think that's enough."

"For now," Kri said. "We will take a break for lunch and then do another round."

Arwel looked at Jin. "How are you holding up?"

"I'm good. Kri is right. After the third or the fourth tether, I stopped thinking and just did it on autopilot. Another round of tethering after lunch is a good idea."

Arwel didn't seem convinced. "Did it become harder the more people you tethered?"

"Not if I released the tether right away. If I kept more than three at the same time, I felt fatigued."

Kri clapped her on the back. "Good job, girl. Your act was very convincing. You looked a little tipsy but not stupidly drunk, and your apologies didn't sound fake."

Jin let out a breath. "Thanks. I was worried about that."

To her, the act seemed forced and her apologies sounded insincere. She was glad Kri thought otherwise, but she wanted another opinion. The one person she knew wouldn't try to be nice and would give it to her straight was Jacki.

"What do you think?" she asked her.

"It was good. But more practice wouldn't hurt. And don't look at the person you are apologizing to. Pretend to be embarrassed and focus on the spilled drink."

Jin nodded. "If I don't look at Kalugal's face, I can pretend that it's not him."

"That too," Jacki said. "But I was thinking more along the lines of him not getting a good look at you. He might recognize you from before."

Kalugal

Rufsur walked into Kalugal's study. "Are we going out tonight?"

"I'm not in the mood." He didn't even lift his head from the book.

The Inca were much more fascinating than chasing tail in clubs.

Last night had been meh. The sisters had been a no show, and the girl he'd picked up had been a bore. She'd seemed so promising but had turned out disappointing on all accounts.

As an English major who loved literature, she should have been well-read and interesting to talk to. But after twenty minutes or so he'd found himself carrying on a monologue because she had nothing to say.

Perhaps he'd intimidated her into silence. That happened sometimes. Not because he was overbearing or condescending, but because he was so knowledgeable.

And the sex had been meh as well. The girl had no spirit.

"You are never in the mood. That's why you have me to drag you away from your musty books and your dusty artifacts. You need to interact with people, and you need to get laid."

Kalugal lifted his head. "I really hate that expression. Getting laid implies passiveness. I'm anything but."

Rufsur bowed low. "My apologies, supreme ruler. Let me rephrase. You need to hunt."

Despite his best efforts to keep a straight face, Kalugal's lips lifted in a smile. One of the main reasons he'd chosen Rufsur as his second-in-command was that the guy refused to take any crap from him and was immune to his bullshit.

"Where do you want to go?"

"I liked the Magnet. Plenty of quality females to choose from, not too loud, and the bar doesn't serve diluted drinks."

Kalugal grimaced. "Let's agree to disagree about what qualifies as quality. Our tastes are different. If I am to abandon this fascinating book, it would be for fascinating company."

Rufsur didn't look happy. "Stanford. That's where you want to go."

"Obviously. Why do you think I chose to live fifteen minutes away from the campus?"

"The startups?"

"That too. You'd be surprised how much more interesting the sex is with a smart woman."

Rufsur shook his head. "I have a rule against schtupping women smarter than me, and I'm not into the mind games that you like to play."

"Not every smart woman is into them either, but I find that the higher the IQ, the more the lady is willing to experiment."

"And the less appealing she is. Brainiacs don't put as much effort into primping."

That was true, but Kalugal didn't like overly done-up females either. "To each his own. But since I compromised yesterday, it's your turn to do so today."

"Can't argue with that. Do you want to include Phinas in our outing?"

"Ask him if he wants to join."

Ideally, Kalugal would have preferred to go out by himself, but his men wouldn't have it, which was quite absurd given that he routinely traveled alone to troubled areas around the world.

They weren't happy about that either, but he'd put his foot down.

After Navuh, Kalugal was the most powerful man in the world, and no one could mess with him. Besides, old Professor Gunter didn't attract attention. And if the unthinkable happened and his plane went down or a bomb exploded right over him, his men would perish with him. He didn't need them for protection.

Still, he needed at least one to accompany him to clubs and bars and such. His shrouds worked only locally. If anyone unaffected by his shroud checked the footage from the surveillance cameras later, or the checkers were in a distant location, they would see his real face, and donning a disguise was not practical for hookups.

Naturally, Kalugal could have taken care of the recordings himself, but it was more efficient to have Rufsur or one of his other men do it for him.

That way, he could concentrate on having fun.

"Phinas is going out with Dandor and Welgost. So, it's only the two of us."

"As it usually is."

On the weekends, Kalugal kept only a minimal guard on the premises, and the rest of the men went out to hunt. On weekdays, they each had two evenings out.

Some complained that it wasn't enough, but Kalugal figured that if it was enough for him, it should suffice for them. After all, he and his older brother were the most pure-blooded immortals out there, and from what he had learned, the more pure-blooded the immortal was, the stronger his libido.

Did it work the same way for immortal females?

Kalugal had been too young to think about sex when he'd snuck into the harem to see his mother.

As always, thinking of her brought about a sharp pang, and he rubbed his chest as if the motion could relieve it.

If only he could talk to her again, see her beautiful face, have her hold him in her arms...

Shaking his head, Kalugal put his book away and rose to his feet. It was absurd for a grown man to long for his mother's embrace.

Arwel

"It's busy at Kalugal's today," William muttered. "More people are living in that mansion than we estimated. I counted eight cars so far."

Each time a car left the gate, Jin and Jacki would be on high alert. Since none of them had been a convertible, they couldn't see who was inside until the car reached its destination and the Guardian following it snapped photos of those getting out.

None had been Kalugal, but they were collecting valuable information about his men. So far, it seemed like there were no females in the compound. Not a single woman had left the place or had gotten in.

Which was odd.

Arwel had expected housekeeping staff, but it seemed that Kalugal's men were responsible for the upkeep. Either that or they kept a bunch of enslaved women in his bunker. Given what Sharim had done in the basement of the monastery, it wasn't such a farfetched scenario.

Arwel flipped through the photos that the watchers had snapped. "Even without following them, it's obvious that none of these was driven by Kalugal. He likes fancy cars."

"We can't be sure of that. A careful guy like him is probably aware of how noticeable those are."

"In this neighborhood, he is not the only one driving an expensive vehicle. Living here, he can get away with it."

"Still, if it were me, I would keep a lower profile. Mercedes and BMW are fine automobiles and don't attract as much attention."

When Jin walked into the office looking like someone else, all Arwel had to do was close his eyes and inhale her familiar essence to reassure himself that everything was as it should be.

The poor girl had been stuck in the costume the entire day, but he'd convinced her to at least take off the layers of clothing. Putting them back on would take a minute, and there was no sense in her and Jacki sweating buckets while waiting for the right car to leave the gate.

"Dinner is ready," she said.

William shook his head. "I'll eat here if you don't mind. I don't want to miss Kalugal."

Jin put her hand on her hip and struck a pose. "You can't sit in this chair all day long and not move. We have watchers upstairs, and they take turns. They will alert us when a car leaves that gate."

"Yes, ma'am." He rolled his chair back and got up.

In the dining room, everyone other than the Guardian on duty was already seated at the table.

"Who cooked?" Arwel pulled out a chair for Jin.

Vivian waved a hand. "Magnus, Kri, and Michael. I only made the salad."

"Thank you."

Regrettably, none of them was a good cook, but Jacki couldn't perform her culinary magic while wearing an itchy wig and tons of makeup. Both girls were uncomfortable, but it was unavoidable.

"I hope this ends tonight," Jin said. "I don't want to spend another day like this. I'm a nervous wreck." She bit into a piece of dry toast.

"Aren't you going to eat the spaghetti?"

She shook her head. "I'm nauseous, and toast is the only thing I can stomach right now."

He took her hand and brought it up to his lips. Her hands and the back of her neck were the only spots not covered in makeup and safe to kiss. "Try to relax."

Jin chuckled. "That's the best I can do."

Jacki had no such problem. She was slurping the spaghetti up one noodle at a time, oblivious to what it was doing to the bachelors watching her.

"Can you stop that?" Jin made a face. "The slurping sounds make me even more nauseous."

Jacki frowned. "Sorry. I didn't realize it was so loud." She looked around the table, finally noticing the men's eyes on her. "Am I grossing you out?"

"Not at all," William said. "I've just never seen anyone eating spaghetti like that."

The discussion that started about the best way to eat noodles was interrupted by William's phone buzzing with an incoming message.

"The Ferrari just left the gate. I'm sure it's Kalugal behind the wheel, but you'd better verify." He passed the phone to Jacki.

"It's him." She handed the phone back. "What face is he shrouding himself in this time?"

"It's the same one from yesterday," William said while texting the info to the Guardians waiting to follow the car. "Apparently, he has several shrouds that he uses for different activities. This one is his hunting face. He needs to look handsome for that."

Jacki pushed away from the table. "We should get in the cars and wait for directions."

Arwel motioned for the others to do the same. "I want everyone in the garage in five minutes. Kri, you are going with Jin and Jacki. Michael and Ewan, you are with me. Magnus and Gregor, you are in the third car."

They hadn't planned on Kri accompanying the girls, but suddenly it seemed like a good idea to him.

Jin would feel safer with Kri around, and if shit went down for some unforeseeable reason, the Guardian was a force to be reckoned with.

Jin

Arwel poked his head through the passenger side window. "He is heading to Stanford. You can start driving in that direction, and as soon as he arrives at his destination, the guys will text you the address."

"You're going to follow close behind us, right?" Jin knew that, but she needed reassurance.

"That's right. And you have Kri with you. She can kick ass just as well as any of the guys."

Jin smiled. "I've seen her in action, and I'm glad she is coming with us."

Behind the wheel, Kri snorted. "You've seen nothing. That was just friendly sparring. I'm a killing machine in a real fight."

Jin leaned away. "Have you ever killed anyone?"

"Not yet. Humans are too easy to kill to bother, and Kian would not let me fight Doomers."

Arwel growled.

Kri had just blurted stuff she wasn't supposed to next to Jacki.

Thinking quickly, Jin lifted her finger. "I've heard about those gangs. The Humans are not nearly as vicious as the Doomers. No wonder Kian keeps you away from the fights. I've heard they do ritual killings, really gruesome, horrible stuff."

Luckily for them, Jacki wasn't an empath. "I've never heard about those gangs. Where are they operating, Chicago?"

"They are all over." Jin turned around. "They are quickly becoming the two largest drug cartels in the States. And there have been rumors about the Doomers getting into trafficking as well."

Jacki shook her head. "I really need to pay more attention to the news."

"You'd better get moving." Arwel leaned and kissed the top of Jin's head. "Good luck."

"Thanks."

As Kri eased out of the garage, a ghost of a smile lifted the corners of her lips. "You are going to be fine."

Jin slumped in her seat. "I hope so."

"Don't think. Just do. Pretend that you are back at the house, training. Do exactly what you did this morning. You were perfect."

"How are we going to do it?" Jacki asked. "We can't go in together because we are all tall and we will attract attention. Especially you, Kri. You are pretty, and with those boots and that leather jacket, you look like a badass. Guys will look at you. Jin and I look like a couple of suburban housewives."

Kri didn't bother to deny it. "We can use that to our advantage. I'll go in first and strut around, maybe flirt loudly with some guys, make a scene and start a fight. Everyone will be looking at me while Jacki enters quietly. Jin, you will come in last."

Imagining Kri knocking guys over and making a scene, Jin shook her head. "Isn't a bar fight too much?"

Kri shrugged. "I'll play it by ear."

"You need to tether me," Jacki said.

"We have earpieces. You can just tell me who he is and where he is standing. That way Kri will know as well."

"I know what he looks like because I saw the picture of who he shrouds himself as." Kri glanced at Jacki through the rearview mirror. "But he might decide to change the shroud for some reason, and then we will need you to find him."

Jin nodded. "That could easily happen if Kalugal sees someone he's been with already and doesn't want her to recognize him while he is hitting on someone else."

"You know what I find really bizarre?" Jacki said.

"What?" Jin tensed, hoping it wasn't about the two gangs she'd made up to cover for Kri's mistake.

"The pictures the guys snap of Kalugal. If he is not in the area, actively manipulating your minds, how come you still see his shroud in those and not his real face?"

"Good question." Jin glanced at Kri. "Maybe the suggestion he plants in our heads stays there. That makes him even more powerful than what we've suspected."

Kri nodded. "Compulsion is a very rare talent. Kalugal must combine it with his shrouds. That's why they hold. I don't know Lokan well, so I'm not sure if he can do that as well, but I would be very surprised if he can."

"I still think that you need to tether me. Shit can happen, the earpieces can malfunction, the reception in the club might be lousy, and Kalugal's men might invade the house and take William hostage. Even a power outage can mess things up. The tether is the most secure connection."

"As unlikely as those scenarios are, you are right about the tether." Jin turned toward the backseat. "Give me your hand."

Jacki shook it. "Done?"

"Yes."

Ten minutes into the drive, Arwel spoke in their earpieces. "Kalugal and his guy just parked at a club. I'm sending you the address."

As the churning in Jin's belly turned from mild to intense, she rubbed a hand over it. "How do I keep from throwing up?"

Kri put a hand on her thigh. "You are not going to puke. You are going to get in there, get a drink, zero in on our boy, and bump into him. He'll be too busy watching me to notice you approach him."

"Are you still planning on starting a fight?"

"I'll wait to see how you are doing. If you hesitate, I'll go up to a random chick and start accusing her of stealing my boyfriend."

Jacki chuckled. "A catfight will attract everyone's attention."

"Yeah, I'll pretend to be drunk. As soon as you tether Kalugal, let me know and I'll apologize, saying that it was a case of mistaken identity."

"Who will leave the club first?" Jacki asked.

"Jin, then you, and lastly, me. I'm not going to leave until I know that both of you are safe."

Arwel

As Kri turned into the club's parking lot, Magnus entered behind her, while Arwel continued driving to the nearest intersection and turned around.

After parking across the street from the club's entrance, he called the Guardians who'd followed Kalugal to the club. "You can leave."

"Good luck," Chester said. "If you need us, we will be in a pub five minutes away from here."

"Thanks. I won't say no to additional backup."

"We are too close," Michael said. "And this is a loading zone. Maybe you should park a little farther down the street."

"I want to be where I can see the door."

"Then backtrack a little. Everyone going in will wonder about three dudes who are just sitting in their car."

"It's fine. The windows are tinted, and even if they can see us, people will assume that we are waiting for someone."

Michael shrugged. "You're the boss."

The club had two egress points. One in the front and one in the back.

To get in, club-goers had to go through the front door and get cleared by the bouncer. But to leave, they could also use the back door to the parking lot, which Magnus and Gregor were watching.

The additional three Guardians Arwel had requested would be arriving shortly, and he debated whether to assign them to guard the back or park farther down the street like Michael had suggested. They were a precaution, so maybe it was better for them to stay out of sight. Together with the two at the pub, Jin had a total of ten Guardians ready to jump in if needed.

The problem was that all of them were useless against Kalugal's compulsion.

As Kri rounded the corner and sauntered toward the entrance, the bouncer gave her a thorough once-over and opened the door with a slight dip of his head.

A few minutes later, Jacki came around, but instead of walking straight in, she glanced around, probably to check where they were parked.

Arwel groaned. That was such an amateur move. He'd thought that not acknowledging their escorts was self-explanatory, so he hadn't bothered warning the girls against it.

The mistake was his, not Jacki's. She was a newbie with no training, and what was obvious to him was not necessarily obvious to her.

When she saw the car, Jacki smiled but thankfully didn't wave, and only then headed toward the club's entrance.

More than ten minutes passed before Jin rounded the corner, huddling into her coat and not looking left or right while hurrying toward the door.

Was it an act? Or was she really cold?

If it was an act, it was a good one because he had the urge to grab his coat and rush to cover her with it.

When the door closed behind her, Arwel's gut twisted with worry.

He tried to reason with himself that Kalugal had only one man with him, and if needed, Kri could take care of the guy, but the problem was Kalugal himself.

They were all defenseless against his compulsion. If anything went wrong and he became aware of Jin and her intentions, they were all royally screwed.

Even if every Guardian on the force was there as backup, it would not make a difference. Kalugal could walk out of there with Jin in tow and no one would be able to stop him.

Given his powers, it was a wonder that the guy had only used them to make money. He could've taken over the damn White House if he wanted.

Thank the merciful Fates for immunes. That was probably the only reason Kalugal hadn't done anything crazy. He must have encountered some over the years and figured that he shouldn't risk it. With the right kind of bullet and a carefully aimed shot to the head or the heart, one immune sharpshooter could incapacitate Kalugal long enough for his teammates to finish the job by either decapitating him or removing his heart.

"You are stressing the hell out of me," Michael murmured. "Relax."

"My mate is in there."

"So is mine, but I know Kri can handle any situation. I've only seen her in action once, and it was awe-inspiring. She took out seven armed humans in seconds."

"I'm not worried about humans. I just wish we had several immune Guardians. As it is, we are defenseless against Kalugal. He could walk right past us or command us to follow him into his bunker."

"Maybe some of the Guardians are immune," Ewan said. "We were never tested."

"We should have been." Arwel turned to the Guardian. "Annani could have tested us."

"Too late for that," Michael said. "Besides, I think you are all worrying too much. Worst case scenario, we can negotiate with him. After all, we have an ace up our sleeve."

Arwel arched a brow. "What?"

"His brother."

"We don't actually have him. He is his own man."

"Semantics. He is not going to refuse to help. Carol would castrate him."

Arwel's lips twitched in an involuntary smile. "I'm not sure about the castrating part, but she might threaten him with bodily harm. The question is whether Lokan can override Kalugal's compulsion. If he can, we have nothing to worry about because he compelled us to refuse Kalugal's commands."

Michael shrugged. "What we can be pretty sure of is that Lokan is immune. If Navuh's compulsion didn't affect him, Kalugal's most likely will not either, and he can negotiate for us."

It wasn't much, but it was better than nothing. Arwel had kept up a confident façade in front of Jin, but the truth was that he was terrified for her.

Closing his eyes, he let his awareness spread wide. If anything went wrong, he would feel it.

Jin

As Jin entered the club, she didn't try to find Kalugal right away. Her eyes went searching for Kri first. The Guardian was her safety net, and just knowing that she was there, watching over her, diminished her anxiety by at least half.

She found her leaning against one of the supporting pillars and holding a bottle of beer in her hand.

No glass for the badass.

The woman was formidable, and not only physically. She had a warrior's attitude, which meant that she wouldn't hesitate to jump in and do whatever she could to help Jin.

"Look to your right," Jacki said in her earpiece. "Do you see the girl with the pink miniskirt?"

Afraid to move her lips, Jin nodded, hoping Jacki could see her.

"The guy she is plastered against is Kalugal."

Closing her eyes, Jin followed the tether to Jacki and looked at the couple through her friend's eyes.

Still, all she saw was the shroud and not Kalugal's real face.

"Can you see the real him?" Jacki asked.

It was weird to hear her in the earpiece and through the tether at the same time.

Jin shook her head.

"So Kri was right. He manipulates everyone around him to see only his shroud, and it sticks no matter what medium is used to look at him."

Jin nodded, then searched for Jacki, figuring her likely position by her viewing angle.

She was sitting on a barstool, holding a large drink in front of her face to hide her moving lips as best she could.

With so many people crowding the space getting to the bar wasn't easy, especially since Jin didn't want to shove people out of the way and attract attention.

It took her what seemed like forever to get there, and then she had to wait for the barman to take her order.

Everything was taking too long. What if Kalugal left, and she missed her opportunity once more?

The thing was, she had a script to follow, one that she'd rehearsed over and over again. If she deviated from it, she might freeze again.

When the barman finally handed her the large mojito she'd ordered, Jin took it and turned around, fearing that

Kalugal would no longer be where she'd last seen him on the dance floor.

Thank God, he was in the same spot with the same blonde girl clinging to him.

Drink in hand, Jin ambled toward the couple. Swaying to the music, she inched toward them the same way she'd practiced at home.

Kri was right. With enough repetition, it almost felt natural, and Jin managed to keep her anxiety at a low simmer, not letting it flare up.

She didn't go straight at them. Instead, she went a little to the left, then a little to the right, never facing them but keeping track of them in her peripheral vision.

Even though she looked very different from what Kalugal saw the day before, he still might recognize her face or her smell.

She'd sprayed herself with enough perfume to knock out an elephant, but then she wasn't dealing with an ordinary immortal. He might be able to smell her real scent under the artificial one.

Stop it!

Those thoughts were needlessly stressing her out. She was very close to him now, and he hadn't even turned his head in her direction.

The blonde with the pink skirt must have been sent by the Fates. With her hands roaming all over Kalugal's back, her big boobs pressed against his chest, and her ass filling his hands, she had his full attention.

As it turned out, Jin didn't even need to fake stumbling into him.

As someone bumped into her from behind, she pitched forward, spilling her mojito all over Kalugal and the blonde and then catching his arm to stop herself from falling.

The training kicked in.

Holding on for a moment longer, she inserted a hook into his mind and attached her tether to it.

It was done in under two seconds.

"You idiot!" the blonde yelled. "Look what you have done!"

"I'm so sorry." Jin patted Kalugal's sleeve. "I'll pay to have it dry cleaned. Someone bumped into me, and I lost my balance. I'm so sorry."

"Don't worry about it," Kalugal said. "Alcohol dries fast."

Pretending to obsess about his ruined shirt, Jin kept her face down. "Are you sure? Let me at least pay for the dry cleaning."

"Forget it. No harm done."

"What about me?" the blonde whined. "She spilled her drink all over my new skirt."

"It will dry out. And if not, I'll buy you a new one."

"Really?" Her tone turned sugary and she put her hands over his chest. "You look sexy with your shirt all wet."

And just like that Jin was forgotten and the couple went back to necking on the dance floor.

Mission accomplished.

Almost. She still needed to check whether the tether worked, and she also couldn't leave right after the incident.

If it had been real, she would have ordered another drink to calm her nerves, as would most girls in her situation.

As she made her way toward the bar, Jacki spoke in her earpiece, "Did you get him?"

Jin nodded.

"Then let's get out of here."

Jin ignored the suggestion until she reached Jacki, who was still sitting on the same stool. Squeezing between her and the guy sitting next to her, she ordered another drink.

"I have to check it out," she said without looking at her friend. "And it would look suspicious if I leave right away."

"You can go toward the bathrooms and continue to the back door," Kri said in the earpiece.

Jin looked at the barman. "I'm waiting for my drink."

"Coming right up. You're next in line."

Leaning against the bar, Jin closed her eyes and followed the tether to Kalugal.

The connection was loud and clear.

"You told me that your ex-boyfriend was working on something interesting," Kalugal said.

"Yeah, he had an idea for an Alexa type device, but then Google came up with something better."

"Did he drop it?"

"I don't know. Why are we talking about him?"

"I'm curious about new technologies."

"Then maybe you should hook up with him instead."

Jin could feel a little of what Kalugal was feeling, which was annoyance and contempt.

Apparently, he wasn't even attracted to Blondie. He only wanted to pump her for information about her ex-boyfriend.

Except, she might have been projecting her own feelings on him. It was rare for Jin to feel her targets' emotions at all.

Except for Arwel.

The connection with him had been amazing, but then what he'd been feeling at the time was intense.

"Let's go," Jacki said in her earpiece.

"I'm still waiting for that drink." Jin smiled at the bartender so he wouldn't get mad at her for pestering him.

Her words were meant for Jacki and Kri.

What Jin really wanted was to hear more about Blondie's ex-boyfriend and his invention. She could try to listen while walking out, but if someone talked to her she might lose concentration and miss some of what was being said. If Kalugal was interested in the technology, then it must be something important, and it might give Kian a clue about Kalugal's future plans.

Arwel

"How long has it been?" Michael lifted his phone to check the time. "Damn, not long at all. Jin only went in thirteen minutes ago. Time moves slowly when the stakes are high."

Arwel nodded.

It felt as if he'd been spreading his mental feelers for at least an hour. Regrettably, he couldn't get a read on any of the three women.

Kri was an immortal, Jacki had thick protective walls, and Jin didn't project her feelings as strongly as other humans did.

Which was excellent for the mission.

Even if she got nervous, Kalugal wouldn't pick up on the intensity. To him, it would feel like the normal emotions of a woman alone in a club. A little apprehensive and a lot hopeful.

His thoughts were interrupted when something dark and nasty registered on the edge of his awareness. Arwel opened his eyes and looked out the window.

The strength of the emotions indicated that the source was human, not immortal, but where was it coming from?

There was no one in front of the car, and the only person at the entrance to the club was the bouncer.

The darkness wasn't coming from his direction.

As Arwel glanced at the rearview mirror, he saw a man walking toward them. His head was bowed, and he was huddled in a heavy coat, holding his arms over its front.

Was he hiding a weapon under there?

The closer the man got, the stronger Arwel felt the turmoil raging inside him. The pain and the hatred were almost too much to bear, and Arwel was only getting it secondhand.

The source was about to explode.

Was he heading toward the club? Arwel waited to see if the guy would cross to the other side.

Even if he had dark deeds on his mind, there wasn't much Arwel could do about it. Intentions, even murderous ones, were not a crime.

Only acting upon them was.

"I feel nefarious intentions," Michael muttered. "Someone is planning to do harm. A human male."

"He is right behind us."

"Should we do something about it?"

"Only if he goes into the club. Intentions don't qualify as a crime, and we are not the police."

Except, when the guy got off the sidewalk and started for the other side of the street, legal or even moral considerations went out the window.

His mate was in that club, and Arwel wasn't going to wait for this bomb to explode anywhere near Jin.

As the guy handed the bouncer what was probably a cash bribe, Arwel opened the driver's side door. "Wait here."

"I'm coming with you," Ewan said.

He didn't need help to handle one human. And if the guy had a bomb under his coat and was planning to murder countless people while committing suicide, Arwel didn't want anyone else to get hurt.

"Both of you stay in the car, and that's an order."

Sensing the human's determination, Arwel yelled into the earpiece, "Take cover. A gunman just came in."

Running toward the entrance, he didn't bother with thralling. Arwel barreled past the bouncer, threw the door open, and leaped just as the guy pulled out a gun.

Sailing over people's heads, he landed on the shooter, tackling him to the ground.

Except, he wasn't fast enough.

The gun fired.

The panic gripping Arwel was like nothing he had experienced before, and if not for his training dictating his moves, he might have first looked up to check on his mate.

Instead, he went for the gun, wrenched it out of the guy's hand, at the same time delivering a blow to his head and knocking him out cold or possibly killing him.

The screaming started a split second later, followed by a stampede.

He couldn't see Jin from where he was, and with the panicked humans all around him, there was no chance of him feeling her either.

It took him another split second to remember that he had an earpiece. "Is everyone okay?"

"Jacki and I are hiding behind the bar."

Arwel felt faint with relief.

"I'm trying to get to you," Kri said. "Damn humans are like a stampeding herd of scared buffalos."

Kalugal

Kalugal hadn't seen the shooter come in, and he hadn't felt his intentions either. He wasn't close enough. Besides, with so many humans around, lusting, envying, plotting, it would have been impossible to isolate one who was crazier than the rest even if he was standing right next to him.

What had alerted Kalugal and made him look over his shoulder, were the blonde's widening eyes and her sudden flare of fear.

He watched the scene unfolding before his eyes as if it was going in slow motion.

One second the shooter was pulling out his gun, and the next a man was sailing in the air over the crowd, his trajectory on a collision course with the guy.

As he landed on the shooter, the gun went off, but not into any of the humans. Somehow the flyboy had managed to knock the gunman's hand up, and the bullet hit the ceiling and went right through the plaster, getting lodged in it.

The screaming started a heartbeat after the shot, which was about how long it had taken the flyboy to get the gun away from the nutcase and knock him out cold.

Unless the guy was an Olympic champion, his speed and power were inhuman.

With people screaming and rushing out, Kalugal could no longer see him, but he was almost certain that Flyboy was an immortal.

Was he one of his father's men?

Sent to protect him?

For a brief moment, Kalugal entertained the absurd notion that his father had known where he had been the entire time and had men watching over him.

Right. More like watching him and reporting back. And the only reason they hadn't attempted to capture him yet was that they were waiting for an opportune moment to catch him by surprise and knock him out before he had a chance to compel them.

Then again, his father might have sent immune warriors after him. Just as there were immune humans, Kalugal had no doubt that there were immune immortals.

Except, Navuh wasn't supposed to know that Kalugal could compel immortals, not unless his mother had revealed his secret.

Was it possible that she had betrayed him?

Regrettably, he couldn't discount that possibility. Areana loved Navuh and thinking that Kalugal was safely out of his reach, she might have told him about his son inheriting the ability to compel immortals.

Whatever the case was, he had to find out. Which meant interrogating that immortal.

"Freeze!" Kalugal shouted over the crowd, infusing his voice with compulsion. "No one move! And no one utter a sound."

The ruckus stopped as if it had never begun.

Moving the blonde aside, Kalugal glanced at Rufsur. His second, who had been on the dance floor right next to him when it had all started, was now frozen like everyone else. "Except for you, Rufsur. You can move."

As Kalugal headed toward where he'd seen Flyboy land, he noticed a woman standing behind the bar who wasn't frozen like the others. Her eyes peeled wide, she gaped at him, and then ducked behind the bar again.

Damn immune.

She looked familiar. Had he seen her before? Perhaps he'd noticed her in his peripheral vision. But why she would register at all baffled him. From one to ten, she was barely a six, and he was being generous.

It didn't matter. No one was going to believe her anyway. They'd think the shock had made her see things.

As Kalugal crouched next to Flyboy, the small hairs on the back of his neck tingled, confirming what he'd suspected. The guy was an immortal.

"Did my father send you? You can answer yes or no."

"No."

Noticing something sticking out of the guy's ear, Kalugal leaned closer and moved his hair aside, exposing it.

"What do we have here?"

He pulled the earpiece out. Obviously, Flyboy wasn't alone, and damage control was required.

Kalugal needed to buy himself time to get away without anyone following him. Activating the device, he put it in his own ear. "Everyone listening, stop talking, texting and any other form of communication. Don't move unless you are driving. If you are, pull to the side of the road and then sit in the vehicle until I tell you to move."

That should do it without causing too much trouble.

For a moment, he debated whether to unfreeze the immortal and tell him to follow, or just lift him up and carry him to the car.

In case the guy tried to resist the compulsion or work around it by dragging his feet, it was better to just carry him.

"Rufsur. Pick him up and carry him to the car. Put him in the trunk."

"He's not going to fit. It's too small."

"Then put him in the back seat."

"Yes, boss."

As his second-in-command heaved the dead weight over his shoulder, Kalugal checked the shooter. The nutcase was still out cold, but regrettably not dead.

He might wake up and start shooting again. Kalugal could take the gun, but the dude might have more hidden under his clothes. It would be quicker to tie him up than search him for more weapons.

Pulling out his belt, Kalugal tied the guy's hands behind his back.

With that done, he got up and looked in the direction he'd seen the immune, but she was still hiding behind the bar.

Good.

He took out the earpiece and put it in his pocket.

"Listen up, everyone," Kalugal yelled to be heard over the music that was still blaring from the loudspeakers. "You are going to forget what you've seen, and in half an hour, you will resume dancing. You'll remember watching a Coldplay concert on the screen in the back."

At the start of the evening, Rufsur had fixed the surveillance cameras, putting them on a loop, so none of what had happened was going to show up on the recording.

With the thrall taking care of the humans' memories of the incident, the only remaining evidence other than the gunman would be the bullet lodged in the ceiling, which no one was going to notice.

Looking down at the shooter, he wondered what to do with him. The best thing would be to throw him into the dumpster out back, but Kalugal had sent Rufsur with the immortal, which meant that he would have to take the trash out himself.

The things he had to do to protect a bunch of insignificant humans.

With a sigh, he wrapped his hand in his shirttail, picked up the gun, and put it in his pocket.

Grabbing the gunman by the belt he'd tied around his wrists, he dragged the piece of human trash out the back door, where he encountered two more males frozen mid-stride.

When the small hairs on the back of his neck started tingling, he took another look at the males. The males could only move their eyes, and the expression in them was more angry than terrified.

They knew what was going on.

He smiled at them. "I apologize for the temporary inconvenience, but don't worry. I'm going to release you as soon as I'm safely away with your friend."

If looks could kill, he would already be dead. Thankfully, he'd never heard of an immortal possessing that power.

Had any of the gods?

His father was the only one who could answer that question, but since he couldn't call Navuh and ask, it was another mystery Kalugal hoped he could solve through research into the past.

Heaving the shooter up, he tossed him in the dumpster. The gun was next. Pulling it out of his pocket using his shirt again, he tossed it inside as well.

With that done, Kalugal turned to assess the two immortals. They didn't look like his father's men. Fair-skinned and light-haired, they looked European. But then many years had gone by since he'd left the island, and his father might have been breeding the Dormants with European men, producing warriors who could more easily blend into the population in the Western countries.

But Flyboy had said that he hadn't been sent by Navuh. Maybe they were Annani's men?

And if so, had they been looking for him, or had it been a coincidence?

He would soon find out.

Jin

The moment Arwel had shouted in their earpieces, Jacki climbed on top of the bar and pulled Jin behind her.

"What are you doing?" the barman yelled at them. "Get down."

"That is what we are doing," Jin yelled back. "Everyone, duck!"

She and Jacki jumped behind the counter and crouched down.

The two barmen did the same. "What's going on?" the closest one asked.

"A shooter," Jacki said.

A moment later, a gun went off and then the screaming started.

As Jin lifted her head to check if anyone had gotten hurt, Jacki grabbed her shirt and pulled her back down. "It might not be safe yet."

"I disabled the gunman," Arwel said in their earpieces.

Jin started pushing to her feet again when she was stopped by one shouted word.

"Freeze!" Somehow the voice overpowered the screaming and the music. It was loud, clear, and infused with command. "No one move! And no one utter a sound."

Immediately, the screaming stopped as if someone had waved a magic wand. Not the music, though. It kept blasting from the loudspeakers.

But that wasn't all. As Jin tried to get back down, she realized that she couldn't move and was stuck in a mid-crouch.

She couldn't talk either.

As the implications sank in, an involuntary shiver seized her. The command had been a compulsion, issued by Kalugal.

Thankfully, Jacki wasn't affected, and she pulled Jin down, making her land unceremoniously on her ass. "We are majorly screwed," she whispered. "I'm the only one the compulsion doesn't work on."

Panic seizing her lungs, Jin wanted to tell Jacki to check on Arwel, but all she could do was blink, which she did rapidly, hoping her friend would understand.

The tether worked only one way, and Jacki wasn't an empath. But she got the message.

Slowly, she pushed up to her feet and then immediately ducked back down. "Damn. He looked right at me. He's crouching next to Arwel, who is lying on top of the gunman, immobilized just like everyone else."

Where were the other Guardians? Were they affected by the compulsion as well?

Her answer came a moment later, delivered by Kalugal's calm voice straight into her earpiece. "Everyone listening, stop talking, texting, and any other form of communication. Don't move unless you are driving. If you are, pull over to the side of the road and then sit in the vehicle until I tell you to move."

Kalugal had just eliminated her last hope.

Help was not coming.

But at least he'd made sure they wouldn't cause accidents by freezing inside moving vehicles.

Trying to force her hand to move, Jin struggled against the compulsion, but disobeying the command proved impossible.

As hot tears started rolling down her cheeks, Jacki wiped them away with her sleeve. "Don't cry," she said quietly. "You won't be able to blow your nose. I can wipe the snot but not blow for you."

She was trying to cheer Jin up, but it wasn't working.

The situation was desperate.

Arwel was at Kalugal's mercy, and no one was coming to help them.

"Wait, maybe you can blow your nose. He just said not to move. Smart guy. He must have a lot of experience with compulsion to make his wording so precise."

Jin didn't want to hear about Kalugal's brilliance. She wanted Jacki to do something, anything.

"Rufsur," Jin heard him call his man. "Pick him up and carry him to the car. Put him in the trunk."

"He's not going to fit. It's too small."

"Then put him in the back seat."

"Yes, boss."

The him could only be Arwel.

Blinking rapidly, she signaled her distress to Jacki the only way she could.

"Okay, I got it. I'll take another look."

Jacki pushed up slowly, only as much as she needed to peek over the bar. "The other guy is carrying Arwel out, and Kal is tying up the gunman." She ducked back down. "I don't know what to do. The pepper spray is in my purse and I dropped it when I climbed on the bar. Maybe I can use a big bottle to hurl at his head?"

Since Jin could see through Jacki's eyes, the spoken update wasn't necessary, but she had no way of reminding Jacki of the tether. The only response she could give her was to widen her eyes.

"I guess it's no. I didn't think so."

"Listen up, everyone," Kalugal said. "You are going to forget what you've seen, and in half an hour, you will resume dancing. You'll remember watching a Coldplay concert on the screen in the back."

"He is so smart." Jacki started pushing up again. "Maybe I can somehow get the shooter's gun."

Through her friend's eyes, Jin saw Kalugal drag the gunman toward the back exit.

He was leaving.

If Jacki didn't do something soon, Kalugal would drive away with Arwel.

Communicating the urgency by darting her eyes from side to side, she hoped Jacki would understand.

Except, how could she possibly overpower two immortal males and free Arwel?

It was hopeless.

Arwel

As Arwel was lifted and swung over the immortal's shoulder, he had never in his entire life felt so helpless.

They passed by Magnus and Gregor, who had been frozen mid-stride. Only their eyes moved, and they reflected the same desperation that Arwel felt.

He was at Kalugal's mercy, his fellow Guardians were just as frozen as he was, and his only possible savior was Jacki, a human girl who could do nothing to help him.

He was screwed, and so was the entire clan.

Arwel was privy to almost everything there was to know, including the village's location. Hopefully, Kian would immediately implement the lockdown protocol to secure the place.

The one good thing was that Arwel didn't know the override codes. They were computer-generated daily, one set going to Onegus and the other to Kian. Both were needed to override the shutdown and access the village.

If only he had a suicide capsule in his tooth like the spies in the movies, he could have killed himself to save the clan. But no one had imagined a scenario in which a head Guardian would be captured by an immortal who could compel him to do anything he wanted.

"Look on the bright side," Rufsur said. "You are getting a ride in a Ferrari. I'm afraid it's going to be a little cramped in the back seat, but at least I don't have to stuff you in the trunk."

He opened the door with a key, moved the chair forward, and dumped Arwel on the tiny back seat. It took some maneuvering, and the guy had to fold Arwel's legs all the way up to his chin before dropping the driver's seat back down.

"I keep telling Kalugal that this car is a joke, but he loves his expensive toys."

Sitting on the driver's seat with his legs outside the car, Rufsur looked at Arwel. "I hope you are not in pain, my friend."

What a surprisingly amiable fellow.

Except, Arwel was under no illusions. When it came time for torture, Rufsur would not hesitate for a moment.

There would be no need for that because Kalugal could compel him to talk, but he might decide to do it for the fun of it.

Where was he?

Why hadn't he come out yet?

Hopefully, he wasn't looking for Jin. Had he connected the two incidents?

Kalugal had asked him if he'd been sent by Navuh, so that was where his mind was going, and Navuh would never have used a woman for his schemes. So, if Kalugal still thought that Arwel was connected to his father, it wouldn't occur to him that the girl who'd bumped into him was with Arwel. She would be just another face in the crowd of frozen humans.

Was he ever going to see her again?

Their story couldn't end like this.

The Fates had not brought them together only to break them apart.

Furthermore, they wouldn't have been arranging matings left, right and center if they knew about the clan's imminent demise.

It was ridiculous to base his hopes on the elusive Fates, but as the saying went, there are no atheists in foxholes, and even a nonbeliever like Arwel found himself praying to a higher power.

Please don't let it end like this. But if you need a sacrifice for your boon, take it out of me, and spare Jin.

William

As soon as Arwel yelled, *take cover*, William opened his channel to the other Guardians so they could hear what was going on.

The problem was that William was operating on blind, and the only information he was getting was through Arwel and the girls' earpieces.

The cameras inside the club had been tampered with, most likely by Kalugal or his guy. William couldn't see the girls going in, nor could he see the shrouded Kalugal.

The same was true for the camera in the parking lot.

By the time he'd hacked into the feed, it hadn't shown the Ferrari or Magnus's car, when he knew that it should.

"Everyone, go in," William shouted as he heard the gunshot through Arwel's earpiece.

"Arwel ordered us to stay in the car," Michael said.

"He didn't say anything to Gregor and me," Magnus said. "We are going in."

"So are we," the Guardian in the backup car announced.

"I'm trying to get to Arwel," Kri yelled. "Everyone is screaming and pushing to get out."

"Are Jacki and Jin safe?"

"They are hiding behind the bar."

A few tense seconds passed, and then William heard another voice coming through Arwel's earpiece. "Freeze! No one move, and no one utter a sound."

William froze with his hand on the control screen, the command affecting him even though he was nowhere near Kalugal.

The air silence from the Guardians meant that the same had happened to them.

The only one he could hear was Jacki, who was talking to Jin. "We are majorly screwed. I'm the only one the compulsion doesn't work on."

William strained, trying to move his hand to open a channel to Onegus, but it refused to cooperate. On second thought, it was a good thing that he hadn't succeeded. Kalugal could have compelled Onegus to freeze as well.

And if he had any doubts, a moment later they were dispelled when Kalugal spoke directly into the earpiece. "Everyone listening, stop talking, texting, and any other form of communication. Don't move unless you are driving. If you are, pull over to the side of the road and then sit in the vehicle until I tell you to move."

Arwel's device went silent, but William could still hear some of what was going on through Kri's earpiece. It was muffled, drowned out by the loud music still blasting as if nothing had happened.

If not for his immortal hearing, he wouldn't have heard Kalugal order his man.

"Rufsur. Pick him up and carry him to the car. Put him in the trunk."

"He's not going to fit. It's too small."

"Then put him in the back seat."

"Yes, boss."

A drop of sweat detached from William's forehead and landed on his desk.

Jacki was right. They were all majorly screwed.

Jin

"Crap." Jacki's eyes darted around. "It's now or never. I need a weapon." She grabbed a stainless-steel cocktail shaker. "Not heavy enough." She tossed it aside and grabbed a large bottle of vodka. "That's good. I need another one." She skirted the barman who was frozen in a crouch next to Jin and went for a second bottle. "I need that damn pepper spray." Jacki left the bottle on the counter, pulled herself on top of the bar, and jumped down on the other side. "Where is my damn purse?"

Through the tether, Jin saw Jacki crawling between people's legs, searching for her purse and the pepper spray. She was wasting time, and in the meantime, Kalugal could be driving off with Arwel.

Jin switched to Kalugal's tether.

Through his eyes, she saw him throw the gunman into a dumpster. Kalugal wrapped his hand in his shirttail and pulled the gun out of his pocket, wiped it, and then tossed it into the dumpster as well.

What was he going to do next? Drive away? Come back and look for her?

Pepper spray in one hand and a vodka bottle in the other, Jacki leaned over the bar. "Wish me luck."

Jin blinked and then closed her eyes to follow the tether to Jacki.

As her friend ran out the back door at full speed, Kalugal looked over his shoulder.

Without a moment's hesitation, Jacki hurled the bottle at his head. If not for his inhuman reflexes, she would have made it.

But he snatched the bottle before it could hit him and smiled at Jacki. "Nice try. Now, be a good girl, turn around, and go back inside."

"Like hell!" She ran at him with the pepper spray aimed at his eyes.

What the hell was she doing? He was going to kill her or tie her up and throw her into the dumpster together with the gunman.

But before Jacki could reach Kalugal, his guy intercepted her, catching her from behind with an arm around her waist, and at the same time wrenching the pepper spray out of her hand and tossing it away.

As he threw her over his shoulder, Jin got just as dizzy as Jacki from seeing things upside down.

"What do you want me to do with her?" Rufsur asked.

Jacki struggled, pounding on his back and kicking her legs.

The guy didn't even grimace. It was as if a child was wriggling to get out of her father's grip. He wasn't hurting her, but he wasn't letting go of her either.

Kalugal looked at Jacki's struggles dispassionately. "Will she fit in the trunk?"

"I think so. She's not as chubby as she looks. It's all clothing."

"Stop!" Jacki yelled at the top of her lungs. "Rape!"

As if that was going to help her.

"You'd better tie her up and gag her." Kalugal gripped Jacki's chin and squeezed. "Is the immortal your boyfriend?" He lifted her face. "You must love him very much to take a stupid risk like that.

Jacki stopped struggling. "Immortal?"

Kalugal smiled indulgently. "You didn't know. He must have liked the challenge of an immune. A woman he couldn't thrall into sleeping with him."

"Let me go. I won't make any trouble."

"I'm sorry, but I can't do that. You are not just a random human who happens to be immune to mind manipulation. You are connected to immortals, and you've seen my real face."

"The clock is ticking," Rufsur said.

"Load her up." Kalugal looked at Jacki, who started struggling again. "It's not a long drive, and you have nothing to fear. No one is going to rape you. You have my word."

Kalugal

"Call security and tell them to move everyone into the bunker," Kalugal said as he pulled out of the club's parking lot.

"Are you going to lock down the bunker?"

Kalugal nodded. "Until we know what we are dealing with. If this was a random coincidence, then a lockdown is not necessary, but if they were after me, it is, and that's the more likely possibility. If he was there alone, I would have been inclined to believe that it was random. But he had backup."

Rufsur glanced at the back seat. "Why don't you ask him?"

"First, I want to get back to the bunker and secure it. His questioning can wait."

Kalugal was worried about the woman in the trunk. She was too quiet. Even though she was tied up and gagged, he'd expected her to kick and thrash.

Maybe there wasn't enough air in there for her to breathe? What if she suffocated?

Humans were so damn fragile, and he didn't want her death on his conscience.

When he heard a thump and then another one, Kalugal let out a relieved breath.

Apparently, she'd been stunned by the revelation that her boyfriend was an immortal and only now had gotten over the shock.

"You'll have to sell the Ferrari," Rufsur said. "The buddies of the guy in the back probably saw us put him inside."

The car was registered to one of Kalugal's subsidiary corporations at a different address, but it was too easy to spot.

Regrettably, Rufsur was right.

"I'll replace it with a different model."

"You should go for a different make. The Aston Martin Valhalla is going to be a sweet ride."

Kalugal chuckled. "You keep complaining about the Ferrari having a joke of a backseat and a small trunk. The Valhalla is a true sports car. Besides, it's not offered for sale yet."

"Aha. So, you were thinking about it."

"Of course. I'm a collector."

And now he was adding an immortal of uncertain origins and an immune human to the rare treasures stored in his bunker.

If the immortal was part of Annani's clan, then he could be used as a bargaining chip. The question was how much the goddess cared about her people. If it were Navuh, he wouldn't even negotiate, not unless the immortal had knowledge that could endanger the island or Navuh himself.

Was the male in the back someone important in the clan?

Kalugal doubted it. An important member of the clan would not rush to save a bunch of humans at the risk of exposing himself. But then his girlfriend was inside, and he'd probably acted on instinct.

He would soon find out, though, so there was no point in speculating.

After the car lift descended into the underground garage, Kalugal parked the Ferrari in its designated spot and killed the engine.

"What do you want to do with the immortal?" Rufsur asked.

"Pick him up and carry him to a holding cell. I'll carry the immune."

Rufsur grimaced. "I'll get one of the men to do it. She's a feisty wench. She'll bite and scratch you."

Normally, Kalugal didn't mind a little rough play, but only if it was in a sexual context and consensual. The woman's heart belonged to another, and he had other things to take care of.

"Make it so."

"Do you want me to put them in the same cell?"

"Yeah. Why not. She was so desperate to save him, I'm sure she'll appreciate being locked up together with him."

It was possible that the two were just teammates, but lovers was more likely. The immortal had exposed himself to protect the immune, and she'd run out to help him with no regard for her own safety.

"Do you want to unfreeze him?"

"He will be released at the same time as the humans in the club. I'm sure he heard the command."

"In case he didn't, maybe you should do it again. If he pisses in his pants because he can't use the toilet, I don't want to have to clean him up."

"Very well." Kalugal turned to the immortal. "Ten minutes from now you can move and talk."

He got out of the car and headed to the security office.

"Has everyone made it back already?" he asked.

Dammal shook his head. "Phinas is five minutes away, and he has Dandor and Welgost with him. But Ruvon and Hivak are all the way in San Francisco. I told them to stay there and get a hotel room. The rest are down here."

"Very well. As soon as Phinas is back, lock the place down and initiate the perimeter's code red security protocol."

"Yes, boss."

"I'll be in my office."

Pushing his hand into his pocket, Kalugal closed it around the earpiece.

Once the lockdown was executed, he would unfreeze the rest of the immortals connected to the listening device.

In the short term, it would be safer for him to leave them frozen. But leaving them in that state guaranteed their exposure, and that was an undesirable outcome that would make his life more difficult in the long term.

Humans should not be allowed to discover the existence of immortals. If they ever did, a witch hunt would start, the scope of which the world had not seen before.

Not only would they feel threatened by a superior race of people living among them, they would also want to get their hands on the secret to immortality.

William

"Hello," Kalugal's voice sounded in William's earpiece. "Everyone listening can move and talk now. Good night."

"Wait!" William called. "What have you done with Arwel?"

He had to act fast and keep the guy talking. Which meant that he had to start the negotiations before Kalugal disconnected the earpiece.

Sweating profusely, William forced himself to concentrate. His fingers flying over the keyboard, he typed up a message to Kian to get his earpiece in and get online.

"Oh, so that's Flyboy's name. I haven't had the opportunity to chat with him and his girlfriend yet."

William's heart skipped a beat. If Kalugal had Jin, they were flying blind. He'd hoped she could tell them what was going on.

The problem was that he couldn't check with her as long as he had Kalugal in his ear.

"Flyboy? And what girlfriend are you talking about?"

His phone pinged with a text message from Jin. *He has Jacki. She and Arwel are locked in a cell in his bunker. He initiated a lockdown of the entire place.*

William had never been more glad of his ability to do several things at once.

He texted back. *Call Kian.*

Magnus already did.

So why the hell hadn't he come on the line yet?

William wasn't a military man, and he knew nothing about negotiating a hostage situation.

Then it dawned on him that Jin and the rest of the team were still connected to Arwel's channel and could hear Kalugal. What if he decided to compel them again?

William cursed soundlessly.

He was no good at handling a critical situation like this. His first action should have been to isolate Arwel's channel.

"Your man sailed over the crowd to knock out the shooter, which was very impressive, but it also gave him away. Then Flyboy's immune girlfriend rushed to save him and fought like a hellcat. But don't worry, we handled them both with care. As you are aware, I don't need to use force to extract information from people."

Brave, stupid girl. What had she been thinking?

"She is not his girlfriend, and we know where you've taken them. As we speak, your place is being surrounded."

He was bluffing, but it was going to be true in a minute or two.

The door to his office burst open and Vivian rushed in in her pajamas. William lifted a hand to stop whatever questions she might have.

"Kri just called me..." She stopped when he pointed to his earpiece.

Kalugal chuckled. "I can just command them to freeze again. Should I do it now?"

"They are no longer connected to this channel. It's just you and me."

"Who am I talking to?" Kalugal asked. "Are you the head of this operation?"

"I'm just the communications guy. The head of the operation is going to join us in a moment."

"Wonderful. I can't wait."

Damn. Maybe it wasn't a good idea for Kian to come on the line. Kalugal could command him to do whatever he pleased.

His fingers flew over the keyboard. *Don't open the channel without Turner next to you. I'll connect Turner's earpiece to Arwel's in a second.*

"If you are planning to compel him as well, it's not going to help you. His second-in-command is an immune."

William hoped that he wasn't revealing the ace up Kian's proverbial sleeve too soon. The trouble was that he had no experience in crisis management, and he was just doing everything he could to keep Kalugal talking.

"How fascinating. I can't wait to hear who your boss is and what he wants with me."

 Jin

Jin used the hem of her dirty T-shirt to wipe her tear-stained cheeks for the hundredth time since Kalugal had unfrozen everyone connected to Arwel's channel. "Wasn't that the right turn?" she asked Kri.

The Guardian had been talking on the phone, and she might have missed it.

"We are not going back to the house." Kri put her phone down. "My instructions are to keep you safe. You are our bargaining chip." The Guardian lifted her hand off the steering wheel. "Not to trade you for Arwel, of course. Just letting Kalugal know that we can see and hear everything he is doing should be a good enough motivator for him to cooperate."

"I don't mind getting traded if it will keep everyone safe. I don't know anything useful, while Arwel knows everything."

"That's very brave of you. But I don't think it will come to that."

"Just let Kian know that it's on the table. Okay?"

If she could save Arwel and the rest of the clan by sacrificing herself, Jin would take it with both hands.

"Where are we going?"

She didn't care what happened to her next, but changing into a clean shirt qualified as public service. Hers was covered with tears and snot that she hadn't been able to wipe off while frozen.

Gross. But who cared about that?

Kalugal had Arwel, and she had no idea how Kian was going to free him.

It had felt awful to drive away without Arwel and Jacki, but it had made no sense to stay in the club either. Kalugal's release was going to kick in in a few minutes, and all those humans wouldn't remember anything from what had happened. About forty-five minutes would be missing from their lives, but they would be under the impression that they'd been watching a concert on the club's big screen.

If not for Magnus filling in the blanks for her and Kri, they wouldn't have remembered any of it either. Luckily, Kalugal had deactivated the earpiece he'd taken from Arwel before issuing his command to forget what had transpired inside the club, so the compulsion hadn't affected the Guardians. Curiously, Magnus's input had triggered the return of their memories, but Kri's were not the same as Jin's. While Jin had been hiding behind the counter and hadn't seen much, Kri had seen everything.

None of the other club goers would remember the gunman, though, or the bullet that had by some miracle missed its target.

Well, not by a miracle. By Arwel. The hero who had saved who knew how many lives tonight and by doing so had sacrificed himself.

She should have left the tether attached to him.

Damn, she should have refused the mission and then none of this would be happening.

She and Arwel would be in the village, working on her transition and planning a wedding.

The one thing keeping Jin from falling into despair was the tethers she had to Jacki and to Kalugal. That was enough to give her a good picture of what was going on. Thinking that Jacki and Arwel were a couple, Kalugal had them thrown into the same cell.

So far, no one had questioned either of them, but that was only because Kalugal was busy talking to William. Hopefully, Kian would take over soon and negotiate something.

What she worried about, though, was that Kalugal would assign one of his men to interrogate Arwel away from Jacki, and he would be tortured. But that didn't make much sense. Kalugal was the only one who could compel Arwel to tell him whatever he wanted, and he could do that without resorting to torture.

He didn't seem like the mean type. So far, the only nasty thing the brute had done was to lock poor Jacki in the trunk of his car. Some other guy had taken her out and carried her tied up to a cell that wasn't as nice as the ones at the keep.

Stopping at a red light, Kri glanced at the rearview mirror for the thousandth time. "Magnus told me to keep driving until he gives me further instructions. He is moving everyone out of the house."

"If they leave, who will watch Kalugal's gate?"

"All the other Guardians who are on their way to surround his compound. In a few minutes, the bastard will be under siege."

"That bastard can walk out of there, and no one will be able to stop him."

"That's true. It's a fucked-up situation. I don't know how Kian is going to handle it."

"He should trade me for Arwel. Once he tells Kalugal that he is tethered, the guy will do anything to get rid of it."

Kri cast her a sidelong glance. "Yeah, and that includes killing you. That's the easiest way to get rid of the tether."

"He is not a killer."

"What makes you think that? Kalugal is an ex-Doomer. Don't think that all of them are like Dalhu. Amanda is his fated mate, and she is the only reason he switched sides and reformed. Before that he was a killer like the rest of them."

Jin passed a shaking hand over her mouth. "Kalugal escaped, which means that he didn't agree with his father's agenda. And his actions so far prove that he is not heartless. Besides, I don't care what happens to me as long as I can free Arwel and Jacki and save everyone else in the village."

"No one is going to trade you, so you can forget about that crazy idea."

Jin had no such intention.

Holding the phone in her pocket, she thought about calling Kian directly and convincing him that this was his best option. Except, right now he was in the midst of managing a crisis, and her call would only distract him.

But maybe she could send him a text?

The moment Jin took the phone out, Kri put a hand on her arm. "Don't."

"Don't what?"

"Text Kian."

"He needs to know that trading me for Arwel and Jacki is an option."

"Wait until he calls you."

"What if he doesn't?"

"He will need you to tell him what Kalugal is doing."

"Right."

Waiting for Kian to call her was better. That way, she wasn't going to distract him. Jin put the phone away.

As the light changed to green, Kri glanced at the rearview mirror before pulling out of the intersection. "You have guts. I admire that."

Jin chuckled. "I'm terrified, and when Kian trades me, I'm probably going to pee in my pants."

Kri cast her a knowing glance. "You must really love Arwel to be willing to do that."

Jin nodded. "I would do anything for him. But this is so much bigger than just the two of us. Even if he wasn't my fated mate, this is the right thing to do."

Kian

As Kian's phone rang, he had a feeling bad news was coming his way, and when he saw Magnus's contact information on the screen, he was sure of it.

"What happened?"

"Kalugal has Arwel and Jacki. You need to lock down the village and evacuate the keep."

Kian's blood ran cold in his veins. This was worse than the worst scenario he'd imagined.

Syssi's panicked expression reflected his own feelings. The only difference was that he was better at hiding them.

"Hold on. I'm going to put Onegus and Turner on a four-way call." He got up from the couch and started walking toward the door while arranging it. "This is an emergency," he said once he had them on the line. "I'm on my way to the war room. Head there while Magnus tells us what happened."

By the time the Guardian finished his report, Kian was halfway to the pavilion, and as he entered the elevator, a text from William arrived.

Kalugal has Arwel's earpiece and he is talking to me. Put yours in. I already have your channel connected. I'll try to keep him on the line for as long as I can.

Kian didn't answer. That would only break William's concentration, and after hearing Magnus's account of what had happened, he had no intention of putting the earpiece in without Turner right next to him.

The motion-activated lights turned on as soon as he entered the war room, and as he booted up the computer, Turner and Onegus rushed in.

"Onegus. We need to lock down the village and evacuate the keep. Whoever is not here will have to find a room in a hotel. Everyone in the Bay Area has to relocate. Find them accommodations. Everyone other than William needs to leave now. All the Guardians are to get in their cars and surround Kalugal's compound."

"I'm on it."

"Do it in your office, and don't listen to the channel."

"Got it." The chief rushed out.

"Turner. If Kalugal compels me, take over." He wrote his override codes on a post-it. "Mine aren't going to work without Onegus putting his in. If I'm compromised, go to his office and lock the door."

Turner took the note and stuffed it in his pocket.

"Get Lokan on the line and tell him what's going on. Call Ella and have her bring Parker over here."

"Good move."

Kian wasn't sure that it was, but he had no choice.

His phone pinged with another text. *Don't open the channel without Turner next to you. I've connected his earpiece to Arwel's as well.*

Way ahead of you, buddy. Kian pulled out his earpiece from his pocket and put it in.

Turner did the same, connecting his to Arwel's channel as well.

"His second-in-command is an immune," Kian heard William say.

"How fascinating." Kalugal sounded like a smug son of a bitch. "I can't wait to hear who your boss is and what he wants with me."

He was in for one hell of a surprise.

"Hello, cousin."

William's sigh of relief was the first response.

The second was Kalugal's. "Who is this?" His tone was no longer smug.

"I am Kian, son of Annani, your mother's sister."

JIN & ARWEL'S STORY CULMINATES

THE CHILDREN OF THE GODS BOOK 37
DARK SPY'S RESOLUTION
TURN THE PAGE TO READ THE EXCERPT—>

JOIN THE VIP CLUB
To find out what's included in your free membership, flip to the last page.

The best-laid plans often go awry...

Kalugal

Kalugal watched the monitor, following the steps as the program ran through the lockdown protocol. Once the bunker was secure, he pulled his immortal captive's earpiece out of his pocket, put it in his ear, and tapped it to activate.

"Everyone listening can move and talk now. Good night."

"Wait! What have you done with Arwel?"

Kalugal paused with his finger a fraction of an inch away from the device.

Should he disconnect? Or should he engage?

A dilemma.

On the one hand, he was eager to start questioning his captive, but on the other hand, this was an opportunity to talk with the team's commander and learn what he had in mind as far as escalating things.

Was the guy on the other side of the connection in charge of the operation?

His quick recovery from compulsion indicated that he had a good head on his shoulders and a strong personality, which were both prerequisites for a command position. Most people would have needed several moments to collect their wits.

This should be an interesting conversation.

Leaning back in his chair, Kalugal crossed his legs at the ankles. "So that's Flyboy's name. I haven't had the opportunity to chat with him and his girlfriend yet."

"Flyboy? And what girlfriend are you talking about?"

Kalugal sighed. He hated it when people played dumb.

"Your man sailed over the crowd to knock out the shooter, which was very impressive, but it also gave him away. Then Flyboy's immune girlfriend rushed to save him and fought like a hellcat. But don't worry, we handled them both with care. As you are aware, I don't need to use force to extract information from people."

"She is not his girlfriend, and we know where you've taken them. As we speak, your place is being surrounded."

Even if the guy wasn't bluffing about knowing the location of Kalugal's compound, there was no way Arwel's pals had made it there so fast. Except, he might have had additional warriors stationed nearby or some that hadn't been connected to Arwel's channel when Kalugal had compelled them to freeze.

His immediate safety was not an issue.

While locked down, the bunker was nearly impenetrable, and they had enough supplies stored to last them for months. The problem would be getting out of there while a large force was surrounding the place.

Two tunnels led in and out of the bunker, but one went into the house, which wasn't going to be helpful as an escape route, and the other led to a grate in the sidewalk on the other side of his property, which wasn't very useful either.

That was the trouble with building a bunker inside an established and affluent community. Digging under existing houses had not been possible.

If the force outside wasn't large, he could just walk out and compel the men surrounding his property to let him through, but there was a limit to how many immortals he could compel at once.

Kalugal wasn't as powerful as his father. Not yet. Twenty or so warriors were the most he could handle at the same time.

With a few quick taps on the keyboard, he flipped through the feeds from the perimeter's cameras and was relieved to find no one outside the compound or on its grounds. That meant that his initial assessment had been correct. The team that had been sent after him wasn't large, and they were all still in the vicinity of the club. Or so he hoped. Whoever had organized this operation might be sending reinforcements.

It was time to issue some threats of his own. "I can just command them to freeze again. Should I do it now?"

"They are no longer connected to this channel. It's just you and me."

Smart move, which Kalugal had anticipated.

"Who am I talking to? Are you the head of this operation?"

"I'm just the communications guy. The head of the operation is going to join us in a moment."

That wasn't good. A small unit didn't need a dedicated communications person, which implied that he was dealing with a large force after all.

The most logical conclusion was that it belonged to Annani's clan. Except, what did they want with him?

He had never bothered them or tried to find them, and they had left him alone as well. Kalugal was surprised that they even knew of his existence.

He was supposed to be dead.

Why the sudden interest? Perhaps they sought his cooperation against his father?

If that was why Annani had sent men to follow him around, she would be disappointed. Kalugal had no such intentions.

He lifted his legs and put his feet on the desk. "Wonderful. I can't wait."

"If you are planning to compel him as well, it's not going to help you. His second-in-command is an immune."

The possibility of compelling the commander hadn't even crossed Kalugal's mind. At this point, all he wanted was to find out why Annani's clan was after him, and then to get them off his back as soon as possible. Which probably meant releasing the warrior and his girlfriend.

He would gladly do that, but only after interrogating them. There was little chance that an opportunity to learn about Annani's clan and what they were up to would present itself again.

Regrettably, once this was over he would have to relocate, and that was a damn shame. Kalugal liked the neighborhood and its proximity to Stanford, and the bunker had cost him a fortune to build, not to mention the hassle it had been. But his location had been compromised, and he couldn't allow the clan to breathe down his neck and interfere with his plans.

"How fascinating. I can't wait to hear who your boss is, and to find out what he wants with me."

"Hello, cousin."

Cousin?

All immortals had common ancestry, but to call him cousin was a stretch.

"Who is this?"

"I am Kian, son of Annani, your mother's sister."

What?

"You heard me right. Areana, your mother, is my mother's sister, which makes us cousins."

Kalugal wasn't aware that he'd voiced his astonishment.

It took a brief moment for the shock to subside and for the gears in his mind to start spinning again. The guy couldn't be talking about Annani the goddess. Many of the clan's daughters were probably named after her.

Had Navuh stolen Annani's sister from the clan?

Was that why they had been stalking him? To get her back?

His mother hadn't said anything about the clan. But then Kalugal had been a young boy the last time he'd seen her, and the subject of the clan and how she'd come to be in Navuh's possession hadn't come up in their conversations.

"Are you still there?" Kian asked.

"I can't help you recover your clanswoman. If I could have, I would have freed my mother a long time ago. Regrettably, she loves my father, and even though I must assume that he kidnapped her and forced her to mate him, she wants to stay with him. I guess Areana is suffering from prolonged Stockholm syndrome."

Kian

Kian felt like scratching his head.

What the hell was Kalugal talking about? Could it be that he didn't know who Annani was?

Navuh had kept Annani's survival secret from her sister, but not from the Brotherhood. Since the very beginning of the conflict, he'd been using her and the supposed evils she and her clan were committing to unify his men behind his so-called cause.

Perhaps Kalugal was suffering from amnesia?

Could it be that he hadn't escaped during WWII but had been buried in stasis for decades, only to revive recently?

It had happened to Wonder, so it wasn't an implausible scenario.

"Do you know who Annani is?"

"I know who *the Annani* is, but naturally, I don't know any of her namesake descendants. If memory serves me correctly, and I'm quite sure that it does, my mother has never mentioned her sister, by name or otherwise."

That explained it.

Kalugal assumed that Kian's mother was an immortal named after Annani, not the goddess herself. And given that Areana hadn't revealed her true identity to her son, Kalugal's assumption made sense.

Unfortunately, the wind had already been knocked out from under the bombastic proclamation that Kian had hoped would have such a profound impact on Kalugal.

How disappointing.

On the other hand, lengthy explanations were precisely what Kian was after. The longer he kept Kalugal talking, the more time he would buy Kri and Jin to get out of the area, and the Guardians to surround the complex.

"No clan females are named after Annani. My mother is the goddess, and your mother is her half-sister."

There was a long moment of silence before Kalugal responded. "What you are saying is impossible. If my mother were a goddess, she would be more powerful than my father, and she obviously is not."

"Areana is a very weak goddess, and Navuh is a very powerful immortal. Still, Navuh doesn't want anyone to know that his mate is a goddess who outranks him in the gene hierarchy. That's the reason he's hiding her in the harem, and that's also the reason he didn't allow her sons to grow up with her."

"He doesn't allow any of his children to be raised in the harem. He thinks that by preventing his sons from being raised in the harem he is protecting them from killing each other over succession rights. If we don't know who our mothers are, we also don't know the hierarchy of who was born to a wife and who was born to a concubine, and Navuh does not play favorites. No one knows who he is going to choose."

Kian shook his head. He'd assumed that Kalugal knew so much more than he actually did, but he should have realized that Areana couldn't have told all that to a five-year-old boy. He'd been too young to understand harem politics and the web of lies and deceit that Navuh had created.

"Navuh has only two sons. You and Lokan. The others were fathered by human males who look like him. I loathe saying anything positive about your father, but he loves your mother and has been loyal to her throughout the years."

As Kalugal processed that nugget of information, there was another long moment of silence.

"Are you saying that the other women in my father's harem are having relations with the human male servants? That means that other than Lokan, my other so-called brothers are not related to me at all."

"That's right."

"I'll be damned. My father actually cares. That's an ingenious way to protect Lokan's and my identity. With numerous fake sons, no one suspects who Navuh's real successors are, or rather is. I have no intention of taking over. Lokan can have it all."

That hadn't been the take-home value Kian had hoped for, but it didn't matter. His main goal was to keep Kalugal talking and asking questions until Turner confirmed that Jin was safe and that the Guardians were in position.

"I'm not sure that you've got it right. Whatever Navuh does serves him and no one else. Technically, you and your brother outrank him as far as godly genes go. While Navuh is the son of a god with a mortal, and therefore only half a god, you and your brother are three-quarter gods. It's just as important for him to keep that information from you as it is to hide his mate's godly identity."

Kalugal chuckled. "Following that logic, unless Annani found a first-generation immortal to mate with, my brother and I outrank you as well."

That was regrettably true, but Kian wasn't going to provide Kalugal with any more information than he absolutely had to.

"You, Lokan, and I are not competing for positions."

"That's true. I'm not interested in your job any more than I'm interested in my father's. So, if that's why you sought me out and sent your warriors after me, rest assured that your clan is of no interest to me. You are not my enemy, and you are not my friend either. Can we leave it at that?"

Albeit mistaken, that was another logical conclusion on Kalugal's part.

The guy was level-headed, smart, and he wasn't easily shaken either. His cousin was a worthy opponent, of whom Kian would be wise to be wary.

"I have no reason to fear you, Kalugal. I sought you out because your mother asked mine to find you. She is worried about you, and she misses you."

Jin

Kri tapped her fingers on the steering wheel. "What if the Guardians surrounding Kalugal's place are given really good earplugs so they can't hear him?"

Jin's heart fluttered with renewed hope. "That's a very good question. His shrouds and his compulsion don't work the same way. It seems that he needs to be heard in order for the compulsion to work. Otherwise, he wouldn't have bothered with Arwel's earpiece. But he can shroud himself without being heard."

Kri nodded. "That's no less problematic than his compulsion. Even if he can't compel them because they have earplugs in, he can shroud himself and his men to be invisible and waltz out of there. The Guardians are not going to see them leave."

"True. But if there is a camera pointed at his gate, and the watchers are all the way back in the village, his shroud is not going to affect them. They will see him and can tell the Guardians."

Kri cast Jin a sidelong glance. "Very clever. I need to call Magnus and have him get everyone the best earplugs he can find. Roni, our hacker, can tell Magnus what to do about installing a surveillance camera." Kri pulled to the side and parked. "Damn. We forgot about Arwel's phone. He has everyone's numbers on it, and Kalugal can start calling people and compel them to do all kinds of shit."

"I can check if he has the phone." Jin closed her eyes and followed the tether to Kalugal. "He is still talking with Kian. I'll check on Jacki." She followed the tether to her friend. "She and Arwel are whispering in each other's ears. They are in a prison cell, but it's not nice like the ones in the keep. It has bars instead of a door, and I can see the toilet. Gross. It doesn't have a privacy wall or anything. It's just there, sitting against the back wall."

Kri grimaced. "It's just getting better and better, isn't it?" She turned to her phone and scrolled through her contacts until she found the right one and placed the call. "Roni. Can you erase Arwel's phone remotely?" A brief moment passed. "Good. I wasn't sure he would think of it."

Disconnecting, Kri huffed out a breath. "Onegus has already told Roni to do that. This is a nightmare. No one's come up with an SOP for dealing with a compeller. We are so unprepared."

The clan had known about Kalugal's ability for a while, and someone should have come up with a protocol before poking the bear. In hindsight, the entire operation appeared amateurish and gung-ho.

"You said that you are going to call Magnus about my idea."

"Right." This time Kri put the call on speaker. "Magnus, Jin and I have some ideas that we would like to run by you."

"Shoot."

"The Guardians surrounding Kalugal's place should have earplugs in, maybe the noise-canceling ones, so he can't compel them to do things. But since he can shroud himself and probably anyone else that he wants to, we need a camera installed somewhere to watch the gate, with the feed going to the village. That's too far for his shroud to reach."

"Good thinking," Magnus said. "I just need to figure out a way to communicate with my men while they are deaf."

"That's easy." Jin waved a hand. "Tell them to put their phones on vibrate and communicate via text messages."

"Excellent solution. Except, I'll have to find a store that sells quality earplugs and rob it, because I can't wait for it to open in the morning."

"You can leave money on the counter with a note," Jin said.

"I can do that. Thank you both for the excellent suggestions. You were thinking outside the box."

Kri lifted her hand for a high five, and Jin slapped it.

"That's why you need women on the force," Kri said.

"You won't hear me arguing against that. But there are no candidates for the position."

Kri nodded. "Wonder would have made a great Guardian, but her heart is not in it."

Jin had no wish to become a Guardian either, but that didn't mean that she couldn't help in other ways. "Please tell Kian that I'm fine with him trading me for Arwel."

"That's not going to happen."

"Please, just tell him that. Trading me for Arwel before Kalugal has a chance to get him to talk will solve the most urgent problem. Later, Kian can figure out a way to get me out, either by negotiating and bargaining or by threatening."

The more she talked, the more convinced Jin became that this was the only solution to the clusterfuck they found themselves in. "Kalugal is not a bad man. He made sure to get the gunman out of the club so he wouldn't shoot people when he woke up, and he told everyone who was listening to pull over before freezing them, so they wouldn't cause accidents. He's not heartless, and he's not going to hurt me. I'm sure of that. Please, Magnus. I appreciate the chivalry, but it would be really stupid on Kian's part not to use me to get Arwel and Jacki out. I beg you to convince him that this is the best option for everyone."

There was a long moment of silence before Magnus replied. "I'll convey your message to Onegus and have him explain the pros and cons to Kian. But just so you know, if we do that, Arwel is never going to forgive any of us."

"Once this is all over, I'll deal with Arwel. Right now, the future of everyone in the village is in jeopardy. That should be our first priority."

"I can't argue with that."

Jin let out a relieved breath. "Thank you."

When Magnus ended the call, she closed her eyes and followed the tether to Jacki. Everything was still the same as it had been the last time she'd checked. They were still alone in the cell, talking in hushed voices. She listened for a few moments, but it felt awkward to spy on them, so she moved to Kalugal.

Jin had no qualms about spying on him, not after he had taken her man and her friend and put them in a freaking prison cell with a damn toilet that was in full view of everyone passing by in the hallway outside.

Arwel

Jacki glanced at the toilet at the back of the cell. "If you need to use the loo, I will look away," she whispered.

"I'm good. You go first." Arwel closed his eyes and leaned against the wall.

"Can you also put your hands over your ears?"

"No problem."

Kalugal's underground bunker was no keep, and the cell they were in looked like what the name implied.

It was a prison.

The front wall was made of bars, two narrow bunk beds were the only furniture, and the toilet had no privacy wall. There was a sink, but no shower, and there were no towels.

Kalugal's men had dumped him and Jacki on the bottom bunk without bothering to untie her. She had to wait for him to unfreeze first so he could release her.

It had been cruel and unnecessary.

Jacki was human, and being tied up for an extended length of time messed up her circulation and caused muscle spasms.

Curiously, Jacki hadn't asked him any questions yet. Since he'd freed her from her bindings, she'd been quietly massaging the stiff muscles in her arms and legs, and other than thanking him, she hadn't spoken at all.

Not typical behavior for someone who had just discovered that she'd gone down the rabbit hole into a world she hadn't known existed.

Could it be that she'd forgotten Kalugal's comment about Arwel being an immortal?

Getting tied up and stuffed in the trunk of a car could mess with anyone's head. Still, even if Jacki didn't remember that, Kalugal almost certainly was going to repeat it at some point, which meant that he probably had no intention of ever letting Jacki go.

No matter on which side of the divide immortals were, they had one thing in common. Keeping their existence secret from humans was necessary for their survival, and since Kalugal couldn't thrall Jacki's memories away, he must either plan to kill her or to keep her imprisoned for life.

The only way things could have been worse was if Kalugal had also captured Jin.

Thank the merciful Fates that the guy hadn't made the connection between the girl bumping into him with what had happened shortly after that.

Jin's tether to Kalugal might help Kian with storming the place. If he had access to everything Kalugal said and did, he might even get from her the override code to unlock the bunker.

As the bed sank under Jacki's weight, Arwel opened his eyes and removed his hands from his ears. "You know that they can see you, right?" He motioned with his head toward the camera mounted near the ceiling.

"I can't do anything about it, so screw them." She flipped a finger at the camera.

"Antagonizing your captors is not a good strategy."

"It doesn't matter." Jacki kicked her shoes off, lifted her feet onto the bed, and wrapped her arms around her knees. "They are going to kill me anyway. Probably you too."

So, she'd figured it out.

Smart girl.

Except, it would have been better for her not to be so clever. As the saying went, ignorance was bliss.

He moved closer to her and whispered in her ear. "The boss is going to get us out."

She arched a brow. "How?"

"I don't know. But between him and his brilliant right-hand man, I'm sure they will figure out something."

Hopefully not by bombing the place, but Arwel couldn't discount the possibility. To keep the clan safe, Kian might decide to sacrifice them. It wouldn't be his first choice, but if everything else failed, this might be a last resort move.

Jacki leaned closer. "I still have Jin's thing, so if you want to say something to her, you can pretend that you are talking to me. Anyway, they assume that we are a couple."

The ability to talk to Jin was the one bright spot illuminating their bleak circumstances. He just wished that the communication went both ways.

Looking into Jacki's blue eyes, Arwel pretended that they were Jin's big brown ones. "I love you. Please don't do anything stupid. Stay safe."

Jacki put her head on his shoulder, probably to maintain the illusion of them being a couple. "What do you think she is going to do?"

He wrapped his arm around her shoulders. "Offer to trade for us."

"Yeah, she might do that. If I were in her shoes, that's what I would do."

That was bad. Jacki had known Jin longer than he had, and if she thought that Jin would offer to sacrifice herself, then she was probably right.

"The boss would never agree to that."

"He might have no choice." She lifted her head off his shoulder and looked at him. "Is Kalugal really his cousin?"

"It doesn't mean much to either of them."

"Are they also immortals like you?"

Damn, she hadn't forgotten.

Arwel nodded.

"Enemies?"

He nodded again, but then tilted his head. "Kalugal's father is our enemy. We don't know whether Kalugal counts himself as one too. I guess we will find out soon."

Jacki leaned against the wall. "You've come up with a good cover story. An organization of paranormally talented people made sense to me." She shook her head. "If you'd told me that you were immortal, I wouldn't have believed you. Is Jin also immortal?"

"No. But I'd rather not talk about it in here."

Even though they were whispering in each other's ears, with the proper equipment their whispers could be amplified.

"Do all immortals have paranormal talents?"

He could answer that. "To some extent. Some are stronger than others. But our mind tricks usually work only on humans. Kalugal and his father are the only immortals we know of who can affect other immortals. That's what makes them so powerful."

Annani could do that too, but that was because she was a goddess, and a powerful one.

Jacki closed her eyes. "We are so screwed. What chance does your boss have against that?"

"There are more of us than there are of them, and we have better weapons." Or so he hoped. "Kalugal can't hide inside this bunker forever, and if he thinks that this place is impenetrable, he is wrong. With the right equipment, any structure can be penetrated."

That had been meant for Kalugal's ears.

There was little chance of Kian launching a massive ordnance penetrator into a bunker located in a suburban neighborhood, but Kalugal wouldn't know that.

Order Dark Spy's Resolution today!

Join the VIP Club
To find out what's included in your free membership,
flip to the last page.

The Children of the Gods Series

Reading Order

THE CHILDREN OF THE GODS ORIGINS

1: Goddess's Choice

When gods and immortals still ruled the ancient world, one young goddess risked everything for love.

2: Goddess's Hope

Hungry for power and infatuated with the beautiful Areana, Navuh plots his father's demise. After all, by getting rid of the insane god he would be doing the world a favor. Except, when gods and immortals conspire against each other, humanity pays the price.

But things are not what they seem, and prophecies should not to be trusted...

THE CHILDREN OF THE GODS

Dark Stranger

1: Dark Stranger The Dream

2: Dark Stranger Revealed

3: Dark Stranger Immortal

Dark Enemy

4: Dark Enemy Taken

5: Dark Enemy Captive

6: Dark Enemy Redeemed

Kri & Michael's Story

6.5: My Dark Amazon

Dark Warrior
7: Dark Warrior Mine
8: Dark Warrior's Promise
9: Dark Warrior's Destiny
10: Dark Warrior's Legacy

Dark Guardian
11: Dark Guardian Found
12: Dark Guardian Craved
13: Dark Guardian's Mate

Dark Angel
14: Dark Angel's Obsession
15: Dark Angel's Seduction
16: Dark Angel's Surrender

Dark Operative
17: Dark Operative: A Shadow of Death
18: Dark Operative: A Glimmer of Hope
19: Dark Operative: The Dawn of Love

Dark Survivor
20: Dark Survivor Awakened
21: Dark Survivor Echoes of Love
22: Dark Survivor Reunited

Dark Widow
23: Dark Widow's Secret
24: Dark Widow's Curse

25: Dark Widow's Blessing

Dark Dream

26: Dark Dream's Temptation

27: Dark Dream's Unraveling

28: Dark Dream's Trap

Dark Prince

29: Dark Prince's Enigma

30: Dark Prince's Dilemma

31: Dark Prince's Agenda

Dark Queen

32: Dark Queen's Quest

33: Dark Queen's Knight

34: Dark Queen's Army

Dark Spy

35: Dark Spy Conscripted

36: Dark Spy's Mission

37: Dark Spy's Resolution

Dark Overlord

38: Dark Overlord New Horizon

Jacki has two talents that set her apart from the rest of the human race.

She has unpredictable glimpses of other people's futures, and she is immune to mind manipulation.

Unfortunately, both talents are pretty useless for finding a job other than the one she had in the government's paranormal division.

It seemed like a sweet deal, until she found out that the director planned on producing super babies by compelling the recruits into pairing up. When an opportunity to escape the program presented itself, she took it, only to find out that humans are not at the top of the food chain.

Immortals are real, and at the very top of the hierarchy is Kalugal, the most powerful, arrogant, and sexiest male she has ever met.

With one look, he sets her blood on fire, but Jacki is not a fool. A man like him will never think of her as anything more than a tasty snack, while she will never settle for anything less than his heart.

39: Dark Overlord's Wife

Jacki is still clinging to her all-or-nothing policy, but Kalugal is chipping away at her resistance. Perhaps it's time to ease up on her convictions. A little less than all is still much better than nothing, and a couple of decades with a demigod is probably worth more than a lifetime with a mere mortal.

40: Dark Overlord's Clan

As Jacki and Kalugal prepare to celebrate their union, Kian takes every precaution to safeguard his people. Except, Kalugal and his men are not his only potential adversaries, and compulsion is not the only power he should fear.

Dark Choices

41: Dark Choices The Quandary

When Rufsur and Edna meet, the attraction is as unexpected as it is undeniable. Except, she's the clan's judge and councilwoman, and he's Kalugal's second-in-command. Will loyalty and duty to their people keep them apart?

42: Dark Choices Paradigm Shift

Edna and Rufsur are miserable without each other, and their two-week separation seems like an eternity. Long-distance relationships are difficult, but for immortal couples they are impossible. Unless one of them is willing to leave everything behind for the other, things are just going to get worse. Except, the cost of compromise is far greater than giving up their comfortable lives and hard-earned positions. The future of their people is on the line.

43: Dark Choices The Accord

The winds of change blowing over the village demand hard choices. For better or worse, Kian's decisions will alter the trajectory of the clan's future, and he is not ready to take the plunge. But as Edna and Rufsur's plight gains widespread support, his resistance slowly begins to erode.

Dark Secrets

44: Dark Secrets Resurgence

On a sabbatical from his Stanford teaching position, Professor David Levinson finally has time to write the sci-fi novel he's been thinking about for years.

The phenomena of past life memories and near-death experiences are too controversial to include in his formal psychiatric research, while fiction is the perfect outlet for his esoteric ideas.

Hoping that a change of pace will provide the inspiration he needs, David accepts a friend's invitation to an old Scottish castle.

45: Dark Secrets Unveiled

When Professor David Levinson accepts a friend's invitation to an old Scottish castle, what he finds there is more fantastical than his most outlandish theories. The castle is home to a clan of immortals, their leader is a stunning demigoddess, and even more shockingly, it might be precisely where he belongs.

Except, the clan founder is hiding a secret that might cast a dark shadow on David's relationship with her daughter.

Nevertheless, when offered a chance at immortality, he agrees to undergo the dangerous induction process.

Will David survive his transition into immortality? And if he does, will his relationship with Sari survive the unveiling of her mother's secret?

46: Dark Secrets Absolved

Absolution.

David had given and received it.

The few short hours since he'd emerged from the coma had felt incredible. He'd finally been free of the guilt and pain, and for the first time since Jonah's death, he had felt truly happy and optimistic about the future.

He'd survived the transition into immortality, had been accepted into the clan, and was about to marry the best woman on the face of the planet, his true love mate, his salvation, his everything.

What could have possibly gone wrong?

Just about everything.

Dark Haven

47: Dark Haven Illusion

48: Dark Haven Unmasked

49: Dark Haven Found

Dark Power

50: Dark Power Untamed

51: Dark Power Unleashed
52: Dark Power Convergence

Dark Memories
53: Dark Memories Submerged
54: Dark Memories Emerge
55: Dark Memories Restored

Dark Hunter
56: Dark Hunter's Query
57: Dark Hunter's Prey
58: Dark Hunter's Boon

Dark God
59: Dark God's Avatar
60: Dark God's Reviviscence
61: Dark God Destinies Converge

Dark Whispers
62: Dark Whispers From The Past
63: Dark Whispers From Afar
64: Dark Whispers From Beyond

Dark Gambit
65: Dark Gambit The Pawn
66: Dark Gambit The Play
67: Dark Gambit Reliance

Dark Alliance
68: Dark Alliance Kindred Souls

69: Dark Alliance Turbulent Waters

70: Dark Alliance Perfect Storm

Dark Healing

71: Dark Healing Blind Justice

72: Dark Healing Blind Trust

73: Dark healing Blind Curve

Dark Encounters

74: Dark Encounters of the Close Kind

75: Dark Encounters of the Unexpected Kind

76: Dark Encounters of the Fated Kind

The Children of the Gods Series Sets

Books 1-3: Dark Stranger trilogy—Includes a bonus short story: **The Fates take a Vacation**

Books 4-6: Dark Enemy Trilogy —Includes a bonus short story—**The Fates' Post-Wedding Celebration**

Books 7-10: Dark Warrior Tetralogy

Books 11-13: Dark Guardian Trilogy

Books 14-16: Dark Angel Trilogy

Books 17-19: Dark Operative Trilogy

Books 20-22: Dark Survivor Trilogy

Books 23-25: Dark Widow Trilogy

Books 26-28: Dark Dream Trilogy

Books 29-31: Dark Prince Trilogy

Books 32-34: Dark Queen Trilogy
Books 35-37: Dark Spy Trilogy
Books 38-40: Dark Overlord Trilogy
Books 41-43: Dark Choices Trilogy
Books 44-46: Dark Secrets Trilogy
Books 47-49: Dark Haven Trilogy
Books 50-52: Dark Power Trilogy
Books 53-55: Dark Memories Trilogy
Books 56-58: Dark Hunter Trilogy
Books 59-61: Dark God Trilogy
Books 62-64: Dark Whispers Trilogy
Books 65-67: Dark Gambit Trilogy
Books 68-70: Dark Alliance Trilogy
Books 71-73: Dark healing Trilogy

MEGA SETS

INCLUDE CHARACTER LISTS

The Children of the Gods: Books 1-6
The Children of the Gods: Books 6.5-10

TRY THE SERIES ON

AUDIBLE

2 FREE audiobooks with your new Audible subscription!

PERFECT MATCH SERIES

Vampire's Consort

When Gabriel's company is ready to start beta testing, he invites his old crush to inspect its medical safety protocol.

Curious about the revolutionary technology of the *Perfect Match Virtual Fantasy-Fulfillment studios*, Brenna agrees.

Neither expects to end up partnering for its first fully immersive test run.

King's Chosen

When Lisa's nutty friends get her a gift certificate to *Perfect Match Virtual Fantasy Studios*, she has no intentions of using it. But since the only way to get a refund is if no partner can be found for her, she makes sure to request a fantasy so girly and over the top that no sane guy will pick it up.

Except, someone does.

> **Warning:** This fantasy contains a hot, domineering crown prince, sweet insta-love, steamy love scenes painted with light shades of gray, a wedding, and a HEA in both the virtual and real worlds.
>
> Intended for mature audience.

Captain's Conquest

Working as a Starbucks barista, Alicia fends off flirting all day long, but none of the guys are as charming and sexy as Gregg. His frequent visits are the highlight of her day, but since he's never asked her out, she assumes he's taken. Besides, between a day job and a budding music career, she has no time to start a new relationship.

That is until Gregg makes her an offer she can't refuse—a gift certificate to the virtual fantasy fulfillment service everyone is talking about. As a huge Star Trek fan, Alicia has a perfect match in mind—the captain of the Starship Enterprise.

THE THIEF WHO LOVED ME

When Marian splurges on a Perfect Match Virtual adventure as a world infamous jewel thief, she expects high-wire fun with a hot partner who she will never have to see again in real life.

A virtual encounter seems like the perfect answer to Marcus's string of dating disasters. No strings attached, no drama, and definitely no love. As a die-hard James Bond fan, he chooses as his avatar a dashing MI6 operative, and to complement his adventure, a dangerously seductive partner.

Neither expects to find their forever Perfect Match.

MY MERMAN PRINCE

The beautiful architect working late on the twelfth floor of my building thinks that I'm just the maintenance guy. She's also under the impression that I'm not interested.

Nothing could be further from the truth.

I want her like I've never wanted a woman before, but I don't play where I work.

I don't need the complications.

When she tells me about living out her mermaid fantasy with a stranger in a Perfect Match virtual adventure, I decide to do everything possible to ensure that the stranger is me.

THE DRAGON KING

To save his beloved kingdom from a devastating war, the Crown Prince of Trieste makes a deal with a witch that costs him half of his humanity and dooms him to an eternity of loneliness.

Now king, he's a fearsome cobalt-winged dragon by day and a short-tempered monarch by night. Not many are brave enough to serve in the palace of the brooding and volatile ruler, but Charlotte ignores the rumors and accepts a scribe position in court.

As the young scribe reawakens Bruce's frozen heart, all that stands in the way of their happiness is the witch's bargain. Outsmarting the evil hag will take cunning and courage, and Charlotte is just the right woman for the job.

MY WEREWOLF ROMEO

The father of my star student is a big-shot screenwriter and the patron of the drama department who thinks he can dictate what production I should put on. The principal makes it very clear that I need to cooperate with the opinionated asshat or walk away from my dream job at the exclusive private high school.

It doesn't help matters that the guy is single, hot, charming, creative, and seems to like me despite my thinly-veiled hostility.

When he invites me to a custom-tailored Perfect Match virtual adventure to prove that his screenplay is perfect for my production, I accept, intending to have fun while proving that messing with the classics is a foolish idea.

I don't expect to be wowed by his werewolf adaptation of Red Riding Hood mesh-up with Romeo and Juliet, and I certainly don't expect to fall in love with the virtual fantasy's leading man.

The Channeler's Companion

A treat for fans of *The Wheel of Time*.

When Erika hires Rand to assist in her pediatric clinic, she does so despite his good looks and irresistible charm, not because of them.

He's empathic, adores children, and has the patience of a saint.

He's also all she can think about, but he's off limits.

What's a doctor to do to scratch that irresistible itch without risking workplace complications?

A shared adventure in the Perfect Match Virtual Studios seems like the solution, but instead of letting the algorithm choose a partner for her, Erika can try to influence it to select the one she wants. Awarding Rand a gift certificate to the service will get him into their database, but unless Erika can tip the odds in her favor, getting paired with him is a long shot.

Hopefully, a virtual adventure based on her and Rand's favorite series will do the trick.

Note

Dear reader,

I hope my stories have added a little joy to your day. If you have a moment to add some to mine, you can help spread the word about the Children Of The Gods series by telling your friends and penning a review. Your recommendations are the most powerful way to inspire new readers to explore the series.

Thank you,

Isabell

FOR EXCLUSIVE PEEKS AT UPCOMING
RELEASES &
A FREE COMPANION BOOK

JOIN MY *VIP CLUB* AND GAIN ACCESS TO THE VIP PORTAL AT ITLUCAS.COM
TO JOIN, GO TO:
http://eepurl.com/blMTpD

INCLUDED IN YOUR FREE MEMBERSHIP:

YOUR VIP PORTAL

- READ PREVIEW CHAPTERS OF UPCOMING RELEASES.
- LISTEN TO GODDESS'S CHOICE NARRATION BY CHARLES LAWRENCE
- EXCLUSIVE CONTENT OFFERED ONLY TO MY VIPs.

FREE I.T. LUCAS COMPANION INCLUDES:

- GODDESS'S CHOICE PART 1
- PERFECT MATCH: VAMPIRE'S CONSORT (A STANDALONE NOVELLA)
- INTERVIEW Q & A
- CHARACTER CHARTS

IF YOU'RE ALREADY A SUBSCRIBER, AND YOU ARE NOT GETTING MY EMAILS, YOUR PROVIDER IS SENDING THEM TO YOUR JUNK FOLDER, AND YOU ARE MISSING OUT ON **IMPORTANT UPDATES,**

SIDE CHARACTERS' PORTRAITS, ADDITIONAL CONTENT, AND OTHER GOODIES. TO FIX THAT, ADD isabell@itlucas.com TO YOUR EMAIL CONTACTS OR YOUR EMAIL VIP LIST.

**Check out the specials at
https://www.itlucas.com/specials**

Printed in Great Britain
by Amazon